THE CITY OF STOLEN LIVES:
THE ADVENTURES OF
PETER THE BRAZEN, VOLUME 1

George F. Worts

Blood Ritual:
The Adventures of Scarlet and Bradshaw, Volume 1
BY THEODORE ROSCOE

Champion of Lost Causes
BY MAX BRAND

The Complete Cabalistic Cases of Semi Dual,
the Occult Detector, Volume 2: 1912–13
BY J.U. GIESY AND JUNIUS B. SMITH

Doan and Carstairs: Their Complete Cases
BY NORBERT DAVIS

The King Who Came Back
BY FRED MacISAAC

The Radio Gun-Runners
BY RALPH MILNE FARLEY

The Scarlet Blade: The Rakehelly Adventures of
Cleve and d'Entreville, Volume 1
BY MURRAY R. MONTGOMERY

Sabotage
BY CLEVE F. ADAMS

South of Fifty-Three
BY JACK BECHDOLT

THE CITY OF STOLEN LIVES

THE ADVENTURES OF PETER THE BRAZEN, VOLUME 1

LORING BRENT

INTRODUCTION BY

WILL MURRAY

ALTUS PRESS
2016

EDITED AND DESIGNED BY
Matthew Moring

PUBLISHING HISTORY
"Introduction" appears here for the first time. Copyright © 2016 Will Murray. All rights reserved.
"Princess of Static" originally appeared in the October 5, 1918 issue of *Argosy* magazine (Vol. 100, No. 1). Copyright © 1918 by The Frank A. Munsey Company.
"The City of Stolen Lives" originally appeared in the October 19, 1918 issue of *Argosy* magazine (Vol. 100, No. 3). Copyright © 1918 by The Frank A. Munsey Company.
"The Bitter Fountain" originally appeared in the November 2, 1918 issue of *Argosy* magazine (Vol. 101, No. 1). Copyright © 1918 by The Frank A. Munsey Company.
"About the Author" originally appeared in the August 2, 1941 issue of *Argosy* magazine (Vol. 309, No. 5). Copyright © 1941 by The Frank A. Munsey Company. Copyright renewed © 1968 and assigned to Steeger Properties, LLC. All rights reserved.

THANKS TO
Gerd Pircher

ISBN
978-1-61827-232-4

Visit *altuspress.com* for more books like this.
Printed in the United States of America.

TABLE OF CONTENTS

WILL MURRAY

ONE OF DOC SAVAGE originator Lester Dent's favorite pulp magazines was *Argosy,* which he read faithfully every week during the years Dent was a telegraph operator, and well into his early pulp writing career. One of his favorite *Argosy* authors was George Frank Worts (1892–1967), who also wrote under the pen name of Loring Brent. As Brent, Worts penned the adventures of Peter the Brazen, a footloose American adventurer operating in the Orient. These had a marked influence on Dent's stories and especially upon his writing style. Not a few Doc Savage novels would owe their inspiration to Worts' numerous *Argosy* serials, which in later years included the exploits of lawyer-sleuth Gillian Hazeltine and vagabond South Seas sailor Singapore Sammy Shay.

Peter the Brazen first appeared in "A Princess of Static," in the October 5, 1918 issue. Like his creator, Peter Moore was a ship's radio operator. In his early exploits, Moore became embroiled with Oriental intrigue, famously battling a Chinese despot named the Gray Dragon. This was followed by a six-part serial, *The Golden Cat,* which takes place after Moore's service in World War I.

After riding roughshod over the wild, untamed country, Peter Moore was forbidden to return to China, where the brash young American "brass-pounder" had picked up his swashbuckling nickname of Peter the Brazen.

And so his Oriental career seemed over. No more was written of Peter for a decade—until Worts brought him back in *The Sapphire Smile* for *Argosy* February 8, 1930, whereupon Moore returns to China and becomes involved with a trouble-seeking girl named Susan O'Gilvie. (Evidently his relationship with Aileen Lorimer during the first sequence of stories had ended.) Thereupon begins an extended series of tales of Peter the Brazen in Asia, in which Moore crosses paths with a delightful group of menacing Oriental villains, such as Ung the Unspeakable, Zarlo the master magician, K'ang of the Green Circle tong, the Octopus of Hong Kong, and Peter the Brazen's recurring enemy, Mr. Lu, the supposedly-immortal Man with the Jade Brain, who was also known as the Blue Scorpion. Throughout these colorful exploits Peter is torn between his love of adventure and the trouble this unquenchable yen—and feisty fiancé Susan O'Gilvie—invariably rain down on his head.

Despite his other nickname of a Ren-Beh-Tung (Mandarin Chinese for the Brass Man or... Man of Bronze), Peter the Brazen is no Doc Savage. He is blond, blue-eyed, and deeply but not metallically tanned. Susan has him wrapped around her finger; he leaves her, they're reunited, then star-crossed lovers become engaged. But their relationship continued to roller coaster over the frantic course of the series, with unforeseen consequences. Peter the Brazen does eventually rise above the level of ordinary pulp adventurer. In the 1933 serial, *The Sapphire Death,* he undergoes exhaustive training to become a physical superman, augmented by Yogic indoctrination, for his final confrontation with the insidious Blue Scorpion. Here, he becomes known as the Man of Chromium. The resemblance to Doc Savage's training is minimal, and this tale was published after *Doc Savage Magazine* had begun. One wonders if this was a response to Doc Savage, whom Worts might have justifiably accused of poaching upon his preserves.

Worts revived Peter the Brazen due to the instigation of editor Archibald H. Bittner. Reportedly, it was he who sought to stem dwindling circulation by reviving well-remembered

recurring characters not seen in a
decade or more. This was too soon after
the stock market crash of October
1929 for the impact of the Great Depression to have triggered it. Pulp
magazines did not begin feeling its
circulation-crushing effects until 1931,
but evidently *Argosy,* with its weekly
freight of multiple serials, was losing
readers ahead of the impending circulation drought. Under his own name,
Worts had been writing the Gillian

*Loring Brent
(George F. Worts)*

Hazeltine stories for Munsey since 1926, and was an *Argosy*
semi-regular. His Dr. Dill stories were appearing in *Blue Book,*
and Worts' byline was all over slick magazines such as *Collier's.*

After supposedly absconding with Munsey funds and a secretary to boot, Bittner fled greater New York late in 1931, later
resurfacing as Wayne Rogers, author of numerous Weird
Menace and *Spider* stories for Popular Publications. *Railroad
Stories'* Freeman H. Hubbard assumed *Argosy* editorship early
in 1930, so Hubbard probably purchased some of the second
group of Peter the Brazen tales. Don Moore, soon to script the
"Flash Gordon" newspaper strip, succeeded both editors and
oversaw the rest. Worts appears to have stopped contributing
to the magazine around the time Jack Byrne took over Munsey
editorial responsibilities in the Spring of 1936.

Although his depictions of China were imaginative, Worts
was no armchair adventurer. During his telegrapher days, he
roamed the ramshackle ports of the exotic side of the Pacific
Ocean. After World War I ended, *Collier's* magazine sent Worts
to the Far East, where the former newspaper reporter covered
China and adjacent Asian nations.

Worts once explained that he took the pen name of Loring
Brent to conceal from his employer that he was writing on the
side. He was then editing *Motion Picture News,* a trade magazine. It is know known what significance, if any, the pseudonym

held for the author. "Loring Brent" first broke into *Argosy's* pages back in 1917, with a short story about a wolf, "By Mercy of Murg," so the writer had come a long way in a dozen or so years. Worts' first hardcover book collected Peter Moore's early novelettes titled *Peter the Brazen* in 1919, for which the author revised and altered the original story sequence.

As the decade turned, under his own name and that of Brent, Worts became a frequent contributor, often cover-featured. When "The Sapphire Smile" was first published, it rated a cover announcement, "Peter the Brazen Returns." No doubt longtime readers of that era kept asking for more of him. During this period the *Argosy* editorial staff was gearing up for its fiftieth anniversary in 1932. Showcasing popular pulp protagonists not seen in several years was part of the celebration strategy.

Between 1930–35, Peter the Brazen ranged the Orient in stories and serials that many aficionados to this day consider among the finest fiction ever to appear in a pulp magazine. This second, unlike the first, verged on fantastic fiction. The *Argosy* editors sometimes used a trick where they took a serial and, rather than run it in five or six parts, broke it down into a shorter serial and ran the remaining segment as a short story or two-part novelette leading into, or out of, the main event. Worts' 1931 short, "Cave of the Blue Scorpion," seems to be one of those. It served as a stand-alone preface to the five-part serial, *Sting of the Blue Scorpion.*

Peter the Brazen bowed out in the 1935 short story, "Over the Dragon Wall," and George F. Worts' bylines vanished forever from the pages of *Argosy* the following year. He moved on and up to the slick magazines, bought a farm in Nevada, later fled to his dream life in Honolulu, served again as a correspondent for *Collier's* during World War II, relocated to Arizona, where he edited *Tucson* magazine, and lived three decades longer than most of his stories' creation, never dreaming that his pulp fiction would resurface in print for successive generations of readers who yearned for the days of colorful between-the-world-wars adventure he chronicled so well.

With this volume, Altus Press kicks off its ambitious program of reprinting the entire Peter the Brazen saga—many installments of which have not seen publication in their original form—or any form—since their original appearances in the pages of the legendary *Argosy*....

I

PRINCESS OF STATIC

CHAPTER I

AN OPERATOR OF SORTS

WHEN PETER MOORE entered the static-room, picked his way swiftly and unnoticingly across the littered floor, and jerked open the frosted-glass door of the superintendent's office, the assembled operators gazed after him with mixed glances of bewilderment and alarm. No one ever entered the chief's office in that fashion. One waited until called upon.

But Moore had privileges. Having "pounded brass" for five useful and efficient years on the worst and best of the ships which minimize the length and breadth of the Pacific Ocean, he could do pretty much as he pleased.

There was a general quieting down of coastwise gossip among the less fortunate members of Moore's profession when the door swung to behind his back.

If human beings can prick up their ears, then that phenomenon actually occurred to the alert organs of those listening operators.

"But great guns, man, I need you!" boomed the authoritative voice of the chief.

Followed then the low hum of the other man's voice as he explained himself.

"Makes no difference," shouted the chief. "Need you. Can't get along right now without you. Short handed. Gotta stay."

When irritated the superintendent always abbreviated his remarks quite as if they were radiograms to be transmitted at dollar-a-word rates.

Then the truth dawned with a dismaying flash, like a tropical sunrise, upon those listeners in the static-room. Moore was resigning! It seemed incredible.

A more daring head pressed its anxious ear tightly against the frosted glass. This was a small, excitable young man, long in the service, but continuing, despite his lengthy record, on one of the intermediate Panama liners. A good operator, but his arm broke, as the saying goes, whenever faced by emergency. He distinctly heard Moore state: "Too much China. God, man—I'll be smuggling opium next! It gets you, you know."

"Rubbish!" snorted the chief.

The Panama Line man waved a pale hand behind him for silence, screwing his features into an expression of concern.

"Want a shore station?"

"No, thank you. But I think I'll rest up and then look around. I've saved quite a bit of money."

"You'll be back. Mark my word. The sea and the wireless house is a winning combination. New ports—new faces—the storms—"

"I've seen them all."

"Bah! You've only begun. When does the *Vandalia* clear for China again?"

"Thursday night. But—"

"I'll hold your berth open till Thursday noon. Intended to break in a new second operator with you. Funny chap. Glass eye! 'Member—Thursday noon."

The frosted-glass door drew back violently. The Panama Line man floundered at the feet of Moore. His white face became pink. The static-room roared with laughter. Picking himself up, the excitable youth retreated to a chair and examined a frayed magazine on the table with pronounced interest.

Moore had been a prisoner in the Pacific coast wireless game. His first assignment was a fishing schooner which ran as far north sometimes as the Aleutian Islands, and he had immediately gained official recognition by sticking to his instruments for sixty-eight hours—recorded by fifteen minute intervals in the log—when the whaler *Walrus* struck a submerged pinnacle rock in the Island Passage and flashed the old C.Q.D. signal for help.

It was brought out in the testimony that the distance at which Moore had picked up the distress signal of the *Walrus* far exceeded the normal working range of either apparatus. When pressed, Moore admitted the possession of a pair of abnormally keen ears. Afterward, it was proved for the benefit of doubters that Moore could "read" a message in the receivers when the ordinary operator could detect only an indistinct, scratching sound.

At that time the captains of ships in the Central American run were complaining of the inability of their operators to transmit and receive important images. This difficulty, the wireless company explained, was due to the intense heat of the tropics, which interfered with the working of the apparatus.

When Moore was placed under command of the skipper who had grumbled the most, complaints ceased. On his very first trip he smashed every record of the southern Pacific. When the *San Felipe* was abreast of Acajutla, Salvador, in one of the dead zones, Moore worked, without difficulty, across the mountains and intervening gulf to Key West, Florida.

Beginning his second year in the company's uniform, Moore was recognized as material far too valuable to waste on the Central American run; and he was stationed on the *Sierra* known in wireless circles as a supervising ship.

This meant that the tremendous power of her apparatus could project out a long electric arm over any part of the eastern Pacific at any point between San Francisco and Honolulu, reprimanding the sluggards who neglected answering calls from other ship or shore stations.

For example, if the operator on an oil-tanker or a coastline ship should neglect his apparatus, it was Moore's duty to din the offender with mighty signals until an answer was forthcoming.

It was whispered that Moore grew tired of the nagging to which his position of supervisor gave him privilege, for he shortly made application for a berth in the Chinese run.

Now, every operator in the Pacific service cherishes the hope that his efforts will some day be crowned by a Chinese run, and there are always innumerable applications on file for those berths. But the superintendent gave Moore his selection without any hesitation, and Moore selected the *Vandalia*, perhaps the most desirable of the transpacific fleet because she remained away from San Francisco the longest.

That the supersensitiveness of his ears was not waning was soon proved by his receipt of a non-relayed message, afterward verified, from the shore station in Seattle, when the *Vandalia* lay at anchor in Hong Kong. That was a record which has never been broken. It was understood that Marconi himself wrote Moore a letter of compliment. But Moore showed that letter to no one. That was his nature.

When the rumor reached the *Vandalia*, couched majestically at her pier, that Moore had handed in his resignation, Captain Jones, after bluntly expressing his disappointment, advanced the argument to the chief engineer that Sparks had "taken the East too much to heart." Whereupon the chief opined that, in his canny estimation, the fangs of China had taken hold.

"He will be back sailing time," said the chief, who had been endeavoring to retire from active duty in that lire for eleven years.

But Moore did not come back to the *Vandalia* for that reason at all.

CHAPTER II

FROM A CHINATOWN WINDOW

COMMUNICATION BETWEEN CERTAIN individuals in China and their relatives and friends in Chinatown must, for political reasons, be conducted in a secret way. In Shanghai, Moore had made the acquaintance, under somewhat mysterious auspices, of Ching Gow Ong, an important figure in the silk traffic.

Moore, so it was said by those who were in a position to know, had once performed a favor for Ching Gow Ong, of which no one seemed to know the exact nature. What was of equal importance, perhaps, was that Ching Gow Ong, who could tabulate his wealth only on the large counting-board, would have willingly given Moore any gift within his power had Moore been so inclined.

But it appears that Moore was not a seeker after wealth, thereby giving some real basis to the common belief that he possessed that rare thing—a virginal spirit of adventure. He cemented this queer friendship by conveying messages, indited in Chinese script, which he could not read, between Ching Gow Ong and his brother, Lo Ong, officially dead, who conducted a vile-smelling haunt in the bowels of Chinatown.

Moore picked his way leisurely through the narrowing alleys, proceeded through a maze of blank walls, down a damp stone stairway, and rapped upon a black iron door. It opened instantly, and a long, clawlike hand reached forth, accepted the yellow envelope from Moore's hand, and slowly, silently withdrew, the door closing as quickly and as quietly as it had opened.

No words were spoken. His errand done, Moore retraced his steps to the wider and brighter lanes which comprised the Chinatown known to tourists.

He walked slowly, with his head inclined a little to one side, which was a habit he had acquired from the eternal listening into the hard rubber receivers. He had proceeded in this fashion a number of steps up one of the narrow, sloping sidewalks when he felt, rather than perceived, a pair of eyes fastened upon his from a second-story window.

They were the aloe eyes of a young Chinese woman, but he sensed immediately that she was not of the river type. Her fine black hair was arranged in a gorgeous coiffure. Gold ornaments drooped from her ears, and her complexion was liberally sanded with rice powder. Her painted lips wore an expression of malignity, as if he had suddenly surprised her in the commission of a covert deed.

In the obliquity of the eyes lurked a solemn warning. Then he became aware that she seemed to be struggling, as if she were impeding the movements of some one behind her.

It is safe to say that in none of his tramps through the winding alleys of Canton, of Peking, of Shanghai, had Moore encountered a Chinese woman of her type. There was a sharp vividness to her features which meant the inbreeding of high cast. She was unusual—startling! She looked into the street furtively, held up a heavily jeweled hand—an imperial order for him to stop—and withdrew. He lounged into the doorway of an ivory shop and waited.

It was quiet in Chinatown, for the time was noon and the section was pursuing its midday habit of calm. The padding figures were becoming a trifle dim, owing to a cold, pale fog that was coming up from the bay. In a moment the woman reappeared, examined the street again with hostile eyes, held up a square of rice paper with a peremptory gesture, and slowly folded it.

Moore nodded slightly and smiled. It was a habit with him— that smile. The sensitiveness of his nervous system found a quick outlet, when he was nervous or excited, by a smile which the keen student would have detected as lacking ingenuousness.

He proceeded to the shop directly underneath her window, observing it to be Ah Sih King's gold shop. The window was rich in glittering splendors from the Orient. He picked up from the sidewalk a crumpled ball of red paper and stowed it away in his coat pocket.

To a close observer the indifference with which Moore turned and pretended to study the gold ornaments in Ah Sih King's window might have seemed a trifle too obvious, and the smile on his lips, one might go on to say, was uncalled for.

As he waited, a soft thud sounded at his feet, coincident with a flash of black and white across his shoulder. He covered the object with one foot as the oily, leering face of Ah Sih King appeared in the doorway. The blanched face surmounted a costly mandarin robe, righteously worn, a gorgeous blue raiment with traceries of fine gold and exquisite gems. At this moment he seemed to exhale an air of faint suspicion.

"Gentleman!" accosted the thin, curled lips in a tone that was well nigh personal.

"Buy nothing," said Moore curtly.

"You see my—my see you," observed Ah Sih King, reverting, as he deemed fitting, to pidgin.

Moore turned his back impolitely, whereupon Ah Sih King did likewise. When he turned again, sharply, the oily smile was vanished, a look of concern having crept into his sly, old face, and the slightly bent shoulders of the much slier young man were several strides distant.

A faint hiss, as of warning, issued from the carmine lips of the Chinese woman, whose shrewd eyes, semi-lidded, peered over the window-ledge. Then the window closed noiselessly, and Chinatown, having paid not the slightest heed to the incident, pattered about its multifarious businesses, none the wiser.

There was an indefinable something in this incident which caused creases to appear across Moore's brow. Why had two notes been thrown? The puzzle sifted down to this possibility: Some one behind the Chinese woman had thrown a ball of red paper, a note, into the street. In all probability it contained a plea for help.

That seemed plausible in view of the struggles of the malignant-eyed Chinese woman to keep some one behind her out of sight.

Then she had beckoned him to wait, had written a second note, perhaps to warn him away. He glanced furtively at the second note, saw that it was written in Chinese, and thereupon decided to call upon Lo Ong for a translation in return for many favors.

Chinatown now was slowly vanishing from perspective, swallowed by the gray blanket of fog which rolled in from the Pacific through the mouth of the harbor. Retracing his steps through the mist, Moore descended the narrow stone stairway and tapped on the oblong of iron with his heavy seal ring. A shutter clinked, sharp eyes scrutinized him, and he heard the bolt slide back, uneasily, hesitatingly. Moore himself opened the door and entered, restoring the bolt to its place.

The room was low, deep and dark under the guttering light of a single dong, which hung from the ceiling at the end of a roped up cluster of fine brass chains. The rich, stupefying odor of opium tainted the heavy air. The orange flame, motionless, as if it were carved from solid metal, showed the room to be bare except for a few grass mats scattered about in the irregular round shadow under it.

To one of these mats Lo Ong, gaunt, curious, even hostile, retreated, squatting with his delicately thin hands folded over his abdomen. A look of recognition disturbed only for the instant the placidity of the ocher features.

"No come buy?" he intoned, as if Peter Moore had never passed under that piercing gaze before.

"My never come buy," said Moore curtly. "Wanchee you come help, savvy."

"Mebbe can do," asserted Lo Ong, in the voice and manner of one who is incessantly pursued by favor-seekers. As if it were detached from his body and governed by some extraneous mechanism, Lo Ong's draped arm indicated a mat. Moore slipped down in the familiar cross-legged attitude, lighted a cigarette and blew the smoke at the belly on the dong.

"You wanchee cumshaw?—" demanded the Chinese, uneasily.

Moore disdained to reply, extracted the two lumps of paper, slid one under his knee and unfolded the other, while Lo Ong looked unfavorably beyond him at the floor. Three rows of Chinese markings were scrawled down it. Lo Ong's body commenced to sway back and forth in impatient rhythm.

"Lo Ong," stated Moore, "my wanchee you keep mouth shut—all atime shut—you savvy?"

"Can do," murmured Lo Ong indifferently. He reached for the rice paper, lifting it tenderly in long, clawing fingers, and held it to the flame. He seemed not to believe what he read, for he twisted the paper over, looked at it upside down, then sat down again, his lean fingers convulsing.

"No can do," he muttered, replacing the paper on Moore's knee. "My no savvy."

The white forefinger of the wireless operator pointed unwaveringly at the flattened nose. "Read that," he ordered.

Lo Ong glanced the other way, as if the subject had ceased to interest him and tapped the floor with his knuckles. "Wanchee money—cumshaw?"

"Lo Ong," declared Moore, losing his patience; "you b'long dead. Now savvy?"

"Mebbe can do," said Lo Ong faintly.

Moore ran his finger down the first row of fresh markings.

"O-o-ey," commented Lo Ong, shifting uneasily. " 'My see you all atime, long ago on ship.' Savvy?"

"What's next?"

" 'You no see my. My see you all atime.' " The long, sloping shoulders seemed to jerk. " 'Keep away.' Savvy?"

"It says that?"

"Take look see," invited Lo Ong, poking his claw nervously down the column. " 'Keep away. Keep away.' One—two times. Savvy?"

Moore nodded thoughtfully.

The Chinese, officially dead, replaced the sheet gingerly on his knees, as if it were an instrument of wickedness. His bony fingers twitched a moment.

"High lady," he added nervously; "velly high lady. You stay away. Hah?"

"Wait a minute." Moore extracted the other paper ball, unfolding it near the orange flame. The inner surface was red, the earthly red of porphyry, and cracked and scarred by the crumpling. Nearly obliterated by the lacework of wrinkles and scratches was an agonized scrawl, evidently scarred into the glazed surface by a knife point. The upper part was unintelligible. On the lower surface he made out with difficulty the single word, *Vandalia.* He carried it to the door, slid back the shutter and let the dim, gray light filter upon it. The other words were too mutilated to be read.

"Hi!"

He returned to Lo Ong's jacketed side. The bony finger was circling excitedly about a smear of black in the lower corner of the rice paper.

"What's this?"

"Len Yang. Len *Yang!* Savvy?"

"O-ho! And who is Len Yang?"

Lo Ong shook his head in agitation.

"Len Yang—city. Savvy? Shanghai—Len Yang—fort' day."

"Fourteen days from Shanghai to Len Yang?"

"No. No! *No!* Fort'."

"Forty?"

"O-o-ey." The flattened nose bobbed up and down. "Keep away—ai?"

"Maskee," replied Moore, meaning, broadly speaking, none of your business.

Lo Ong unbolted the door, to hint that the interview was concluded. "You keep away—ai?" he repeated anxiously. Moore grinned in his peculiarly ingenuous way, swung open the black door, and a long, gray arm of the fog groped its way past Lo Ong's tense, fulvid countenance.

CHAPTER III

THE TARDY PASSENGER

THE JUNIOR OPERATOR toyed with the heavy transmitting key while Moore, who knew the behavior of his apparatus as he would know the caprices of au old friend, adjusted helix plugs, started the motor generator, and satisfied the steel-eyed radio inspector that his wave decrement was exactly what it ought to be.

Then the inspector grunted suspiciously and wanted to know if the auxiliary batteries were properly charged. With a faint smile, Moore hooked up the auxiliary apparatus, tapped the key, and a crinkly blue spark snapped between the brass points above the fat rubber coil.

"I reckon she'll do," observed the inspector. "Aerial don't leak, does it?"

"No," said Moore.

"Ground connection ain't shook loose, has it?"

"No," said Moore.

The government man took a final look at the glittering instruments, and withdrew. Wherewith the junior operator swung half around in the swivel-chair and exposed to Moore an expression of mild imploration. Two gray lids over cavernous sockets lifted and lowered upon shining black eyes, one of which seemed to lack focus. Moore recalled then that the chief had said something about a second operator having only one eye, the other being glass.

"This is your first trip?"

The sallow face was inclined slowly and the pallid lips moved dryly.

"I just came from the school. I'm pretty green. You see—"

"I see. We'd better let me take the first trick. I'll sit in till midnight. After that there's very little doing. You may have to relay a position report or so. Be sure and don't work on navy time. We have the odd half-hour, you know."

"Yes; they told us that at the school."

"The only other important matter is the log. Sign your initials at the top of each page, and keep a fifteen-minute record. Write down the initials of every station you hear, no matter how far away they are. The chief will watch you closely for long distance. The farther you work, the better he'll like it. How's the air? Have you listened in?"

"Do you mean—static?"

Moore grunted.

"I heard a little. Seemed pretty far away, though. Weather man said an electric storm would break around Eureka. Perhaps that's it."

Moore adjusted the nickeled straps about his head and pressed the rubber disks tight to his ears. He tilted his head slightly. A distant but faint rasping, as of countless needlepoints grating on glass, occurred in the head phones. This was caused by charges of electricity in the air, known to wireless men as "static." Percolating through the scratching was a clear, bell-like note. The San Pedro station was having something to say to a destroyer off the coast.

With delicate fingers Moore raised the tuning-knob a few points. The junior operator, hands clutched behind him, stared with the fearful adoration of an apprentice watching his master. He seemed to be making a mental notation of every move that Moore made, for future reference.

Moore deposited the phones on the scarred mahogany ledge, just then the telephone communicating with the pilothouse jangled. A voice, apparently unused to telephones, because of the roar of it, boomed into the wireless house.

"Everything O.K., Sparks?" They were the Lancashire accents of Captain Jones.

"All O.K. here, sir."

"Other operator on hand?"

"Yes, sir."

"Is he a mutt, like the last one?"

"No, captain." Moore cast a sidelong look at the junior operator, who was anxiously clutching the helix strap with both hands. "Looks to me like a good man."

A pause followed. Then:

"We're casting off in five minutes. Say, Sparks—"

"Yes, sir."

"Drop in for a smoke when you get time." A snap and a pop occurred in Moore's receiver as the other was closed.

The junior operator regarded him dizzily.

"Do you—*smoke*—with the *captain?*" he managed to ask.

"Oh, we're pretty good friends. By the way, what's your name?"

"Andrew Rover Dale. Want to see my license?" The junior operator unfolded, from a long official envelope, an engrossed document, signed by the Secretary of Commerce. "Ah—do you mind if I ask a few questions? You see, I'm kind of green."

"Go ahead!" said Moore.

"Where do I eat? With the crew? I hear that lots of these ships make you eat with the crew."

"No. In the main dining-saloon. The purser will take care of you. See him at six thirty."

A deep, monstrous shudder, arising to a clamor, half roar, half shriek, issued from the boilers of the *Vandalia*.

"It's rather interesting to watch us pull out," said Moore when the noise had ceased. "But be careful. There's no rail around this deck."

To the junior operator there was nothing stale in leaving port. Besides, he hoped that his sister would be down on the pier to wave him good-by.

Moore had plenty to do until it was time for sending in his report to the San Francisco station. The motor commutator needed sandpapering, and the high-power spark-gap was pretty badly worn down. Then, too, the battery cells should be refilled. The vigilant radio inspector had overlooked that detail.

He was on his hands and knees with a pad of sandpaper between his fingers when the tremulous voice of the junior operator sounded in the doorway.

"Mr. Moore, come on out. There's some excitement on the dock."

Moore followed the narrow shoulders to the starboard side and looked down. The *Vandalia* was warping out from the pierhead with a sobbing tug at her stern. He noted that the head-lines were still fast. A straggling line of passengers' friends, wives, husbands, and sweethearts was moving slowly toward the end of the pier, for a final parting wave.

Something seemed to be wrong at the shore end of the gangplank, for, despite the fact that the *Vandalia* was swinging out, the plank was still up. In the midst of an excited crowd a taxicab purred and smoked. There was a general parting in the crowd as the door was flung open. Two figures emerged, were lost from sight, and reappeared at the foot of the plank. An incoherent something was roared from the bridge.

One of the figures appeared to be struggling, clutching at the rail. For an instant she seemed to glance in his direction. But her face could hardly be seen, for it was shrouded by a heavy gray veil. A gray hood covered her hair, and a long cloak reached to her shoe-tops.

Patiently urging her was a Chinese woman in silk jacket, trousers, and jeweled slippers. A customs officer tried to break through the mob, but somehow was held back. The gray-hooded figure suddenly seemed to become limp, and the Chinese woman half lifted, half pushed her the remaining distance to the promenade deck.

Moore was then conscious of a staring, lifeless eye fixed upon his.

"What do you make of it, Mr. Moore?" the junior operator wanted to know.

"Of that?" said Moore. "Nothing—nothing at all. By the way, I neglected to tell you that the captain has issued strict orders that no sub-officers use the starboard decks. Always, when you're going forward or aft, walk on the port side."

CHAPTER IV

STATEROOM NUMBER FORTY-FOUR

WHEN MOORE TURNED over the log-book and the wireless house to Dale, the second operator, a few minutes before midnight, he knew what to expect. A green operator's first experience with commercial apparatus, when he is given time to think over the position he is placed in, is nerve racking, ghastly.

Perhaps Dale had had his long, white fingers on the rubber knob of a high-power key during his training at the wireless school. Perhaps not. At all events he had never previously felt the weight of responsibility which sitting behind a high-power commercial machine imposes upon a man.

Dale knew that Pacific operators were uncannily swift, and he was aware, from listening to the air on former occasions, that they quickly became irritable when a "ham" could not keep abreast of their signals. And Dale frankly admitted that he was scared. His fingers trembled as he adjusted the nickeled band about his head.

"Everything's cleared up," said Moore from the doorway. "The static is worse, and KPH may want you to relay a message or two to Honolulu. If you have trouble, let me know."

"Yes, yes," replied Dale, looking over his shoulder nervously. "I will. Thanks." And Moore knew that he was praying for strength, fortitude.

Moore climbed down the iron ladder, which jutted through a hole in the afterdeck's canvas covering, and went below to his stateroom. But he did not undress, for he was reasonably sure that disrobing for bed, with that worried youth at the key, would be sheer futility. He laid down on the lower bunk—the upper was Dale's—and snapped off the light at the press button near his head. He did not intend to go asleep.

The light in the corridor projected an odd, truncated pattern through the opened ventilator above the door upon the white enameled ceiling of the stateroom. The twin reciprocating engines throbbed and shook the elastic fabric of the *Vandalia* as she strode through the quiet, starlit night. There was an odor of fresh paint in the vibrant air, and the room smelled close because of it. Moore's thoughts marched on to more distant things.

Who, he asked himself, and of what nature was the individual who had scratched the hurried message on the glazed red paper? And why, he went on to demand, had the Chinese woman gone to such pains to warn him away? Were they on this ship now? And where? What relation did they have, if any, to the strange pantomime he had glimpsed on, the gangplank that afternoon, when the *Vandalia* was warping out from the pierhead? Where had the two figures gone? And was the silk-jacketed-and-trousered woman the same that tossed the rice paper at his feet in front of Ah Sih King's gold shop?

He rehearsed the incidents, trying to arrive at some logical conclusion. But the solution evaded him. The whole affair had the involved and twisted aspects of a riddle that baffled decision. The regular monotone of the engines dulled the edge of his analysis. He was endeavoring to puzzle out Lo Ong's actual or fancied fear when sleep came.

The patient throb of the woodwork came back to his senses leisurely, reluctantly, and his awakening was not unlike an emergence from hypnosis. He felt the tightening influence of some ominous presence, the weight of a prescient eye.

Contracting his lids lightly, be stimulated sleep. Light from the partly opened doorway streamed redly upon his closed lids. Nervous fingers fumbled for the pressbutton, and a snap followed as the fingers discovered it. The redness increased to blood-orange. Some one paced the length of the stateroom, returned and hovered above him. For some unknown reason, he felt impelled to laugh, but he inhibited the impulse. Some one coughed feebly.

"Mr. Moore, I-I'm sorry but—but—"

Moore's eyes opened drowsily, and hc appeared to be endeavoring to readjust himself.

"Oh, Dale? What's wrong?" His legs slid over the cedar weather-board, and he sat up, rubbing his eyes.

"Static's much worse, Mr. Moore. Frisco's sent me the same message three times now. It's for Honolulu. He says he won't repeat it again." The pale Ups trembled in misery. "And there seems to be a funny sort of static in the receivers. The dynamos in the engine-room may cause it."

"That's funny," frowned Moore, slipping on his blue coat. "There's never been any induction on board as far back as I can remember. Does it hum—or what?"

"No, it grates, like static. Sounds like static, and yet it doesn't. Kind of a hoarse rumble, like a broken-down spark-coil."

Two even rows of white teeth drew in the trembling lip and clung to it.

"I'll take a look," said Moore. "What did KPH tell you when you asked him to repeat the last time?"

"He said—he said: 'Go to hell.'"

Moore led the way through the empty, narrow corridors, through the darkened smoking-room, out upon the after-deck, and up the narrow iron ladder to the wireless house on the boat-deck. The *Vandalia* was entering a zone of pale, thin mist, which created circular, misty auras about the deck-lights. The tarpaulined donkey-engine beneath the after-cargo booms rattled as the *Vandalia's* stern sank into a hollow, and the beat of the engines seemed to become muffled and deeper. A speck of white froth glinted on the black surface and vanished astern.

The wireless house seemed warm and cozy in the glare of its green and white lights. An odor of cheap cigarette-smoke puffed out as he opened the door.

Moore slipped the hard rubber-disks over his ear, and tapped the slider of the tuner. Static was bad to-night, trickling, exploding and hissing in the receivers. He glanced up at Dale, who was leaning over him anxiously.

"Static. No induction," he said quietly.

The electric lights sank under the strain of the heavy motor, as Moore slid up the starting handle. The white-hot spark exploded in a train of brisk dots and dashes. Moore snapped up the aerial switch and listened.

KPH—the San Francisco station rang clear and loud through the spatter of the electric storm. Moore flashed back his O.K., tuned for the Kahuka Head station at Honolulu, and re-transmitted the message. He swivelled about the awed Dale with a comforting grin.

"The first time, you're scared; after that it comes easy."

"For you," amended Dale hastily. "But me? Gosh! I'm a ham!"

Moore left him to the mercies of the static and the irritableness of KPH. As he descended the iron ladder to the promenade-deck, he thought he saw some one moving underneath him. The figure, whoever, whatever it was, slid around the white wall and vanished as his foot felt the deck. He hastened to follow.

As he stepped into the light a long, low, sibilant whisper reached him. At the cross corridor doorway he was just in time to see the flicker of a vanishing gray garment and a sandaled foot on a naked ankle flash over the vestibule wave-check. He shook open the door and followed.

A vertical stripe of yellow light cleaved the dark of the long, narrow corridor as a door was quietly shut. He heard the faint, distant click of a door-latch. Counting the entrances to that one, and sure that he had made no mistake, he rapped. The near-by clank of the engine-room well was the reply. He tried the handle. It was immovable. Striking a match he mentally annotated the number. It was stateroom forty-four.

Whoever the retreating figure was, he argued, had run away at sight of him; therefore was subject to suspicion. Somehow the unaccountable flight linked itself up in his mind to the momentary confusion on the pierhead and the tossing of the two notes in Chinatown.

For this reason, as he descended the stairway to the purser's office, he made up his mind to keep his eyes open and his mouth shut.

Light rippled through the wrinkled green, round window, as Moore had hoped. He tapped lightly, and a cloaked voice bade him to enter.

Hazard the purser, dwarfed, wizen, perpetually stoop-shoul-dered, looked up from a clump of cargo reports and blinked through convex, thick, steel spectacles at his interrupter. His eyes were red and dim with the gray-blue, uncertain definition which always reminded Moore of oysters. Stiff, white hair grew sparsely above a wrinkled, compact brow. The wireless man could carry the unpleasant simile a step further. Hazard had been purser of the *Vandalia* for thirteen years, and Moore knew that the man possessed the linguistic habits of the oyster as well.

"Well, well!" observed Hazard in the crisp, brittle accents of senility; "so you're back again, eh? Well, well, well." There was no emphasis laid on the words. They were all struck from the same piece of case-hardened metal.

"Here I am!" agreed Moore with mild enthusiasm. "The bad penny returns!"

"Ha, ha! The bad penny returns!" The exclamation died in a futile cough. "What are you prowlin' around ship this time o' night for, eh? After three bells, Sparks. Time for respectable people to be fast asleep. Or, are you leavin' the radio unwatched?"

"I'm looking for information." Moore drew himself by stiffened arms upon the purser's single bunk.

"Lookin' for information?" The thin voice suffered the attrition of surprise, the quavering inquiry of decrepitude. "Funny place to be lookin' for that commodity. What's on your mind? Eh?"

"Chinamen!"

Hazard tilted the rusted spectacles to his forehead, and the motionless gray orbs seemed to glint with a half-dead light. "Chinamen? What Chinamen?" The spectacles slid back into place.

"One, a woman, came aboard as we were pulling out this afternoon. Who is she? Where is she? Where's she from? Where's she going? Who's with her? That's what I want to clear up."

"Is *that* all?" squeaked Hazard. His wrinkled, dried lips seemed to be struggling as if with a curious indecision. A veiled, a thinly veiled conflict of thoughts or emotions apparently was taking place behind that ancient gray mask. "What—what for?" was the final outcome in a hesitant half whisper.

"My private information," smiled Moore. "Just curious, that's, all. Didn't mean to pry open any dark secrets." He made as if to go.

"Sparks! Don't be in a hurry. I'm not *so* busy."

"Well?"

"What's botherin' you? Maybe I could straighten you out."

Through his crafty expression of frankness, of willingness to be of help, indeed, of eagerness to confide, Moore saw plainly the motif of selfish curiosity.

"Who are the occupants of stateroom forty-four?" he retaliated.

Again the expression shifted like water smitten by an evil wind.

"Forty-four!" The words were mild explosions.

"Yes, Mr. Hazard. Forty-four."

A long cardboard sheet with blue and red lines was extracted from a noiselessly opened drawer.

"The passenger-list. We shall see." Hazard's red, shiny forefinger clawed down the column of names, halting at the numeral forty-four. The space was blank. "You see."

"Empty?"

"Empty." A restrained note of triumph was unquestionably evident in the purser's cracked voice.

"I'll bother you with just one more question. What is Len Yang?"

A look of doubt, of incredulity bordering upon feeble indignation, settled upon the serrated countenance. But Hazard only shook his head as if he did not comprehend.

Moore slipped down from the bunk. "Then I guess I'll take a turn on deck, if the fog's lifted, and roll in. G'night, purser."

Hazard started to say something, evidently thought better of it, and retrieved his pen. As he dipped the fine point into the red ink by mistake he flung another quizzical frown over his shoulder. The wireless man lingered on the threshold, swinging the door tentatively.

"G'night, Sparks."

CHAPTER V

OUT OF NOWHERE

THE *VANDALIA* WAS wallowing majestically through long, dead black swells. The fog zone had been kicked astern minutes ago. Deck lights, excepting those that peered over vestibule ways, were extinguished. Moore poked his way up forward to the solitary lookout in the peak and glanced overside.

Broad, phosphorescent sworls broke smoothly with a rending, rushing gurgle over the steep cutwater.

His eyes darted hither and thither over the void as his mind struggled to straighten out this latest kink.

The mystery now possessed five intangible, perplexing aspects. Five glittering promises like the facets of a partly exposed, monstrous gem. The elusive relationships, if relation actually existed, served only to tantalize him.

What facts of importance he might have discovered from Hazard were overshadowed in significance by the purser's suspicious attitude. Hazard knew who were the tenants of stateroom forty-four, and Hazard, for some reason, did not choose to divulge. This made matters more interesting, even if slightly more complicated.

He was now reasonably sure of several things, without really having definite grounds for being sure. The malignant-eyed Chinese woman and whoever she had successfully concealed behind her in the loft above Ah Sih King's were now aboard the *Vandalia*. He was quite positive that he had recognized her in the woman who had come aboard in company with the gray-cloaked figure at the last minute before sailing-time.

Therefore, he argued, it must have been the woman in the gray cloak who had thrown the red note, advising him that she would sail on the *Vandalia*. Against her will? Perhaps. The second note, warning him away, had followed.

The Chinese woman, it began to appear, was taking the woman in the gray cloak some place against her will. Where? To that distant, vague place called Len Yang? Possibly. He could not be sure.

It seemed obvious, in view of Hazard's agitation, that he was sponsoring the Chinese woman's cause. That had an unpleasant ring.

This, Moore decided, could easily prove to be a faulty line of reasoning. But he could test it quite as easily by breaking into stateroom forty-four. Furthermore, if the woman in the gray cloak had really asked for help in that scarred red note, she would ask again. In all probability she had seen him before she dropped the note; so that she would easily recognize him again.

He recalled the scene on the pierhead, and it occurred to him in a vague way that the eyes behind the gray veil, before she was whisked up to the deck and from his sight, had fastened upon him for a long breath. Had she recognized him then? That maddening "perhaps" seemed to be the only logical answer. If she were confined by force, what methods could she employ to signal to him? The only solution to this perplexing possibility appeared to be an occult one; and Moore was a gross disbeliever in all things occult.

"Four bells, all well!" bawled the lookout as four clanging strokes rang out from abaft the wheel-house.

And Hazard had proved that stateroom forty-four was unoccupied.

Moore became conscious that he was suddenly wide awake, suspicious. Perhaps the purser was lying! Had Hazard proved it? He would borrow a master key in the morning, perhaps from the chief engineer, and make sure.

With the feeling that he was on the verge of discovering, something which did not exist, he prepared to turn in.

Hardly was he undressed when the lock grated, the door lurched open, and the pale visage of Dale teetered at his shoulder. An attempt at grinning ended in a hissing sob of in-taken breath. The limp frame flung itself in the bunk beside Moore, and Dale's white, perspiring face was buried in palsied hands.

"Feel the motion?" Moore pulled down one of the hands, gently uncovering the expressionless eye.

"I wish I was dead!"

"Want me to finish your trick?"

Dale's face disappeared in the pillow. A moment he was stark. His head partly revolved, profiling a yellow, pointed nose against the white of the linen.

"That awful staticky sound's been going again. And the Rover's calling us." He groaned miserably, "I couldn't answer either of them. I was lying on the carpet!"

"Get some sleep," advised Moore. "When you feel better come on up and relieve me. If I were you I wouldn't smoke cigarettes when you think it's rough."

"I won't smoke another cigarette as long as I live!"

Moore slipped into his uniform, draped an oil-skin coat about his slender shoulders, and made his way up to the wireless house. The receivers were lying on the floor.

He listened in. The ether was soundless. Sensitizing the detector, he slid up the tuning handle for high waves. A little static, far removed, trickled in. Then a faint, musical wailing like a violin's E-string pierced this. The violin was the government station at Arlington, Virginia, transmitting a storm warning to ships in the South Atlantic. For five minutes the wailing persisted. Sliding the tuning handle downward, Moore listened for commercial wave-lengths.

A harsh grinding, unmusical as emery upon hollow bronze, rasped stutteringly in the head phones. Were these the sounds that had frightened Dale? Laboriously, falteringly, the grating was cleaved into clumsy dots and clashes of the Continental code, under the quaking fingers of some obviously frightened and inexperienced operator. For a time the raspings spelled nothing intelligible. The unknown sender evidently was repeating the same word again and again. It held four letters. Once they formed, *H-L-J-X*. Another time, *S-E-L-J*. And another, *L-P-H-E*.

The painstaking intent, as the operator's acute ears recognized, was identical to each instance. Frequently the word was incoherent altogether, the signals meaning nothing.

Suddenly Moore jerked up his head. Out of the jumble stood the word, as an unseen ship will often stand not nakedly in a fog rift. Over and over, badly spaced, the infernal rasp was spelling *H-E-L-P*.

He waited for the signature of this frantic operator. But none occurred. Following a final letter "p" the signals ceased.

For a minute or two, while Moore nervously pondered this wretched plea, the air was silent. Then another station called him. A loud, droning purr filled the receivers. Moore gave the "k" signal. The briskly clipped, ethereal voice of the transport Rover droned:

"I can't raise KPH. Will you handle a M-S-G for me?"

"Sure!" roared the *Vandalia's* stridulent spark. "But wait a minute. Have you heard a broken down auxiliary asking for help? He's been jamming me for fifteen minutes. Seems to be very close. K."

"Nix," replied the Rover breezily. "Can't be at all close or I would hear him too. I can see your lights from my window. You're off our port quarter. Here's the—S-G."

Moore accepted the message, re-transmitted it without difficulty to the alert KPH operator, then called the wheelhouse on the telephone. Quine, first officer, answered sleepily.

"Has the lookout reported any ship in the past hour excepting the Rover?"

"Is that the Rover on our port quarter?" Quine's voice was gruffly amazed. Like most mariners of the old school, he considered the wireless machine a nuisance. Yet its intelligence occasionally caught him off guard.

"Only thing in sight, Sparks."

Moore made an entry in the log-book, folded his hands and shut his eyes, to concentrate. The Leyden jars rattled in their mahogany sockets as the *Vandalia* climbed a wave, faltered, and sped into the hollow. Far removed from her pivot of gravity, the wireless house behaved after the habits of an express elevator as the bows plunged and reared. But the wireless house chair was bolted to the floor.

Had another misshapen link been forged to the apparently endless chain? Wrinkles of perplexity creased his forehead. Had this stuttering static anything in kind with those other formless events? If not, what terrified creature was invoking his aid in this blundering fashion?

A simple test would prove if the signals were of local origin. He hoped anxiously for the opportunity. And in less than a half hour the opportunity was given him.

Incomprehension grew as the mystifying statements of the uneasy Hazard recurred, and anger at the unseen, malign forces which seemed to be creeping about him promised to displace his perplexity.

A tarred line scraped the white belly of the life-boat which swelled up from the deck outside the door, giving forth a dull, crunching sound with each convulsion of the engines. The square area above it danced with reeling stars, moiled by a purple-black heaven.

Moore, who had been studying the tarred rope, swung about in the chair and dropped an agitated finger to the silvered wire which rested against the glittering detector crystal. A tiny, blue-red flame snapped from his finger tip to the crystal line chip!

He checked his thoughts as the broken stridulations took on the coherence of intelligible dots and clashes. The former blundering was absent, as if the tremulous hand of the sender was steadied by the brutish grip of a dominant necessity; the signals clarified by the pressure of terror.

"Do not try to find me," it stammered and halted.

Some maddened pulse seemed to leap to life in Moore's throat. His fingers, writhing at the base of the tiny instrument, were clammy with perspiration.

"You must wait," labored the rasp, *"You must help me!"*

"God—God! I will. I will!" cried Moore, half aloud.

"Danger," rasped the unknown sender, faltering. *"You are watched."*

For a breath there was no sound in the receivers other than the beating of his heart.

Click! Snap! Sputter! Then: *"Wait for the lights of China!"*

"It's on board!" he muttered profanely. "Some one—"

The receivers rattled to the red blotter, and Moore rushed out on deck. Slamming the door, he stared dazedly at the spurting streams of white in the racing water. Indescribably feminine was the fumbling touch of that unknown sender!

A grating—hollow, metallic—occurred in the lee of the wireless cabin. As Moore turned, a footfall sounded, coincident with the heavy collision into his side of an unwieldy figure, whose hands, greasy and hot, groped over his. Both grunted.

" 'Sthat you, Sparks?" They were the German gutturals of Luffberg, one of the oilers on the twelve-to-six watch. "Been fixin' the ventilator. Chief wondered if you were up. Wants to know why you ain't been down to say hello."

Moore decided to lay a portion of his difficulties before Minion.

CHAPTER VI

A QUESTION ANSWERED

THE FIRST OPERATOR had developed for himself at an early stage of his occupancy of the *Vandalia's* wireless house the warm friendship of the chief engineer. A wireless man is far more dependent for his peace of mind upon the engine-room crew than upon the forward crew. The latter has only one interest in him: that he stick to his instruments; while the engine-room crew strictly is the source from which his blessings flow, his blessings taking the invisible, potent form of electric current.

Wireless machines are gourmands of electricity. They are wastrels. Not one tenth of the energy sucked from the ship's power wires finds its way through the maze of coils and jars to the antenna; between the mastheads.

The *Vandalia's* engine-room equipment was installed long before wireless telegraphy was a maritime need and a government requirement. Hence, her dynamos protested vigorously against the strain imposed upon them by the radio machine.

Inevitably, the result was deterioration. Any electric engine is unlike any steam engine. Steam engines will do so much work—no more. Dynamos or motors will do so much work—and then more. They can be overloaded unsparingly. But the strain tells. Stout, dependable parts become hot, wear away, crumble, snap. Effect more work for the engine-room crew.

In the typical case of the *Vandalia,* the question of whether or not the wireless men should be provided with all of the current they required, was narrowed down, as always, to the point of individuals.

If Minion had disliked Moore he could have slowed down the dynamos at the critical times when the operator needed the high voltage; which would necessarily have placed him at a disadvantage while saving the dynamos from wear and tear.

But Moore had had encounters with chief engineers before. Surreptitiously, he had at first courted Minion's good graces with fair cigars, radio gossip and unflagging courtesy. And on discovering that the chief was a sentimentalist at heart and a poet by nature, he had presented him with an inexpensively bound volume of his favorite author. Daring, but a master stroke! He had not since wanted for voltage, and plenty of it.

As he prepared to accompany Luffberg below decks, he pondered the advisability of taking Minion entirely into his confidence. He was half decided to await more illuminating developments as he followed the sweated, undershirted shoulders to the engine-room galley, and thence across the oily grill of shining steel bars which comprised one of the numerous and hazardous superfloors which surrounded the cylinders.

He was still undecided as they went down the last flight of steep steel steps into the engine pit, the atmosphere growing hotter, more close and humid, oilier with each yard of descent.

Minion was nursing a stubbornly warm bearing in the port shaft alley.

The fat cylinder revolved with a pleasant ringing noise, the blurring knuckles of the frequent joints vanishing down the yellow, vaulted alley to a point of perspective, where the shaft projected through the hull. The floundering of the great propellers seemed alternately to compress and expand the damp atmosphere.

The sad, white face of Minion arose from the dripping flanks of the journal as he caught sight of Moore in the arched bulkhead entrance. A pale smile flickered at his lips as he wiped his hands on a fragment of waste. He bade him to enter.

The chief did not in any wise reflect his monstrously heaving and clanking, oil-dripping surroundings. He was a small, deliberate man, with oceans of repressed energies. His skin had the waxy whiteness of a pond lily. An exquisitely trimmed black moustache adorned his mouth. Deep brown eyes of a perpetual visionary rested beneath the gentle, scythe like curves of thin and pointed eyebrows.

"You look tired, nervous," vouchsafed Minion as their hands met. His quiet voice had a clarity which projected it with remarkable ease through the bedlam of engine-room noises. "Why are you up so early—or so late? Is anything wrong?"

Moore took out a cigarette and nervously lighted it at the sputtering flame Minion held for him. "Mr. Minion, something's in the wind," he complained, and hesitated. He was at the verge of telling what he had seen on the promenade deck, of the confusion on the pierhead, of the unaccountable behavior of the woman in the window above Ah Sih King's, of the suspicious attitude of Hazard, of the recent plea for help. Again something checked him, and he held his tongue.

The chief engineer, regarding his hesitancy with musing interest, said nothing.

"Mr. Minion, what is Len Yang. And where is it?"

The scythe like brows contracted. Minion's lucid, brown eyes rested on his lips, seeming to await an elaboration of the query. His features suddenly had stiffened. His whole attitude appeared on the moment to have undergone a change, from one of friendly interest to a keen defensiveness.

"Len Yang is a city in China. Why?"

The operator began to suspect that Minion was sparring for time to arrange his replies.

"Precisely where is Len Yang?"

"Do you mean, how does one reach Len Yang?"

"Either. What do they do there? I understand it is about forty days inland from Shanghai."

"Mr. Moore"—the suspicion fell from Minion's expression, leaving it calm and grave—"you have discretion. You are not an amateur. I believe I can trust you with answers to your questions. The man, who controls Len Yang is the *Vandalia's* owner!"

"Why, I understood she was held by the Pacific and Western Atlantic Transport Lines!"

Minion's head shake was gravely contradictory. "This man—"

"What is his name?" interrupted Moore, glancing through the bulkhead door at Luffberg, whose blackened hand was flying up and down with the low pressure piston as he tightened an oil cup.

"He is Chinese. I do not know. I have never seen him. One of the richest of China's unknown aristocrats, the central power of the cinnabar ring. You have never remained aboard when we reached Shanghai and went on up the river to load at Su-Chow Fu?"

Moore shook his head. "Cinnabar from his mines is smelted, brought down the Whang-poo on junks and transferred at Su-Chow Fu, I presume."

Minion seemed not to be listening. His eyes were stagnant, with an appalling retrospect. "It was terrible—horrible! Five years ago I visited Len Yang. Hideous people with staring eyes, dripping the blood-red slime of the mines! I went up the great river as *his* guest. Trouble with the seepage pumps. Hundreds of them drowned like rats.

"Len Yang is near the trade route into India. Marco Polo traveled that highway! Ten days by the best of buffalo carts from the upper falls. Leprosy—filth—vermin! God! you should have seen the rats! Monsters! They eat them. Poor devils! And live in holes carved out of the ruby mud."

He tore the clump of waste from his left hand and ground it under heel.

"And in the center of this frightfulness—his palace! Snow-white marble, whiter than the Taj by moonlight. But its base is stained red, a creeping blood-red from the cinnabar, damn him!"

The white face writhed, and again, for a reason that he could not then lay his finger on, Moore restrained his impulse to tell Minion what he had seen., Startling, even alarming, this new information did not clarify his possessed facts, nor miter with them, no matter how arranged.

Their conversation drifted, due to a feeling of restraint, to general shipboard matters. Tactfully, as he was leaving, Moore borrowed the chief engineer's master key on the excuse that he had locked himself out of the wireless room.

CHAPTER VII

THE IDEOGRAPH

BESIDES A STIFFENING head wind the ship was now laboring into piling head seas. Far beyond the refulgence of the scattered lights stars shone palely. Flecks of streaming white were making their appearance at the toppling wave crests.

A hail of stinging spray, flung inboard by a long gust, struck Moore's face sharply as he struggled forward. The needlelike drops were icy cold. The elastic fabric of the *Vandalia* shivered as her broad nose sank into a succession of black mountains. Peak gutters roared as the cascading water was sucked back to the untiring surface.

Another shower of spray was seized from the frothing cut-water, catapulted aft the length of the promenade deck, rattling like small shot against the vizor of his cap and smarting his eyes.

Gaining the cross corridor entrance, he braced his strength against the forces of wind which imprisoned the door, and crept stealthily down the passage.

His heart pounded with irrepressible violence as his groping fingers outlined the cold iron numerals on the panel. Nervously, he inserted the master key into the door lock, and paused to listen.

Rhythmic snoring moaned from an opened transom near by. What other night sounds might have been abroad were engulfed by the imminent throbbing in the engine-room well.

Stateroom forty-four's transom was closed. What confronted him behind that mute panel? Would the malignant Chinese woman offer resistance? Scream for help? Would he find there the one who had entreated him to wait for the lights of China? Would he be shot at? Stabbed? The lock yielded. The door yawned soundlessly. A round, portentous eye glimmered on the opposite wall. An odor of recently wet paint and of new bed linen met him. The excited pulsing of his heart outsounded the engines.

He shut the door cautiously, not to awake the occupants of the berths.

He fancied he could again hear the warning sibilance of the whisper, but in sleep, perhaps drawn through unconscious lips.

Eagerly, his hand slipped over the enameled wall and found the electric switch. Turning, to cover all corners of the stateroom, he snapped on the light.

Stateroom forty-four, through whose doorway he could have sworn to have seen a sandaled foot vanish less than three hours previous, was empty!

The blue-flowered side curtains of the white enameled bunks were draped back in ornamental stiffness. Below the pillows the upper sheets were neatly furled like incoming billows on a coral beach. He threw open the closet door. Bare! Not one sign of occupancy could he find, and he looked everywhere.

As he made to leave the room a small oblong of white paper was thrust under the door. He hesitated in surprise, stooped to seize it and flung open the door. A gust of night wind—the slamming of a door—and the messenger was gone.

Tremblingly, he unfolded the paper. His eyes dilated. There was no direct, decipherable message. Hastily scrawled in the lower right-hand corner of the otherwise blank leaf was a replica of the blurred sign that had caused such consternation on the part of Lo Ong.

The ideograph had twice been scrawled for his express attention. Apparently its purpose was to strike fear into his heart. It was explicitly a solemn warning. Should he heed it? He felt that he was watched. But the port-hole glowed emptily.

Lighting a cigarette, he dropped down to the bunk, cupped his chin in his palms, and frowned at the green carpet.

Inexorably, he was being frustrated, thrust back, by persons of adroit cunning, by powers whose identity maddeningly eluded him. The love of the game was gone. This had ceased to be an adventurous lark. It was to become a fight with sons of darkness, against weapons whose sole object seemed to be to guard the retreat of some evil spirit.

It occurred to him suddenly that he should be grateful upon one score at least: He had not lost the trail, for the symbols were unchanged.

But from that point the trail vanished—vanished as abruptly as if the creators of its preliminary design had been wiped off the earth! Sharp eyed and eared, alertness night after night availed him nothing. And not until the twinkling lights of Nagasaki were put astern, when the *Vandalia* turned her nose into the swollen bed of the Yellow Sea, did the traces again show faintly.

CHAPTER VIII

THE FACE AT THE PORT-HOLE

THAT A RECRUDESCENCE of the lives of those involved in the murky affair might be imminent was the thought induced in Moore's mind as the green coast of Japan heaved over the horizon. With each thrust of the *Vandalia's* screws the cipher was nearing its solution. Each cylinder throb narrowed the distance to the shore lights of China—the lights of Tsungmin Island. And then—what?

Apparently drowsy, he puffed at his cigarette and watched the poker players as he drummed absently upon the square of green cork inlaid in the corner table. The vermilion glow of the skylight dimmed and died. Lights came on. A clanging cymbal in the energetic hands of a deck steward boomed at the doorway, withdrew and gave up its life in a far away, tinny clatter.

The petulant voice of a hardware salesman, who was secretly known to represent American moneyed interests in Mongolia, drifted through the haze of tobacco smoke at the poker table.

"—that's what I'd like to know. Damn' nonsense—Saving steam, probably—Off Wu-Sung before midnight—if—wanted to throw in a little coal—Means I miss the river boat to-morrow—Not another—Saturday. Dammit!"

Moore drew long at the cigarette and glanced thoughtfully at the oak-paneled ceiling.

Chips clicked. The petulant voice continued:

"—rotten—Forty-four—Seventy-five—"

Moore's eyes withdrew from the beams and examined the speaker, a fat, gray man with double chins. What was that he had said about forty-four?

"—rottenest luck ever had." Evidently he was referring to his losses. "Rotten line—rottener service—Miss my man—Mukden—" The petulant voice ceased as its owner half turned his head, magnetized by the intentness of the operator's gaze. Moore glanced away. The salesman devoted himself to the dealer.

The *Vandalia* was bearing into a thin mist. The night was cool, quiet. Had he been on deck Moore would have seen the last lights of Osezaki engulfed as if at the dropping of a curtain.

During the voyage he had haunted the smoking-room, hoping that by dint of patient listening he might catch an informative word dropped carelessly by one of the players. No such luck. The players were out-of-season tourists, bound for South China or India, or salesmen, patiently immersed in the long and strenuous task of killing time.

"—thirty—thirty-five—forty—forty-five—" The fat man was counting his losings.

Faint, padding footsteps passed the port doorway. Moore shortly became aware of an elusive perfume-scented rice powder—

"—seventy-five—eighty—eighty-five—ninety—"

A pale, malignant face was framed momentarily in one of the starboard windows.

Petrified, Moore blinked, then bounded after. The salesman impeded his progress and grudgingly gave way.

The deck was empty, slippery with the wet of the mist.

He gripped his fists, tightened his muscles against he knew not what, and crept forward close to the cabin. Were the furtive magi stirring again?

He was suddenly aware that one of the ports, in the neighborhood of the stateroom he had entered, was ajar. Nervously he halted, gasping as a long, trembling hand, at the extremity of a spectral wrist, plucked at his sleeve!

Blanched as an arm of the adolescent moon, it fumbled weakly at his clutching fingers—and was swiftly withdrawn!

The staring eyes of a white, gibbous face sank back from the hole. Below the nose the face seemed not to exist.

Its horror wrapped an icy cord about his heart. He plunged his arm to the shoulder through the round opening, struck a yielding, warm body; then descending claws steeled about his wrist and deliberately forced him back.

The brass-bound port-hole glass squeezed shut on his fingers. He wrenched them free, crushed, throbbing, and warmly wet. The anguish seemed to extend to his elbow. Then, suddenly, the gruff, seasoned voice of the captain descended from space behind him. "Sparks, come to my office."

As Moore followed the brutish shoulders to the forward companionway he endeavored to aline and clarify his thoughts. Some explanation was due the captain for this incident. What should he say? Mild confusion prevailed in Moore's mind when Captain Jones closed and locked the door of his spacious stateroom behind them and dropped heavily into one of the cumbersome teak chairs.

CHAPTER IX

AN INTERVIEW WITH THE CAPTAIN

HE WAS A hardened, brawny chunk of a man, choleric in aspect and temperament, brutal in method, bluntly decisive in opinion. Iron was his metal. "Starboard Jones" was one of three living men who had successfully run the Jap blockade into

Vladivostok during that bloody tiff between the black bear and the island panther.

Reddened sockets displayed keen, blue eyes in a background of perpetual fire. His large, swollen nose had a vinous tint, acquiring purplishness in cold weather. Tiny red veins, as numerous as the cracks in Satsumaware, spread across both cheeks in a carmine filigree.

His office was ornamented chiefly by hand-tinted photographs from the yoshiwaras of Nagasaki, of simpering, coy geishas. Souvenirs of their trade, glittering fans, nicked teacups, flimsy sandals, adorned the available shelf room. Cigars as brawny and black as if their maker had strived to emulate the captain's own bulk were scattered among waybills and clearance papers on his narrow desk.

He reached clumsily for one of these brown cylinders now, neglecting to remove his glance of gloating austerity from the operator's tense face. Captain Jones was never a man to withhold the cards.

"Haven't seen much of you lately, Sparks," he observed, applying a steady match flame to the oval butt. He spoke in his usual tones, with a gruffness that balanced on a razor edge between rough jocularity and official harshness. "What's new? Have one of my ropes?"

Moore studied the glowing end narrowly. "Had a little trouble first night out. No, thanks. Not smoking to-night." His bruised finger-tips were curled up tenderly in his coat pocket.

"What's at?" The steel eyes were motionless beneath half-lowered lids.

"Some one used an electric machine. Jammed my signals."

The choleric face dipped knowingly. What Captain Jones did not comprehend he invariably pretended to comprehend. "Noticed anything else?" His ruddy face was now weighty with significance.

Moore sat up abruptly. "What!"

A thick, red forefinger threatened. "Lis'n to me, Sparks. You're a overgrown, blundering bull in a china-shop. You're—"

"Well?" There was a trace of anger in Moore's suave inquiry. His face became stony white. A spot of color appeared at either cheek.

"I mean: keep your damn' nose out of what don't concern you. Savvy?" The heated words spilled thickly from the captain's red lips. "I mean: Butt out of what concerns Chinese women and—and—other words, mind your own particular damn' business! Duty on this ship's to mind the radio. What goes on outside your shanty's none of your damn' concern!"

Captain Jones's mouth remained open, and the butt of the black cigar slid into it.

Moore raised a restraining hand. His lips trembled. His eyes seemed to snap in a rapid fire between the eyes and mouth of the big man slouched down in the chair in front of him. "Wait a minute," he spat out. "Since you do know that somebody is being kidnaped on this ship—"

"What in hell do you mean?"

"Exactly what I say. A Chinese woman, no matter who she is—I don't know, don't care—is hiding some one, a woman, somewhere on this ship. That woman—that woman who's being held—grabbed my hand not five minutes ago. It's your duty—"

"Keep your hands where they belong. You're talking like a fool. Kidnaped? You're crazy. My duty? You're a fool! You're talking baby talk."

"So you're in on the deal, are you?" Moore's tones were sarcastic. "You know all about it. Afraid of the Chinaman in Len Yang, are you? On his pay-roll, eh?"

Captain Jones sprang from his chair. "You're on this ship to tend the wireless," he bawled. "You're under oath to keep your mouth shut. Any one back there?"

"No!"

"Don't you know it breaks a government *rule* when that room's empty—at sea?"

The mist-laden wind shrilled through the screen door abruptly thrust back. Captain Jones slammed the stout inner door. Moore turned up his coat collar, bound a clean handkerchief about his aching fingers, climbed agilely over the life-rafts, passed the roaring, black funnels, and entered the wireless house.

CHAPTER X

THE JUNK

THE LOW, INTERMINGLING whine of Jap stations was broken by an insistent P. and O. liner, yapping for attention. Shanghai stiffly droned a reply, advising the P. and O. man to sweeten his spark.

Moore tapped his detector and grunted. Shanghai was loud—close! The *Vandalia* must be nearing the delta.

"—Nanking Road. Stop. Forty casks of soey—" yelped the P. and O.

Nearing the great river! Out of the mist a faint blur would come—the first lights of China!

"—Thirteen cases of tin—" The P. and O.'s spark remained unsweetened.

Would the lights be Hi-Tai-Sha—Tsungmin?—Port or starboard?

Far below decks a bell jangled faintly. The throbbing of the engines was suddenly bushed. The bell resounded distantly, through a portentous silence.

Moore glanced at the clock. Half past twelve.

The silence was shattered by a turbulent, stern lifting rumble as the screws reversed. The *Vandalia* wallowed heavily, and lay with the yellow tide.

Extinguishing the lights, Moore slipped out on deck, leaned over the edge, and peered into the murk. His heart pumped with nervous acceleration.

At first all was blank. Then a misty, gray-white glow seemed to swim far to port. Murkily, it took form, vanished, reappeared and—was swallowed up again.

But these were not the lights of Tsungmin. They were in the river. He knew those lights well. Even now the *Vandalia* was slipping down with the current abreast of Wu-Sung! The first lights of China! But what was happening?

He dashed to the starboard side.

Out of the mist there arose a tall, gaunt specter. A junk. Perhaps a collision was decreed by the evil spirit of the Whang-poo. But the usual shriekings of doomed river men were absent. The gray bulk floated idly with the steamer. The silence of death suspiciously permeated both craft.

At a loss to account for this queer coincidence, this mute communion, Moore suddenly recalled the rasping plea for help.

Elbowing over the edge, dangerously high above the water, he slid down a stanchion to the promenade deck.

Simultaneously every light on that side of the ship was ex-tinguished. As his feet struck the metal gutter, several unseen bodies rushed past him, aft.

He was grabbed from behind and hurled to the deck. Spring-ing up, he heard the thick breathing of his unknown assailant. He lunged for the sound, met flying fists, smashed his man against the rail. The blow knocked the wind from his antagonist, or broke his back.

Moore did not pause to make inquiries. As the limp body thudded to the wood, the operator sprinted after the vanished figures.

A lone light on the after spar illumined a dim confusion in the cargo well. The stern of the junk was backed against the rail. Oars flashed faintly as the crew of the junk strove to keep her fast against the steamer's side. But where was the crew of the *Vandalia?* Had Captain Jones consented to and perhaps aided in arranging this mid-river tryst?

Another source of illumination, sprang into being. A dong was burning yellowly on the junk's poop deck, casting a plentitude of light upon the scene.

As Moore dropped down the precipitous ladder into the well, he made out two figures struggling against the rail. From the junk, imploringly, a giant Chinese with pigtail flapping about held out his long arms. Silent, his face was writhing with the supplication to hurry.

Moore drove in between the two figures, one of which suddenly collapsed and lay inert. The other sprang at his neck, sinking long claws into his throat. Slit eyes glinted close. Before his wind was shut off he caught the oppressive fragrance of a heavy perfume. A woman!

He struck the clawing hands loose, and she stemmed a scream between convulsing lips. The woman proved to be the one above Ah Sih King's!

He hurled her back, and she staggered against the iron flank of the well. A chatter of Chinese broke from her lips. Shaking, she extracted an envelope from her satin blouse and pressed it into his hands. Thoughtlessly he stuffed the envelope into his pocket, not reckoning what it might contain.

The junk swung out, closed in with a smart smack, and the giant on her deck crouched to spring. He squealed, a high-pitched ululation of anger. Another sound was abroad, the jangling of the engine-room bell.

Moore struck the groping hands of the woman down and sprang to the rail, bracing his feet on the smooth iron deck-plate as the Chinese leaped. A knife glinted. Moore seized a horny wrist with both hands, bent, and wrenched it. The knife struck the water with a sibilant splash. The *fokie* lost his balance. His legs became entangled.

He gibbered with horror as he slipped—slipped—

The Chinese woman sprang at Moore with the frenzy of a pantheress.

A weltering splash—Moore dimly saw the bobbing head before it was driven below the surface as the junk, yawing in, crowded the swimmer down.

A life? Nothing to the turgid river, draining all effluvia from the yellow heart of this festering land.

With a hissing sob, the woman drove Moore backward, raining blow after blow on his chest.

The engines pounded briskly. A boom rattled.

Despairingly, Moore's antagonist shifted her tactics, surprised him by flinging herself to the rail.

The junk was veering away as the *Vandalia's* blades took hold.

She poised on the top rail, drew herself together, and leaped!

The junk slid into the mist.

CHAPTER XI

A RESCUE

MOORE WAS CONSCIOUS of a hot stickiness at his throat where the claws had taken hold. Then he concerned himself with the gray shape that lay quite still on the iron deck at his feet.

New enemies from other quarters, he realized, might strike at any instant.

Gathering up the limp form, he climbed the ladder to the darkened promenade-deck and up another flight through the tarpaulin cover to the boat-deck.

Opening the wireless house door, he deposited his burden gently upon the carpet, and switched on the light. Then he turned the key in the lock, and examined his find.

A long, gray bag of some heavy material swathed the small figure from head to feet. There was no sign of life.

As he bent down to untie the silken knot, some one pounded on the door. He sprang up, trembling.

The pounding was repeated. A gruff voice demanded entrance.

Moore searched the room wildly. His eyes fell to the giant transformer-case beneath the shelf—a mahogany case filled with coiled-up miles of copper wire, as large as a small coffin. When the massive key was pressed, low voltage current entered that case and sprang out—a thunderbolt!

"Open that door!"

He dragged out the case, lifted the dead weight in the gray bag, rolled it into the deep shadows behind, and pushed the case back.

Sitting down, be clapped the receivers about his head, then leaned over and unlocked the door.

"Well! What—what—"

Captain Jones's face was steaming red with anger.

"Sh!" Moore held up his hand in a peremptory gesture for silence, which even captains of ocean liners learn to respect. "Shanghai is calling—with message."

"I don't believe it!"

Moore slipped the disks from his head and held them to the captain's ears. The steel-blue eyes rolled thoughtfully.

"Answer him!"

As his hand reached for the motor-starter, Moore's face went white. Dared he risk the life of that unconscious body which lay in such dangerous proximity to the terminals of the mighty coil?

"Why don't you answer him?" demanded the captain belligerently.

Moore compressed his lips, snapped up the handle, and reached for the key. Did he dare? Captain Jones hovered about him threateningly.

Crisply he sent out Shanghai's call, listened, and exposed a grave face to the captain.

"What does he say?"

"He says"—Moore hesitated—"anchor off Wu-Sung and wait for orders."

And the door banged behind Jones.

The engines became silent as that spurious order was executed.

Yelping arose from the river. It was still dark. The sampan coolies were out early. Moore listened, becoming thoughtful as a solution seemed to present itself to his problem.

He went out on deck and beckoned to one of them to stand by.

But darkness prevented their seeing him. Encircling the nearest davit with his fingers, he leaned far out, cupped his left hand above his mouth, and called.

The groan of heavy chain and a distant splash as the broad flukes of the anchor sank into the river distracted the coolies' attention.

He shouted again with official imperativeness. He dared not risk remaining aboard another hour. And the only opportunity for escape lay in the hazardous route of a sampan to Shanghai.

"No one but a fool will risk his life in a Whang-poo sampan after dark."

A swaying body in the stern of the nearest craft caught sight of him.

"Hie! Hie!" The wagging paddle became mad. The sampan slipped under the towering shadow and brought up with a smack against the black hull.

Moore pried up the tarpaulin life-boat cover, dragged out a coil of dirty rope, made one end fast at the foot of the davit, and tossed the other end overside. The coolie caught it and clung for dear life.

Reentering the wireless room, he dragged out the transformer case and rolled the gray bag from behind it. The body stirred feebly.

He extracted his pocket-knife and slit the cord at the head.

A mass of curly, brown hair flowed out upon the carpet. There was a silken lisp of underskirts. A faint sigh.

Moore suddenly became conscious of the aura of an unseen presence. He turned his head. Black, glassy eyes were riveted upon his from the after window. They vanished.

He jumped up, bolted to the deck, and stood still, listening, darting his eyes nervously from left to right.

The scuffle of a foot sounded on the port side. Some one was running forward. They would report what had been seen. An alarm would be given. And he would be caught—and ordered to explain!

He plunged after.

The footsteps stopped sharply coincident with a dull smash, a frantic grunt, and a thud. The pursued reeled to the deck, groaning.

Moore pounced upon him, grabbed his collar, and dragged him across the deck into the wireless house.

"Mr. Moore, the captain told me—" whimpered Dale.

Moore knocked him into the chair, opened the tool-box, and extracted a length of phosphor-bronze aerial wire. Binding the wiggling arms to the chair, he made the ends fast behind.

Snapping out the lights, he gathered the gray bag into his arms, and deposited it on the deck in the narrow space between the life-boat and the edge.

He looked overside. The coolie was staring up, clinging to the rope, dumbly waiting.

His nervous fingers gripped the closed end of the bag, and he jerked. The bag slipped down half-way.

A warm, moist hand clutched at his wrist. A faint moan issued from the unseen lips.

He jerked again. The bag came away free, and he tossed it overboard. The yellow current snatched it instantly from sight.

The hand clung desperately at his wrist.

"Don't let them—" began a sweet voice in his ear.

He wrapped his legs around the rope and worked his way over the edge.

"Arms around my neck!" he commanded hoarsely. "Hold tight!"

Soft, enfolding arms obeyed him. They dangled at the edge.

The coarse rope slipped swiftly through his fingers, scorching the palms, seeming to rake at the bones in his hand.

A wild shout came from the wireless house. An echo, forward, answered.

They slipped, twisting, scraping, down the rough strand. His hands seemed hot enough to burst.

Maddened blood throbbed at his eyes, his ears, and dried his throat.

Dimmed lights of the promenade-deck soared upward. A glimmering port-hole followed.

For an eternity they dangled, then shot downward.

Something popped in his ears. His feet struck a yielding deck. He staggered backward, sprawled. The rope was whipped from his hand. The warm arms still clung about his neck.

As the world wheeled and careened, a drunken universe, black, shut down. A sullen voice yelped at his ear. The arms loosened.

The *Vandalia* twinkled closely and was swept into the mist, a blur, a phantom. His bands blazed with infernal fire.

He sat up and looked behind him. The river was murderously dark. Water gurgled under the flimsy bow. The dull tread of feet and a watery flailing behind him advised Moore that the coolie was struggling madly against the rushing current.

Slowly he became conscious of a weight upon his breast, a low sobbing. A delicate, feminine odor brought him to earth, unraveled his tangled wits.

He was sitting upon the wet floor of the sampan's low cabin. His captive had crept close to him for protection.

Protection! He snorted, wondering if the coolie was licensed.

"Hai! Hai! Wu-Sung way." The retort was villainously stubborn.

"Shanghai-way. Man! Man!" he shouted.

"Shanghai-way," roared Moore. A sigh escaped from the girl. She snuggled closer. "Wu-Sung. No can do. Savvy?"

"Hai! Mebbe can do." The sampan reared, braving the direct onslaught of the Whang-poo's swift tide.

A myriad questions in his brain strove for utterance.

But the girl spoke first.

"Who are you?" she whispered. "I am Aileen Lorimer."

"I am—I was the wireless operator of the *Vandalia*."

The coolie paused a moment for breath, then the mad plunging of the paddle sounded again.

"The wireless operator? You heard my call?"

"Been waiting for China's lights—ever since. But how—what?" he demanded.

She was silent a moment. "How did I signal you?"

He grunted.

"I know the code. My brother owned a private station. We lived in Pasadena ages ago. It does seem ages." She stirred feebly. "You don't mind?"

"No, no," he protested.

"I am afraid—such a long time. Weeks? Years?" She shuddered. "I do not know. Oh—I want to go home!"

The coolie broke into a working singsong as he struggled. The tide should shift before long.

"Were you in the loft above Ah Sih King's?"

"I was tied to the bed. But the ropes were loose."

"The red note?"

"I scribbled with a nail, and threw it before she knocked me down. That woman was a demon!"

A pale, yellow glow seemed to body forth from the enshrouding mist. Dawn was breaking. Soon the great river would be alight.

"School-teacher," the girl was murmuring. "A wedding present for her—in Ah Sih King's." A small hand fumbled for his, and found it. "In the back room they began gibbering at me. And this demon came. Meaningless words—Ah Sih King leered. Called me the luckiest woman in China."

"But how did you know?"

An empty freighter with propellers flailing half out of water pounded through the yellow mist close to them.

"Hie! Hie!" shrilled the coolie's warning.

Light seeped through the doorway. The outlines of a dark skirt were silhouetted against the scrubbed white floor.

"He said when I saw the lights of China I would go aboard a beautiful ship. She watched you. Three times our stateroom was changed—at night."

"You used a coil?" Moore was professionally interested on this point.

"She had some affliction. A San Francisco doctor said the electric machine would cure it. And I pretended to use it, too. But it broke down that night."

The yellow light was diluted with white. The furnishings of the squat cabin came forth—a crock of rice and fish, a corked jug—perhaps samshu, a bundle of crude chopsticks bound with frayed twine, a dark mess of boiled seaweed on a greasy slab.

He glanced down. The girl moved her head. Their eyes met.

Timid, gray eyes, innocently unblinking, searched his face. Hair of an indescribable dark hue billowed down either side of her pale, oval countenance. Her rosebud of a mouth trembled in the overtures to a smile.

In the realization of that moment Moore shaped his course. And his next thought was that he was penniless!

He delved into his pockets, bringing to light a handful of change. Less than one dollar, disregarding four twenty-cent Hu-Peh pieces; hardly enough to pay off the coolie with a decent cumshaw.

His charge sighed helplessly, thereby clinching his resolution. "I haven't a penny."

He tried the side-pocket of his coat, hoping against grim fact that he had not changed his bill-fold to his grip. Surprise showed in his expression as his fingers encountered an unfamiliar object.

The struggling pantheress flashed into his mind. And the wrinkled envelope she had drawn from her satin jacket and pressed into his hand. Past dealings with Chinese gave him the inkling, correctly, that he had been unknowingly bribed.

A scarlet stamp, an unintelligible monograph, was imposed in the upper right-hand corner of the pale-blue oblong.

"Money—Chinese bills. Full of them!" gasped the girl. "I saw it."

"Jet-te-e-ee!" The coolie swung the oar hard over. The sampan grated harshly against a landing. "Shanghai-way. Cumshaw! Cumshaw!"

Through the irregular hatchway Moore glimpsed the masts of cluttered shipping.

"Fifty one-thousand-dollar Bank of China bills!"

Excited yelpings broke out on the landing. The rickshaw coolies were dickering for their unseen fare.

Moore tossed the sampan boy all of the coins he had, and left him to gibber over them as he lifted the girl to the jetty.

She clung to his arm, trembling, as the rickshaw coolies formed a grinning, shouting circle about them. Moore raced in from the muddy bund.

"What are we going to do?" she moaned.

"We are going to the American consul!" cried Moore, swinging her into the most comfortable rickshaw of the lot. "We are going to cable your mother that you are coming home by the first steamer. The *Mongolia* sails this afternoon."

"But what will become of you?" she demanded piteously.

Moore gave her his ingenuous smile. "I will vanish—for a while. Otherwise I may vanish—entirely!"

She laid her little hand on his sleeve. "I-I won't see you again? Ever?" Her rosebud mouth seemed to quiver.

Moore glimpsed a very yellow, very supercilious face, swing in his direction from the padding throng of the bund. He knew what it might mean.

"But I like you," the faltering voice continued plaintively.

The yellow face reappeared and was swallowed again by the crowd, as a speck of mud is effaced by a river.

For a moment Moore had forgotten his obligation.

"Not likely," be rejoined in a rather impersonal voice. "Your way lies there"—he pointed down-river, toward the sea. "For the present mine lies here"—and he jerked his thumb in the general direction of Shanghai's narrow, muddy alleys. "You see, I may have to hide for a while."

For no apparent reason the sentence of the wireless chief popped into his mind:

"A winning combination—new ports, new faces."

II

THE CITY OF STOLEN LIVES

CHAPTER I

THE GIRL OF THE RICKSHAW

"When menaced by danger," runs an old Chinese proverb,
"go to the very heart of it; there you will find safety."

THE BUND OF Shanghai was striped with the long, purple
shadows of coming night, a night which seemed to be creeping
out of the heart of the land, ushering with it a feeling of subtle
tension, as though the touch of darkness stirred to wakefulness
a populace of shadows, which skulked and crouched and whispered, comprising an underworld of sinister folk which the first
glow of dawn would send scampering back to a thousand evil-
smelling hiding-places.

The rhythmic chant of coolies on the great river ended.
Mammoth go-downs, where the products of China flowed on
their way to distant countries, became gloomily silent and
empty. Handsome tall Sikhs, the police of the city, appeared in
twos and threes where only one had been stationed before; for
in China, as elsewhere, wickedness is borne on the night's wings.

With the descent of the velvety darkness Peter Moore, late
wireless operator of that transpacific greyhound, the *Vandalia*,
slipped out of an obscure, shadowy doorway on Nanking Road
and directed his steps toward the glittering bund, where he was
reasonably sure his enemies would have difficulty in recognizing him.

Peter Moore's uniform, which he had worn officially on the
Vandalia, now reposed on a dark shelf in the rear of a silk-shop.

He had no desire to be stabbed in the back, which was a probability in case certain up-river men should find him. The
Chinese gentleman who conducted the silk-shop was an old
friend, and trustworthy. Besides, he was somewhat indebted to
the young adventurer for having had his precarious old life
saved on one occasion.

Now Peter Moore wore the garb of a Japanese merchant.
His feet were sandaled. His straight, lithe figure was robed in
an expensive gray silk kimono. Jammed tight to his ears, in good
Nipponese fashion, was a black American derby. His eyebrows
were penciled in a fairly praiseworthy attempt to reproduce the
Celestial slant, and he carried a light bamboo cane.

Yet the ex-operator of the *Vandalia* was not altogether sure
that the disguise was a success. If the scowling yellow face he
had detected among the throngs on the bund that morning
should have followed him to the silk-shop, of what earthly use
was this silly disguise?

He padded along in the lee of a moneychanger's, keeping
close to the wall. By degrees he began to be aware that he was
followed; and he endeavored to credit the feeling to imagination, to raw nerves. A ghostly rickshaw flitted by. The soft chug-
ging of the coolie's bare feet became faint, ceased. A muttering
old woman waddled past.

He looked behind him in time to see a gaunt face, illuminated by the dim glow of a shop window, bob out of sight into
a doorway. Moore proceeded, as though he had not noticed the
furtive escape. Turning swiftly again a moment later, he saw
the man dive into another doorway.

Peter Moore ran to the dark aperture, seized a muscular,
satin-covered arm, and dragged a whispering Chinese, a big,
brawny fellow, into the circular zone of the yellow streetlight.
Quickly recovering from his surprise, the Chinese reached
swiftly toward his belt. Moore, hoping that only one man had
been set on his trail, gave vent to a murderous yell, and at the
same time drove his fist into a yielding paunch.

With a groan of pain the Chinese staggered back against the shop window, caving in a pane with his elbow. He chattered a remonstrance in the up-river dialect. Moore raised his fist to strike again.

Then a monumental figure, with a fresh white turban coiled about his head, strode austerely into the circle of yellow light.

"Thief," said Moore simply, indicating the broken shop window.

"H-m!" growled the Sikh. He seized the luckless window-breaker by both shoulders, backed him against an iron trolley-post, and strapped him to it.

With a jovial "Allah be with you!" Peter Moore continued his stroll toward the bund. Now that the trailer was out of his way for the night at least, he could make his way in peace to the Palace bar and find out what might be in the wind for him.

As he crossed Nanking Road where it joined the bund, a frantic shout, mingled with the scream of fear or of warning, impelled him to leap out of the path of a rickshaw which was making for him at breakneck speed.

A white face, with a slender gloved hand clutched close to the lips, swept past.

Peter Moore gasped aloud, not in anger or fright, but in surprise quite as staggering as if the girl in the rickshaw had slapped him across the face. He shouted after her. But she went right on, without turning.

"Licksha?" A grinning coolie dropped the shafts of an empty rickshaw at Peter Moore's heels.

"Yes!" snapped Peter Moore.

He ceased being angry as a softer glow crept into his veins. The rickshaw turned to the right, following the other, which occupied the center of the almost deserted bund, and speeding like the wind.

"Man—man!" shouted Peter Moore. The girl seemed to be headed for the bridge. But why? A number of questions stormed futilely in his brain. Why had the girl ignored him? Why had she not gone aboard the *Manchuria,* as she had promised?

He was a little sore at her disobedience, and he was a little pleased to know that she was still in Shanghai. Since the morning, with hours to himself to ponder over her loveliness, her gentle, straightforward belief in him, he had become rather sorry because she was going away.

The coolie jogged along, his naked legs rising and falling mechanically. The wireless operator drew the folds of the kimono more closely about his throat, for the night air blowing off the Whang-poo was chill and damp.

At the bridge the rickshaw ahead suddenly stopped, waiting. Peter Moore drew alongside, and leaped to the ground.

The near-by street-light afforded him the information that he had made a mistake. Undeniably similar to the girl he had sent away on the *Manchuria* that morning was the young lady in the rickshaw. She had the same white, wistful face, the same alert, appealing eyes, the same rosebud mouth.

Any one might have made such a mistake. It was very embarrassing.

An obscure shadow, which had seemed to be a part of the river scenery, suddenly moved to action as Peter Moore approached the rickshaw from the opposite side. Such events are not at all uncommon in Shanghai after nightfall.

The shadow, coming to life, crept to the vehicle and clutched the side rail. He was a river coolie, and he flavored the air with the odor of stale opium.

The rickshaw coolie hesitated and became frozen. He was too frightened even to call for help. The river man reached clumsily for the girl's hand. She jerked it away.

Peter Moore crossed behind the rickshaw, grabbed the ropy neck of the river man, drove up his knee into the small of the muscular back, and sent the coolie reeling out over the bridge. He recovered his balance, but he did not return. Peter Moore looked into the girl's eyes and found them ablaze with anger.

"Why are you following me?" she demanded.

"I thought I knew you. I am sorry. I'll go at once."

"No! Wait." Her voice relented. It was a fresh young voice, not indeed unlike that of Aileen Lorimer's. "That is hardly convincing. Why are you dressed up as a Japanese?"

"I am sorry," faltered Moore, retreating. "I have made a terrible mistake. You are not the girl I-I expected. I might say," he added dryly and in a more confident tone, "that it is not especially safe for a girl to be on the streets of Shanghai alone at this time of night. Sayonara!"

"*Please* don't run away," said the girl with a soft laugh. "I'm not afraid, or I would have run instead of waiting, when you followed me. I've just come up from Amoy—alone. And I leave to-morrow for Chungking—alone."

Peter Moore edged away an inch or two. He imagined he had detected a hint of invitation in the sweet voice, and felt himself at a disadvantage. This girl was pretty, alluring; but he had extricated himself only this morning from one affair, and it had been difficult—it had hurt—and he was not going to rush headlong into another, not if he could help himself!

Peter Moore was susceptible to girls of a type; and Aileen Lorimer had filled every specification. But to him, Aileen and all other nice girls, including the one who was now smiling at him musingly from her high perch in the rickshaw, meant but one thing.

He had argued this all out earlier in the day. Sooner or later, in some reckless moment, he would marry some girl such as Aileen Lorimer. Marriage meant permanency, and Peter Moore loathed the very idea of it. At heart an adventurer, his way was the open road, the rolling sea, the zest and flavor of change, of romance, of new lands—freedom!

She was softly inquiring his name! He sighed quite audibly, and gave her the desired information.

"Ah, American!" she murmured. "But why the Japanese—disguise?"

"In China," said Moore, rather curtly, "one doesn't ask leading questions." He began to feel somewhat irritated, as if this bright-faced girl were trying to impose upon him.

She disregarded his aloofness. "Mr. Moore, I'm an American, too. I used to live in New York, on Riverside Drive. Oh! It must have been long, long ago!"

"Why?" asked Peter Moore unguardedly.

"I haven't met one of my countrymen in perfect ages! And to-morrow I go up the great river, way beyond Chungking, way beyond Szechwan!"

"Bad traveling on the river this time of year," said Moore politely. "She's out of her banks up above Ichang, I have been told."

"Yes," replied the girl sadly. "If I could only have just one evening of fun—a dance or two, maybe—I-I wouldn't mind half so much. I-I—"

Peter Moore advised himself as follows: I told you so. Aloud he said:

"I believe there's a dance at the Astor Hotel. If we can get a table—"

"Oh, how lovely!" exclaimed the girl. "Do—do you mind very—much?"

"Tickled to death," declared Peter Moore amiably.

CHAPTER II

A REQUEST

LUCKILY FOR THE ex-operator of the *Vandalia*, the dance at the Astor Hotel was a costume affair. His Japanese kimono fitted him quite nicely. At least it was not conspicuous.

Seating himself at a small round table in the end of the room over which hung the orchestra balcony, Peter Moore found himself in the presence of two disarming gray eyes, which drank in every detail of his good-looking young face, including the penciled eyebrows.

Miss Vost—Miss Amy Vost—gave him to understand that she was really grateful for his hospitality, rushed on to assure him that it was not customary for her to meet strange young men as she had met him, and then frankly asked him what he was doing in China. Every time she thought of him her curiosity seemed to trip over the Japanese kimono.

Influenced by his third glass of Japanese champagne, he almost told her the truth. He modified it by saying that he was a wireless operator; that he had missed his ship, and that his plans were to linger in China for a while. He liked China. Liked China very much.

Miss Vost caressed the tip of her nose with a small, pink thumb. She was not the kind who hesitated.

"You can do me a favor," she said, and halted.

Peter Moore nodded. It has been said that he did not pretend to be able to cope with any pretty woman. His nod was an unqualified consent, a gallant "I shall!"

The Philippine orchestra burst into a lilting one-step. Miss Vost arched her eyebrows. Peter Moore arose, and they glided off. It developed that Miss Vost was exceptionally well qualified as a dancer. There was divineness in her youthful grace; she put her heart into the dance. It seemed probable to Peter Moore that she put her heart into everything she did.

"You spoke about my doing a favor," he suggested, glancing sternly at a dark-eyed Eurasian girl who seemed to be trying to divert his attention.

"There is a man in Shanghai I want you to try to find for me to-night. Last time I saw him—this morning—he was drunk. He was the first officer on the steamer that brought me up from Amoy. Perhaps you know him. He's only been on the coast a short while. Before that he ran on the Pacific Mail line between San Francisco and Panama. His name is MacLaurin, a nice boy. Scotch. But he drinks."

"MacLaurin? I know a man named MacLaurin—Bobbie MacLaurin."

"No!" gasped Miss Vost. "I suppose I ought to make that old remark about what a small world it is! Do you know where Bobbie MacLaurin is?"

It was quite plain that Miss Vost was deeply concerned over the probable fate of one of Peter Moore's best friends!

"No," murmured Moore. "Why, is he drunk? He never touched the stuff when I knew him."

"That is a matter," replied Miss Vost, somewhat distantly, "that I prefer not to discuss. Will you try to find him for me? He threatened to be—be the captain of the river-boat, the *Hankow*, that I leave on to-morrow for Chungking. I'd rather like to know if he intends to carry out his threat. Do you think he is capable enough?"

"Bobbie MacLaurin could sail the *Hankow* from Nanking to Chungking blindfolded! He's a pilot by instinct!"

"Will you find out, if you can, if he is going to be sober enough to make the trip—and let me know?" requested Miss Vost, as the music stopped. "I'd rather he wouldn't, Mr. Moore," she added quickly. "He—he's too impulsive. But I do wish you were going to make the trip. I'd love to have you!"

The ex-operator of the *Vandalia* experienced a warm suffusion in the vicinity of his throat. In the next breath he felt genuinely guilty. That very morning he had made the vow, to his sacredest inner self, that if ever he permitted himself to love any woman, that woman would be Aileen Lorimer.

As he looked deep into the anxious, appealing gray eyes of Miss Vost, and recognized the emotions which caused her fine, rosy lips to twitch, he cursed himself for being, or having the tendencies to be, a trifler; and in his estimation a trifler was not far removed from the reptile class. Yet somehow, damn it, that trip to Chungking on the *Hankow* appealed to him now as a most profitable excursion.

And Chungking was removed only by a few hundred miles by caravan from Len Yang, home of the "Gray Dragon," the man whose life he had sworn some day to take! Even now in this ballroom there might be spies of the Gray Dragon set to watch him—to murder him!

At the thought, Peter Moore did not look around. He muttered, as they regained their seats.

"I missed that," said Miss Vost, with an adorable smile. "What was it you said?"

"I said," replied the wireless operator, "if you will pardon me, I'll leave you now and take a look-see for Bobbie MacLaurin."

CHAPTER III

BOBBIE MACLAURIN

A NEEDLE ONE and one-half inches in length and so thin as to be invisible at a distance of ten paces will kill a man. So will a few drops of poison ingeniously administered. So will an automatic revolver!

Knowing well what he was about, Peter Moore took a rickshaw to the silk shop on Nanking Road, stepped quietly over the sleeping watchman in the doorway, and entered the dark room, which exhaled the perfume of China's costliest silks.

There was no danger of his being apprehended as long as the watchman did not awake. He knew that the watchman, and all watchmen in northern China, belonged to a gild of thieves. The watchman was merely a representative of this enterprising gild, a symbol which meant that the silk merchant paid yearly dues to the gild and was thereby afforded protection. Had he hired a legitimate watchman, that watchman would have been murdered forthwith, and the shop looted!

Peter Moore wanted his automatic revolver, quite sure that once he again linked arms with that daredevil of a MacLaurin, he would have no time, no opportunity, to select his weapons for a probable encounter with the Gray Dragon.

Previously Peter Moore had not directly pitted himself against the Gray Dragon; he had simply been drawn into an adroitly laid net unknowingly, and had cunningly slipped out of it, spoiling one evil intention of the Gray Dragon, depriving the monarch of that lovely captive, Aileen Lorimer. He had yet to match his strength and wits against the monarch of Len Yang.

Something of the futility of a mongoose marching bravely but blindly into a den of monster cobras characterized Peter Moore's intention to penetrate the stronghold of the cinnabar king. Undeniably it was a noble impulse that inspired him to the deed; and it was a typical one. His hunger for adventure was not a pose; it was generated by a spirit that did not countenance fear; a spirit which had been tested by the acid and fire of more than one critical situation.

It must have been the light of the crusader which glowed in Peter Moore's eyes as he fumbled on the dark shelf under his uniform and encountered the chilly steel of his revolver. Now that his mind was made up to seek out the Gray Dragon, he did not underestimate the power and the cunning of his adversary. He knew that the chances in favor of his entering Len Yang alive were pitifully small. Yet the whole of the Chinese Empire was no safer for him now.

The Gray Dragon had paid him the compliment of recognizing in him an enemy; and it was evident that the Gray Dragon would not sleep easily until he was removed from China utterly—or the world. He had had previous testimony that the gray tentacles reached beyond the seas. If such were the case, in fact, Peter Moore blithely admitted to himself that his life, no matter where he elected to roam, would be safer in a den of hyenas. Indeed, now that the cards were spread before him, if he desired to run away from the danger, in which direction could he run?

"When menaced by danger, go to the very heart of it; there you will find safety."

Now that his course was decided, his thoughts drifted, perhaps reluctantly, to that captivating person, Miss Vost. Her teasing gray eyes, her spontaneous, silvery laughter, seemed to reproduce themselves in the darkness of the silk-laden shelves, as he dropped the revolver into the long baglike sleeve of the kimono.

Was his undeniable interest in Miss Vost aroused, maybe, by a reflection? Wasn't it true that Miss Vost only suggested to his still poignant memory the lovely girl whose last sentence still rang in his mind? It was a hungry little sentence, accompanied by a hungry little look. "I like you!" she had murmured, when he had said he could not return to America, but must remain in China, "until the smoke had blown away."

Because the world, and China and women, particularly women, baffled Peter Moore's young mind to the point of numbness, he jerked the black American derby over his ears until they were horizontally inclined, snapped the door behind him, stepped over the recumbent watchman, and proceeded with angry strides toward the bund.

It lacked a few minutes of midnight when Peter Moore entered the Palace bar by the bund side. Only a few lights were burning, and the exceedingly long teak bar—the longest bar east of Suez—was adorned by a few knots of men only. Tobacco smoke was thick in the place, nearly obscuring the doorway into the hotel lobby.

He scanned the idlers, looking for the cloth of sailormen; for he was comfortably assured that if Bobbie MacLaurin happened to be awake and on his legs he could be found only in the Palace bar. Bobbie MacLaurin was a gentleman of elevated tastes. Even in San Francisco he would no more have thought of entering a water-front saloon on the Embarcadero than he would have thought of eating terrapin with a spoon!

Peter Moore's quest was ended. Bobbie MacLaurin was there, disposing of all of the imported Scotch whisky that came convenient to his long and muscular reach.

In a deep and sonorous voice he was insisting to a group of uniformed sailors, emphasizing his point with a clublike forefinger with which he pounded on the edge of the teak bar, that while he rarely drank off duty, he never drank when on. This claim Peter Moore had reason to know was the truth, and the whole truth.

The wireless operator edged his way to MacLaurin's side, and touched his arm, making a whispered remark which the Scotchman evidently did not comprehend. For MacLaurin wheeled on him and bestowed upon him a red, glassy, and hotly indignant stare.

Bobbie MacLaurin was, in the language of the sea, a whale of a man. His head seemed unnecessarily large until you began to compare it with his body; and his body was the despair of uniform manufacturers, who desire above all things to make a respectable percentage of profit. He was like a living monument, two and a half hundredweight of fighting flesh and blood, which, when all of it went into action, could better be compared to a volcano than to a monument. Otherwise he was an exceedingly amiable young giant.

The redness and hotness of the stare he imposed upon the friend of more than one adventurous expedition slowly receded, leaving only the glassiness in evidence. Reverting again to the language of ships and the men who sail them, Peter Moore was forcibly impressed with the notion that Bobbie MacLaurin was "soused to the gills."

"Well, Bobbie," he managed to say quietly, "you don't seem over-glad to see your old *compañero* again."

Bobbie fidgeted uneasily.

"Damn my hide!" he roared genially. "Your face is familiar! It is! It is! Where have I seen that face before? Aha! I know now! I had a fight with you once."

"More than once," corrected Peter Moore, grinning. "The last time was in Panama. Remember? I tripped you up, after you knocked the wind out of me, and you fell, clothes and all, into the Washington Hotel's swimming tank!"

"Peter Moore!" gasped Bobbie MacLaurin, and Peter Moore was forthwith smothered in loglike arms and the fumes of considerable alcohol.

Extricating himself at length from this monstrous embrace, Peter Moore permitted himself to be held off at arm's length and be warmly and loquaciously admired.

"My old side-kick of the damn old *San Felipe!*" announced Bobbie MacLaurin to the small group of somewhat embarrassed sailors. "The best radio man that God ever let live! He can hear a radio signal before it's been sent. Can't you, Peter?"

"Sure thing!" agreed Peter Moore.

"Boys, take a long look at the only livin' man who can fight his weight in livin' sea serpents; the only livin' man who ever knocked me cold, and got away with it! Boys, take a long, lastin' look, for the pack o' you're goin' out o' that door inside of ten counts! Ain't he a young devil? God bless 'um! Just look at that there Jap get-up! Sure as God made big fish to eat the little fellows, Peter Moore's up to some newfangled deviltry, or I'm a lobster!"

"Sh!" warned Peter Moore, conscious that in China the walls, doors, floors, ceilings, windows, even the bartenders, have ears.

"Out with the lot of you!" barked MacLaurin. "There's big business afoot tonight. We must be alone. Eh, Peter?"

The sailors seemed to vanish. The distant door swung on the back of the last of them. They did not pause. They went!

And Peter Moore was firmly convinced that business could not be talked over tonight. Of one thing only did he wish to be certain.

"You're taking the *Hankow* up-river tomorrow?"

"That I am, Peter!"

"Have you signed a wireless man?"

"I want you, Peter! No one else can hear these funny Chinese signals half so far as you!"

"Then we take the express for Nanking to-morrow morning."

"Aye—aye! sir!"

"Then we'll turn in now. Otherwise you'll look like a wreck when Miss Vost sees you on deck."

"Miss Vost!" exploded MacLaurin. "When did you see Miss Vost?"

"A little while ago, Bob. Shall we turn in now?"

"Miss Vost is why I'm drunk, Peter," said Bobbie MacLaurin sadly. "She treated me like a dog."

"So she admitted. To-morrow we'll talk her over, and other important matters."

"As you say, Peter. I'm the brawn, but you're the brains of this team—as always! The bunks are the order. I'm staying here—the Astor's too drafty. My room is one-seven-seven."

WHEN Bobbie MacLaurin's not unmusical snore proceeded from the vast bulk disposed beneath the white bedclothes, Peter Moore again descended to the lobby, let himself into the street, and hailed a rickshaw.

The mist from the Whang-poo, had changed to a slanting rain. The bund was a ditch of claylike mud. Each street light was a halo unto itself.

He lighted a cigarette, suffered the coolie to draw up the clammy oilskin leg-robe to his waist, and dreamily contemplated the quagmire that was Shanghai. His active young imagination escorted him on the wildest of trips up the River of Golden Sands to Chungking, to Len Yang—to the very heart of the white marble palace where the Gray Dragon held forth.

Having wound up the long, evil life of the Gray Dragon with a well-placed shot from his automatic revolver, Peter Moore permitted his vision to rest upon the happy scene of a little cottage, perhaps in lower California, with bliss and Aileen Lorimer and himself as the occupants; but his vision appeared to have a will of its own. It dwelt brazenly upon the lovely small face of Miss Vost, and there faithlessly it lingered.

The rickshaw crossed the garden bridge, veered from the bund and drew up, dripping, under the porte-cochère of the Astor Hotel, where a majestic Sikh door-tender emerged from the shadows, bearing a large, opened umbrella.

Contrary to her promise, Miss Vost was not awake, waiting for his message. However, she sent back word by the coolie, that she would dress and come down, if he would wait. Peter Moore pondered a moment, and decided not to wait. A glimpse of Miss Vost at this time of night meant nothing to him. Or was he hungry for that glimpse? Nonsense!

He dashed off a hasty note, sealed it in an envelope, and gave it to the room-boy to deliver.

He pictured her sleepy surprise as she opened it, and read:

> Bobbie seems much put out. We take morning express to Nanking. Try to make it. Well have tea, the three of us, at Soochow!

At Soochow! There he was—at it again! A trifler!

"Damn my withered-up sense of honor, anyway!" observed Peter Moore to himself, as he climbed into the rain-soaked rickshaw.

CHAPTER IV

THE GRAY DRAGON'S MAN

WITH THE PRISTINE dawn, Robert Malcolm MacLaurin arose from his bed like a large, yellow mountain; for his pajamas—every square yard of them—were of fine Canton silk the color of the bulbous moon when it reposes low on China's horizon.

Satisfying himself at length that the bedroom had another occupant, he drained the contents of a fat, white water-jug, then tossed the jug upon the incumbent of the bedroom's other bed.

At such times as this critical one, the smiling destiny which held the fate of Peter Moore in the hollow of her precious hand was ever watchful; and the white water-jug caromed from his peaceful figure with no more than an unimportant thud. The jug bounded to the floor and ended its career against the hard wall. Peter Moore sat up, rubbing his eyes.

"Dead or alive, Peter?"

"You nearly broke my back."

"Serves you right, old slug-abed! I indistinctly recall your tucking me in last night with the warning that we pick up the early morning express for Nanking."

"Quite so," admitted Peter Moore thickly. In the past two days he had managed to set aside altogether four hours for sleep; and he felt that way. He examined his roommate, but was not surprised at what met his glance.

Bobbie MacLaurin, disregarding the fact that he had not yet shaved, looked as fresh as a rose. His endurance was like that of a range of mountains. His sea-blue eyes were cannily clear, his complexion was transparent and glowing. The ill effects of last night had been absorbed with about as much apparent effort as a gigantic sponge might display in absorbing a dewdrop.

Discreet knuckles rattled the door. It opened silently, admitting a room-boy, who crossed the room as softly, as stealthily as a panther. He bore a chipped red lacquer tray, upon which was nicely arranged, a coffee-pot, steaming, two cups; buttered toast, and two fresh copies of the North China News, that estimable political publication which says so much and tells so little.

"Gentleman!" The Oriental bowed as Bobbie MacLaurin seized the coffee-pot and poured both cups with steady hand. "*Cumshaw?*" murmured the youth shyly.

"Peter, give the kid a ten-cash piece. Bobbie no have got. Savvy that, Peter? I'm busted." He resumed shaving.

Peter Moore flipped a white coin to the boy, who dived into a clinking pouch for change.

"Maskee," said Peter. "Run along."

The door closed as softly as it had opened.

"Why did you jump when the kid came in?" inquired MacLaurin, endeavoring to extricate, with a coffee-spoon, a spot of lather which floated on the smoking black liquid in the cup.

"Chinamen's eyes and Chinamen's knives have been running through my dreams. Am I afraid? It looks that way."

"Cheer up! The pirates are thick above Ichang. We'll both have our worthless necks slit a dozen times before we make Chungking. Bloody traveling, I'm informed." He turned from the miniature mirror. His sea-blue eyes glared through a white lake of lather. "Hurry up and shave, you loafer! We'll miss that train."

"I'm not going to shave for six months!"

"Election bet?"

"Bobbie, when you've had your heart broken as many times as I have—"

"Poppycock!"

"When your utterly worthless life has been endangered as many times as—"

"What you need is a drink, my lad!"

"When you have positive, specific evidence that the greatest, the most heartless criminal-at-large wants to have you stuck like a pig—"

MacLaurin swung his big frame about and stared. "You're not serious!"

"I am referring to the Gray Dragon."

The razor in the large, red hand of Bobbie MacLaurin flashed. It came away from his cheek. A broad trickle of crimson spread down the lathered jaw. But he did not curse.

"We must hurry for that train," rumbled his big voice. "We must talk this over. We must hurry, Peter," he said again.

MISS AMY VOST was not in evidence when the two rickshaws rattled up to the platform of the red brick station.

Peter Moore paid off the coolies and shoved a handful of large, green assignats on the Bank of Shanghai and Hong Kong into the ready fist of MacLaurin. There was bustle and confusion.

While MacLaurin ran in to buy the tickets, Peter Moore gave the station and its environs a careful search. Miss Vost was not to be found. Perhaps she had changed her plans, and had given up the trip to Chungking. Perhaps she would arrive in Nanking by later train. In that event she might miss connections with the river steamer. On last thought, perhaps she was already on the train!

MacLaurin reappeared with the tickets. "Have you seen Miss Vost?"

Peter Moore shook his head. "Perhaps she's waiting for us in the coach, holding seats for us."

"Just like her," said MacLaurin. "She's a little peach!"

Peter Moore entered the compartment first and scanned the heads for the auburn tresses of Miss Vost. The only tresses in evidence were the long, black shining ones of a bejeweled Chinese lady. The other passengers were men.

Bobbie MacLaurin stood up to inspect the handful of occupants of the second-class compartment. The Nanking express was divided into five cars: one coach of first and second class, several thirds, and a baggage-car. Miss Vost would not be traveling third, nor could he conceive of her riding in the baggage-car.

"There will be no tête-à-tête in Soochow," observed Peter Moore to his conscience.

"I'd go to hell for that girl!" declared Bobbie MacLaurin simply, as he sat down at Peter Moore's side. "Now, tell me what you were doing in that Jap rigging. Two years, isn't it, since we were chased out of Panama City by the *spigotties?*"

"I came over on the *Vandalia.*"

"And didn't go back, I gather."

"She sailed up-river for Hankow yesterday. No, I won't go back. Bobbie, I started something on that ship, and I'm on my way to Chungking—and way beyond Chungking—to finish it!"

"It will be beautifully finished, Peter! Or your name's not Peter Moore."

"There was a girl, a beautiful girl—"

"There usually is." MacLaurin stared reminiscently out of the window at the fields of paddy and blue-coated coolies, soft and blurred by the mist and rain. He sighed deeply.

"I saw her first—a white, terrified face in the loft window above Ah Sih King's gold shop in Chinatown, just before we cleared Frisco I saw her again. And she saw me. A Chinese woman half-dragged, half-carried her up the gangplank. Then she disappeared."

"Where?"

"She was held in a stateroom by the Chinese woman, a tool of the Gray Dragon."

"Ah!"

"I tried to find her. The purser, Hazard—you know the old fox—knew nothing. Froze up. But the girl knew the radio code. There was an electrical machine, a medical apparatus of some sort in the stateroom. She flashed a call. But her sending was bad. At first her signals were only a blur, a low, harsh grating, like emery on bronze. Then I caught the word, 'h-e-l-p.' A little later, 'wait for the lights of China.' Just that! She knew what was afoot.

"I waited. For ten days! The lights came. They were Whang-poo's lights. A yellow junk towered out of the mist. All the starboard lights were cut out. I ran aft to the cargo well. Some one carried a gray bag to the rail, where the junk swung in. I grabbed the bag—the girl was inside! Then there was a fight!"

"God, Peter; why wasn't I there!" moaned MacLaurin.

"When the junk pulled clear, the Chinese woman jumped. I had the bag and the girl! I called a sampan. Came to the custom's jetty. The river was thick yellow Whang-poo mist. When morning dawned I saw—her face."

"A beautiful face, Peter?"

Peter Moore gazed bitterly at the scenery flitting evenly past the window: groves of feathery bamboo, flaming mustard fields, exquisite gardens, and graves—graves beyond count.

"Perhaps she is passing through the Inland Sea by now. Bobbie, I wanted her to go home. She was—she was that kind of a girl. She wanted to stay. Bobbie, that girl could have made a man of me! She—she even told me she—liked me!"

"They have a way of doing that," commented Bobbie sadly.

Several miles rolled by before either of the men spoke.

"Why is Miss Vost making the trip to Chungking?"

"You'll have to find that out for yourself, Peter. I was too busy letting her know how bright my life has become since she entered it!"

The square, red jaw swung savagely toward Peter. Of a sudden the sea-blue eyes seemed a trifle inflamed.

"She's probably going to Chungking on serious business. She's like that. She's not like you."

"What do you mean?" said Peter.

"You're going to try to break into Len Yang; that's what I mean!"

"Well, what of it?"

"Some day, on one of these reckless expeditions of yours, Peter, you're going to run plumb into a long, sharp knife!"

"Better run into a knife than have it stab you from behind."

"You believe the Gray Dragon is as interested in you as all that?"

"I certainly do."

The ivy-clad walls of ancient Soochow appeared through the gray rain.

"If I could head you off, I would."

"You can't, Bobbie. My mind is made up. I'm unsafe anywhere in China, because the Gray Dragon knows I'm here, knows that I'm aware of his methods."

"Get out of China."

"That would be cowardly and foolish. He wants my life, if only in revenge. Wherever I went, I'd still be in danger."

"There's truth in that. But why enter the lion's den? You're too confiding, too trusting, too young. Even now you may be in the presence, in the very hands, of agents of the Gray Dragon."

Peter cast an anxious, a furtive look about the compartment. The Chinese woman with the shining black hair was smiling at him.

"Please don't joke."

"I'm not joking, Peter. I repeat, at this instant you are virtually brushing elbows with one of the Gray Dragon's men. That's how wise you are!"

Peter's hand dipped swiftly into the long sleeve-pocket of the kimono. The warm butt of the automatic revolver was in the palm of his hand.

"Point him out!" he whispered.

"Promise not to shoot!"

"I promise nothing!"

"Then blaze away, *compañero!* The Gray Dragon is paying my salary! He owns the *Hankow!* In duty to my conscience, I oughtn't to let you go. But I know you'd walk or fly or swim if I tried to head you off."

"I certainly would," agreed Peter.

CHAPTER V

THE PASSENGER DELAYS

NO MEMBER OF the earth's great brotherhood of dangerous waterways is blessed with quite the degree of peril which
menaces those hardy ones who dare the River of the Golden
Sands.

Bobbie MacLaurin's steamer, the *Hankow*, was the net result
of long ship-building experience. Dozens of apparently sea-
worthy boats have gone up the Whang-poo, not to return. After
years of experiment a somewhat satisfactory river-boat has been
evolved. It combines the sturdiness of a harbor tug with the
speed of a torpedo-boat destroyer.

The *Hankow* was ridiculously small, and monstrously strong.
Chiefly it consisted of engines and boilers. The accepted type
of river steamer to be found on the Mississippi, the Ganges,
the Nile, the Indus, the Amazon, and the Magdalena, would
undergo the experience on the Whang-poo that an autumn-leaf
is indulged in by a violent windstorm.

Despite their security, despite the shipwrecks and deaths that
have been poured into their present design, Whang-poo river-
boats sink, a goodly crop of them, every season.

But the world of commerce is an arrogant master. There is
wealth in the land bordering the upper reaches of the river. This
wealth must be brought down to the sea, and scattered to the
lands beyond the sea. In return, machinery and tools must be
carried back to mine and farm the wealth.

Little is heard, less is told, and still less is written of the men
who dare the rapids and the rocks and the sands of the great
river. They are not a race nor a type, but individuals. The red
blood of explorers runs in their veins, the blood of ancestors,
probably, who were not afraid to take a chance. Gamblers all.

Sometimes the spirit of adventure sends them up the Whang-poo. Frequently, as is the case with men who depart unexplainedly upon dangerous errands, a woman is the inspiration, or merely the cause.

Miss Amy Vost, of New York City, but more recently of Amoy, China, province Fu-Kien, was the generator in the case of Bobbie MacLaurin.

When Miss Vost tripped blithely aboard the *Sunyado Maru*, anchored off the breaks of Amoy, and captured, at first blush, the hearts of the entire forward crew, from the staid British captain to the wheelsman on the dog-watch, Bobbie MacLaurin was the most eager prisoner of the lot.

Perhaps she took notice of him out of the corner of her glowing young eyes long before he became seriously and mortally afflicted. Certainly the first mate of the *Sunyado Maru* was no believer in the theory of non-resistance.

He thought he was a fast worker. Given two hundred and fifty pounds of tall, strong, finely proportioned human flesh; place this in a uniform of beautifully tailored white ducks; allow the uninterrupted friendship of two full weeks with a susceptible young woman, and the outcome is all in favor of the two hundred and fifty pounds.

Had Miss Vost been a susceptible young woman, it is safe to assume that Bobbie MacLaurin would not have accepted command of the *Hankow* from tide-water to that remote Chinese city, Chungking.

He wooed her in the pilot-house—where passengers were never allowed; he courted her in the dining-room; and he paid marked attention to her at all hours of the day and night, in sundry nooks and corners of the generous promenade-deck.

Miss Vost sparred with him. As well as being lovely and captivating, she was clever. She seemed to believe in the rule of the old philosophers, that conversation was given to mankind simply for purposes of evasion. By the end of the first week Bobbie MacLaurin was earning sour glances from his staid

British captain, and glances not at all encouraging from Miss Vost.

He informed her that all of the beauty and all of the wonder of the stars, the sea, the moonlight, could not equal the splendor of her wide, gray eyes. She replied that the moon, the stars, and the sea had gone to his head.

He insisted that her smile could only be compared to the sunrise on a dewy rose vine. He added that it was godlike. She retorted, with severity, that he was endangering his chances of getting to heaven by being sacrilegious.

He threw his big, generous heart at her feet a hundred times. Being fair and sympathetic, she did not kick it to one side. She merely side-stepped.

He closed that evening's interview with the boast that he would follow her to the very ends of the earth. She gave him the opportunity, literally, by observing dryly that her destination was precisely at the world's end—in the mountains beyond Chungking, to be exact.

He took the breath out of her mouth by saying that he would travel on the same river-boat with her to Chungking, if he had to scrub down decks for his passage. She told him not to be a silly boy; that he was, underneath his uncouthness, really a dear, but that he didn't know women. He replied that he knew one of the deadly species just well enough to follow her wherever she went, world without end, amen.

"You are insane," she said, a little frightened.

"About you," replied Bobbie, trying hard not to kiss her.

When the *Sunyado Maru* dropped anchor off Woosung, Miss Vost let Bobbie hold her hand an instant longer than was necessary, and stubbornly refused to accompany him in the same sampan—or the same tug—to the customs jetty. Summarily, she went up the Whang-poo all alone, while Bobbie, biting his finger-nails, purposely quarreled with the staid British captain, and was invited to sign off, which he did.

Through devious subterranean channels Bobbie MacLaurin found that the berth of master on the *Hankow* was vacant, the latest incumbent having relinquished his spirit to cholera. Was he willing to assume the tremendous responsibility? He was tremendously willing! Did he possess good papers? He most assuredly did!

WHEN the Shanghai express rolled into the Nanking station, Bobbie MacLaurin climbed into a rattling rickshaw and clattered off in the direction of the river-front, registering the profound hope that Miss Vost had somehow managed to reach the *Hankow* ahead of him. Peter Moore, who knew China's ancient capital like a book, struck off in a diagonal direction on foot.

He made his way to a Chinese tailor's, who bought from him the Japanese costume and sold him a suit of gray tweeds, which another customer had failed to call for. While not an adornment, the gray tweeds were comfortably European, a relief from the flapping, clumsy kimono.

Half confident that Miss Vost might have come to Nanking by the slower train, which left Shanghai an hour or so ahead of the express, he ventured to the Bridge Hotel and made inquiries.

It developed that Miss Vost, or a young lady closely in harmony with the description he gave to the curious clerk, had come, breakfasted, and departed for parts unknown. She left no forwarding address, nothing indeed but good Shanghai silver to pay for the food she ate.

He waited a while, hoping that she might return. In the courtyard English song sparrows and cooing doves gave expression to their musical temperaments; and a wheelbarrow squeaked by. But Miss Vost did not return.

He wanted to have a little talk with her before she saw Bobbie MacLaurin again. He had so much affection for Bobbie that he wanted to ask Miss Vost to, please, not be unnecessarily cruel with him. He did not know that Miss Vost was never unnecessarily cruel to any living creature; for he made the mistake there of classifying women, without modifications, into the good and the cruel, of which Miss Vost seemed to be among the latter.

As a matter of fact, Miss Vost was simply a young woman very far from home, compelled to believe in, and on occasion to resort to, the primitive methods of self-defense.

Peter waited at the Bridge Hotel until the afternoon was half spent. Then he took a rickshaw to the river.

He picked out the *Hankow* among the clutter of shipping, anchored not far from shore, and out of reach of the swift current which rushed dangerously down midchannel. Black smoke issued from her single chubby funnel. Blue-coated coolies sped to and fro on her single narrow deck.

With professional interest Peter Moore searched the air between the two spars until his eye caught the bronze glint of the aerial wires. He followed the single black line, indicating the "lead in" wires, which dropped from the forward end of the aerial to a small cabin on the top deck, located directly aft of the pilot-house. Here he caught sight of Bobbie MacLaurin's dominating figure. The captain of the *Hankow* seemed to be searching the jagged shore-line with some intentness. Perhaps Miss Vost had not yet arrived.

Peter Moore left the massive wall of Nanking behind him, taking a sampan, for which he dickered briefly in the coolie's own tongue.

Bobbie MacLaurin leaned far out across the rail as the sampan slapped smartly alongside. The coolie thrashed the water into yellowy foam. Peter Moore drew himself up on the lower rung of the Jacob's ladder.

"Have you seen Miss Vost?" shouted MacLaurin above the hiss of escaping steam. "We pull out in an hour, Miss Vost or no Miss Vost. That's orders."

Peter Moore, reaching the deck, scanned the pagoda-dotted shore-front.

"Not a sign of her," he said. "But she's in Nanking. I just missed her at the hotel. Had breakfast and vamosed. She'll be here."

Pu-Chang, the *Hankow's* pilot, a slender, grayed Chinese, grown old before his time, in the river service, sidled between them, smiling mistily, and asked his captain if the emergency steering-gear had been delivered. While MacLaurin went to make inquiries, Peter Moore climbed into the little cabin behind the wheel-house and inspected his wireless equipment.

When he returned to the deck a sampan, bow on, was floating down-stream, with the intention, evidently, of making connections with the *Hankow's* Jacob-ladder. On her abrupt foredeck was a slim figure of blue and white.

Startled a little by recollection, Peter Moore leaned far out. For a moment he imagined the white face to be that of Aileen Lorimer. The demure attitude of Miss Vost's hands, caught by the fingertips before her, gave further grounds to Peter Moore for the comparison. Her youth and innocence had as much to do with it as anything, for there was undeniably an air of youth and extreme innocence about Miss Vost.

Something in the shape of a triumphant bellow was roared from the engine-room companionway. Whereupon the companionway disgorged the monumental figure of Bobbie McLaurin, grinning like a schoolboy at his first party.

He seized Miss Vost by both hands, swinging her neatly to the deck.

She panted, and fell back against the rail, holding her hand to her heart, and welcoming Bobbie MacLaurin by a glance that was not entirely cordial.

"The sampan boy hasn't been paid," she remarked, opening her purse. "It's twenty cents."

While MacLaurin pulled a silver dollar from his pocket and spun it to the anxious coolie, Miss Vost turned with the warmest of smiles to Peter Moore. Rarely had any girl seemed more delighted to see him, for which, under the circumstances, Peter found it somewhat difficult to be entirely grateful.

He experienced again that dull feeling of guilt. He felt that she ought to show more cordiality than she had to Bobbie MacLaurin. Here was Bobbie, trailing after her like a faithful dog, on the most hazardous trip that any man could devise, and he had not been rewarded, so far, with even the stingiest of smiles.

Women were like that. They took the fruits of your work, or they took your life, or let you toss it to the crows, without a sign of gratitude. At least, some women were like that. He had hoped Miss Vost was not that kind. He had hoped—Miss Vost laid her small, warm hand in his, and she seemed perfectly willing to let it linger. Gazing softly up into his troubled eyes, she gave him to understand, without the crudity of speech, that she was happy now—now that she was again with *him*.

Her lips were parted in a smile that was all but a caress. She seemed to have forgotten that the perplexed, the baffled young man who had stared so fixedly at the back of her pretty, white neck had ever existed. She was all for Peter. That was evident.

It was quite embarrassing for Peter. Nevertheless, a warm glow stole without rights into his guilty heart. The feeling of the warm, little hand that lay so confidingly, so intimately, within his, sent an electric shock into his brain.

Then, aware of the pain in the face of Bobbie MacLaurin, a face that had all suddenly gone white, and realizing his duty to this true friend of his, he pushed Miss Vost's hands away from him.

CHAPTER VI

THE SECOND PASSENGER

THAT GESTURE SERVED to bring them all back to earth.

"Aren't you glad—aren't you a little bit glad—to see me—me?" said the hurt voice of Bobbie MacLaurin.

Miss Vost pivoted gracefully, giving Peter Moore a view of her splendid, straight back for a change.

"Of course I am, Bobbie!" she exclaimed gently. "I'm always glad to see you. Why—Oh, look! Did you ever see such a Chinaman?"

They all joined in her look. A salmon-colored sampan, riding swiftly to the *Hankow's* riveted steel side. With long legs spread wide apart atop the low cabin stood a very tall, very grave Chinese. His long, blanched face was more than grave, more than austere. To its celestial majesty and mystery was added a grimace of malignity, a look of downright villainy.

Peter Moore stared and ransacked his memory. He had seen that face, that grimace, before. His mind went back to the shop front, on Nanking Road, last evening, when he was skulking toward the bund from the friendly establishment of his friend, the silk merchant, Ching Gow Ong. Yet Chinese were indisputably alike. It had taken Peter years to distinguish a Cantonese from a Pekingese.

This man was neither Cantonese or Pekingese. His long, rather supercilious face, his aquiline nose, the sudden flare of his nostrils, the back-tilted head, the high, narrow brow, and the shock of blue-black hair identified the Chinese stranger, even if his abnormal, rangy height were not taken into consideration, as a hill man, perhaps Tibetan, perhaps Mongolian. Certainly his features were sharply, acutely Mongoloid; certainly he was no river man.

Yet was he the man who had trailed him, dodging from one shop doorway to another along Nanking Road, until Peter had tricked him into the hands of a Sikh.

It seemed improbable that the window-breaker could have been released by the heartless Shanghai police so quickly; yet Peter himself was aware of the powers of Chinese "squeeze"; out of his own adventurous past he could remember more than one occasion when a bribe had saved him from embarrassing consequences.

There was no constraint in the pose of the man on the sampan's flat roof. With carelessness bordering upon outright indifference his narrow gaze flitted from the face of Bobbie MacLaurin to that of Miss Vost, and wandered on to the stern, sharp-eyed visage of Peter Moore.

Here the casual gaze rested. If he recognized Peter Moore, he gave no indication of it. He studied Peter's countenance with the look of one whose interest may be distracted on the slightest provocation.

An intelligent and wary student of human nature, Peter dropped his eyes to the man's long, clawlike fingers. These were twitching ever so slightly, plucking slowly it may have been meditatively at the hem of his black silk coat. At the intentness of Peter's stare, this twitching abruptly ceased.

The sampan whacked alongside. The big man tossed a small, orange-silk bag to the deck. He climbed the ladder as if he had been used to climbing all his life.

"I don't care for his looks," remarked Miss Vost, looking up into Peter's face with a curious smile.

"Nor I," said Bobbie MacLaurin.

The richly dressed stranger vaulted nimbly over the teak-rail, recovered the orange bag, and approached MacLaurin. His head drooped forward momentarily, in recognition of the authority of the blue uniform.

He said, in excellent English:

"I desire to engage passage to Chungking. I trust there is room."

"There is," replied the *Hankow's* captain. "This way."

"You seemed to recognize him," said Miss Vost to Peter, when they had the deck to themselves.

"Perhaps I was mistaken," replied Peter evasively. He suddenly was aware of Miss Vost's wide-eyed look of concern.

Impulsively she laid her hand on his arm. She had come up very close to him. Her head moved back, so that her chin was almost on a level with his.

"Mr. Moore," she said in a low, soft voice, "I won't ask you any questions. In China, there are many, many things that a woman must not try to understand. But I-I want to tell you that—that I think you are—splendid. It seems so fine, so good of you. I-I can't begin to thank you. My—my feelings prevent it."

"But—why—what—what—" stammered Peter.

"Oh, Mr. Moore, I know—I know!" proceeded Miss Vost tenderly. "Like all fine, brave men, you are—you are modest! It—it almost makes me want to cry, to think—to think—"

"But Miss Vost," interrupted Peter gently and gravely, "you are shooting over my head. I don't know what you're talking about!"

In the rakish bows of the *Hankow* arose the clank and clatter of wet anchor-chains. A bell tinkled in the engine-room. The stout fabric of the little steamer shook and shuddered. The yellow water began to slip by them. On the shore two pagodas moved slowly into alinement. The *Hankow* was moving.

Miss Vost strengthened her gentle hold upon Peter's unreluctant arm. Her bright eyes were a trifle blurred.

"Last night, when we met on the bund," she went on in a small voice, "I knew immediately—immediately—what you were. A chivalrous gentleman! A man who would shelter and protect any helpless woman he met!"

"That was nice of you," murmured Peter.

Like Saul of Tarsus, he was beginning to see a bright light.

"And it was true!" exclaimed Miss Vost musically. "Now—now, you are risking your life—for poor, unworthy little me! Please don't deny it, Mr. Moore! I only wanted to let you know that I-I understand, and that I am—g-grateful!"

Her eyelids fluttered over an unstifled moistness. The rosebud mouth was very close to his lips, and very inviting.

But Peter Moore's thoughts had gone back to the sweet young face that bore such close resemblance to the blushing features before him; and his memory gave him the hungry little sentence of the other girl.

"It—it isn't fair," he blurted.

Miss Vost opened her eyes on a look that was hurt and humiliated. He had insulted her. He had wounded her sensitiveness, which in Miss Vost was as delicate as a violet. She stepped back, slowly relinquishing his arm.

"It isn't fair to him. It isn't fair to Bobbie. He loves you. He'd do anything in the world for you. He told me so. He told me—"

"What?"

"He'd go to hell for you!"

"He's an overgrown boy. He doesn't know what he says. That's nonsense," declared Miss Vost, looking away from Peter in shame. "I know his type, Mr. Moore. He falls in love with every pretty face; and he falls out again, quite as easily."

"You don't know Bobbie the way I do," said Peter stubbornly.

"I don't have to. I know his kind—a girl in every port."

"No, no. Not Bobbie!"

For a moment it seemed that they had come to an impasse. Miss Vost was blinking her eyes rapidly, appearing to be somewhat interested in a junk which was poling downstream. Peter seemed to be in a panic.

She looked up with a wan smile. Tears were again in her eyes.

"Mr. Moore," she said in a broken voice, "what you've told me about Mr. MacLaurin, Captain MacLaurin, moves me—deeply!"

"Do try to be nice to Bobbie," begged Peter. "He is the finest fellow I know. He is true blue. He would give his life for your little finger. Really he would, Miss Vost!"

The bright eyes gave him a languishing look.

"I'll try," she said simply.

CHAPTER VII

THE INCREDIBLE WAVE

AFTER DINNER PETER ventured up to the wireless shack, to give it a more particular look-see. He tested out the various instruments, discovered a dusty hydrometer, found that the specific gravity of the batteries was too high, and wondered where he might find some distilled water with which to dilute the solution in the cells.

While this process of thought was taking place his eyes wandered to the receiving apparatus, a little glistening heap of polished rubber and copper, which straggled down the whole length of the mahogany ledge. All of a sudden he stopped thinking, and he sat bolt upright as something out of the or-dinary in connection with the woodwork behind the ledge caught his attention.

Projecting out from the wall, along the entire span of the ledge, was what appeared to be a deep, heavily enameled wood panel. This measured about eight feet in length and three feet in height. It projected only an inch or so from the wall, partook of its color, and would not have attracted Peter's attention had he not noticed a number of exceedingly fine copper wires pro-truding from small holes along the bottom.

He unscrewed the panel and lifted it gingerly away. This revealed a depression in which it was given Peter to look upon the most gigantic coil of fine copper wire he had ever imagined. He had never seen such a coil. It was all of two meters in length, and all of one meter in diameter, and wound throughout with a single glistening ruddy coil of pure copper!

Peter stared at the coil, which represented miles of copper hair-wire, and knitted his brow into dark, deep furrows, wonder-ing what on earth (although he employed a different locality in describing his feelings) this monster of coils could have been placed there to do.

But Peter was not of the kidney which wonders overlong. He knew at least what *he* could do with that glowing mass of wire, and he did not lose very many moments in idle contemplation.

This light-hearted adventurer, as readers of his previously recorded experiences may recall, had been, before his forced retirement from active service in Shanghai, one of the crack operators of the Pacific.

His first berth had been a small and dejected fishing schooner which tottered up and down the rock-bound coast as far north, when the weather wore a particularly kind smile, as the Aleutian Islands.

By sticking coolly to his instruments for a seventy-two-hour watch on one of these uncertain voyages, he had managed to keep in communication with a steamer aground in the Inland Passage, which is a somewhat precarious channel frequently patronized by ships running between Vancouver and Alaskan ports.

Growing out of this trying seventy-two-hour vigil, Peter's ability, his reliability, and his intelligence, all were recognized and subsequently rewarded. He was placed in charge of wireless cabins on many ships before he came to China.

In the course of this time Peter had become something of an inventor. Probably his most valuable contribution to the science was a self-adjusting detector, which eventually found its way into the most important of the Marconi stations.

Many idle moments are given to wireless operators, whose chief function at sea is to sit and listen. But Peter's was a restless disposition. He experimented constantly. There was always an eager willingness on the part of operators to take Peter's place when he left for another ship. They were sure to find the equipment at the highest pitch of smooth-working efficiency.

With this splendid coil, and with all the time in the world on his hands, Peter felt that he was in a position now to perform an experiment that had long been denied him.

For the sake of clarity and understanding, let us consider for a moment the wireless means for transmitting intelligence. Wireless signals are transmitted from one station to another by means of invisible electric waves. These waves of electric energy, not unlike the waves on the ocean's surface, are of various sizes. The wireless machine on a small ship sends out a small, or short, wave. Larger ships send out larger, longer waves. Shore stations, because of the tremendous amount of wire they have in the air, send out exceedingly long waves.

For example, the wave-length of the *Hankow's* diminutive apparatus was somewhere in the neighborhood of three hundred meters. The wave-length of the Federal wireless stations at San Francisco and Honolulu is nearly ten thousand meters.

Now, in order for Peter Moore, with his diminutive apparatus, to hear wave-lengths as great as ten thousand meters, it would be necessary for him to supplement his equipment with many, many coils.

This he was now prepared to do. On the ships where he had worked previously, he had never been given the opportunity to listen for long wave-lengths. That was not necessary, from a commercial point of view. All Marconi and government stations that he held communication with transmitted on either the three-hundred-meter or the six-hundred-meter wave.

But now, in the spirit of the explorer, Peter desired to reach into the heavens, to pluck down and to listen to those gigantic electric waves which rose higher than the peaks of the Himalayas. In order to accomplish this rather interesting feat, all of those surplus coils lying behind the narrow mahogany ledge were necessary.

He experienced a sort of thrill as he set about this task. It seemed like old times—the glitter of the instruments, the faint buzzing of distant ships in the receivers clamped to his ears—the substantial pounding of the *Hankow's* mighty propeller.

The man who has known what wanderlust means—that tremendous tugging at the heart-strings by remote, strange lands—can appreciate the love that Peter Moore had for his craft; for it carried him directly to these remote, strange lands; and it uncovered for him the wells of romance and adventure.

In plumbing the higher altitudes for what these regions might have to offer, Peter Moore's thrill took on definite shape. Perhaps he had the thrill of the man who, having used a shotgun all his life, was given the privilege of pulling the electric trigger of a fourteen-inch gun, or the sensation that Isaac Walton might have experienced had he angled for tarpon.

Peter expected to land big fish; nor was he disappointed. Several hours winged by that might have been minutes. With pincers and knife he hooked up the many coils of fine wire to his receptor. Finally, he listened in, slowly swinging the handle of his tuner. He heard nothing.

The *Hankow* was pounding speedily upriver, the deep vibrations of her great engine keeping every loose object in the wireless cabin in motion. Hearing was difficult. Yet Peter was the possessor of a pair of hypersensitive ears. More than once he had heard distant signals in the receivers when the average operator could hear nothing. But now there was nothing in the receivers.

He took pencil and paper out of the drawer and did some figuring. He frowned, then grinned. No wonder! He had attached enough coils of wire to intercept a wave of thirty thousand meters! No station in the entire world used such a monstrous wave-length! But still.

He clamped the hard rubber receivers so tightly to his ears that a vacuum was formed. He had heard—or was it imagination?—a high, faint wail, like a silvery note on the night wind. The signals were too faint for deciphering. Yet they were there. He slid down the tuning handle, thereby cutting out one hundred meters of wire. The signals were gone!

Beads of cold sweat leaked out upon his forehead. His heart out-drowned the engines. He had made a vastly important discovery, a discovery that he would keep to himself. Some station, he knew not where, was transmitting signals on a thirty-thousand-meter wave! It was unbelievable—incredible!

It meant but one thing. Some one was making use of gigantic waves which were not intended for ordinary ears. Some one, evidently aware of the secrecy that could be had in transmissions on this enormous wave-length, was carrying on a wireless conversation that would pay listening attentively to!

So he listened, shoving back the tuning handle to its original position. Like the whining of a mosquito, he heard a weak answering wail. Distinctly he made out the signals. An experienced operator was at that far-away key. The signals spelled "O K.—O.K. Good night."

What did it mean? A chain of mysterious wireless stations operating in the heart of China? Monstrous! But what could they be used for?

Peter sat back in his chair, shivering. He looked out of the doorway and into the smiling vision of Miss Vost, who had been standing there, he knew not how long, witnessing his excitement.

A pink scarf, snapping in the breeze, was wound about her throat. As she met his glance, her smile was replaced by a straightness of lips which lent some emphasis to the silky whiteness of her face and to the look of longing in her wide, gray eyes.

"Hearing things?" she inquired softly.

Peter observed that she wore a long, loose-fitting gray coat, which was exceedingly becoming. It would have been difficult to picture her in anything that was not becoming.

He dropped the receivers to the mahogany ledge and shook his head.

"Then come out on deck. Do come out! It's so stuffy in this little coop. You should see the big, golden moon, riding along the wall of China! It's entrancing. I'm lonely. Won't you come out of your den, Mr. Monster, and talk a wee little bit?"

Mr. Monster observed that Captain MacLaurin was certainly capable of supplying this deficit.

"Bobbie's in the pilot-house, learning, as he says, the soul of the terrible river, by feeling its pulse!"

The banks of the great river were gray and mysterious under the effulgence of a top-heavy yellow moon. The search-light on the peak pierced out the fact that a low, swirling mist was creeping up from the river's dulled surface.

The air was damp with the breath of the flat, dim land. Occasionally the gentle puffs of the wind bore along the water the flavor of queer, indistinguishable odors; pungent, sweet smells that stirred the imagination, but gave no satisfactory answer. Sour or sweet, they partook of the mystery, the troubled yearning, that alone is China's.

Elbow to elbow, glancing down at the hissing water, Miss Vost and Peter stood for a number of sweet, meditative moments in silence. At length Miss Vost slipped her arm through his.

"Sometimes," she murmured, inclining her head until it almost rested against his shoulder, "I feel lonely—terrible! Especially on such a night as this. The moon is so impersonal, isn't it? Here it is, a great, gorgeous ball of cold fire, shining across China at you and me. In Amoy it came up and shone and went away again. I was ill, and it seemed to frown at me. Now—it seems to smile. The same moon!"

"The same moon!" whispered Peter as her warm hand somehow slipped down and snuggled in his.

"Don't *you* ever feel lonely—like this?" demanded Miss Vost suddenly.

Peter sighed. "Oh, often. Often! The world seems so big, and so filled with things that are hard to learn, that keep—that keep moving farther and farther away from you as you try and try to grasp them. Especially at night!" He wondered what she thought he meant.

"I-I feel that way," Miss Vost's absorbed voice replied. "I try—and try—to reason these things out. But they are so baffling! So elusive! So evasive! Here is China, with its millions of poor, wretched ones, struggling in darkness and disease. They are so many! And they are so hard to help. And out beyond there, not so many miles beyond that ridge, lies Tibet, with her millions, and her ignorance, and her disease. And to the left— away to the left, I think, is India.

"If a person would be happy, he must not come to China or India. Their problems are too overwhelming. You cannot think of solutions fast enough, and even while you think, you are overcome by the weariness, the hopelessness, of it all. I wish I had never come to China!"

"We are young," said Peter gravely.

"Yes," breathed Miss Vost, "we are young. But you agree with me, don't you?"

"By all means!" he reassured her. "To me, you have a fine and very beautiful mind."

"Ah!" she said with a confiding little laugh. "You wonder why I like you so. I suppose you are astonished every time a woman makes love to you."

"I would hardly say that," gasped Peter. "You—I—"

"I'll tell you why. You have understanding. You credit me, and you probably credit other women you meet, with minds— with souls! We like to know that we're something other than pretty little dolls."

"Of course," agreed Peter hazily; "Yes, indeed! Of course!"

"We like to talk of the things that stir and move the world, perhaps as much as men do. We feel the forces of life. Perhaps we don't express them well enough—"

"You express them beautifully," disagreed Peter.

"We feel the ache and the sorrow of years that have gone. We do feel the bitterness—yes—the rottenness—of nations that are marching blindly to ruin. China is honeycombed with immorality. Do you agree with me?"

"In a way." It was on Peter's lips to tell her of the most glaring sample of immorality that had so far been brought to his attention. He was thinking of the Gray Dragon, of the indescribable poverty and wretchedness of Len Yang and the cinnabar mines of Len Yang.

"I happened to be in Fu-Chow not long ago," Miss Vost continued. "There is in Fu-Chow a tower that illustrates what I mean. It is called the baby tower. Girls, you know, aren't thought much of in China. At the bottom of the tower is a deep well. Women to whom are born baby girls go to the baby tower—" Miss Vost shuddered. "The babies are thrown into the well. I have seen them. They are quite heartless, quite ruthless about it. Poor—poor, little creatures. Squirming, moaning, dying like that!"

"It is cruel," said Peter sadly.

Miss Vost sniffled to herself for a moment. Brightly she said: "I like to talk to you, Mr. Moore. You're so—*so* sympathetic!"

"I try to be," said Peter, not knowing how it could be possible to be otherwise.

A great, dark shadow bulked up against the rail alongside Peter.

"Good evening, folks!" declared the pleasant bass voice of Bobbie MacLaurin.

"We were just talking about you, Bobbie," said Peter affably. "As I was telling Miss Vost, you're the most sympathetic man I ever knew! Good night, Miss Vost. Night, Bobs!"

CHAPTER VIII

THE MARK ON THE DOOR

WHEN PETER DESCENDED the stairway into the narrow vestibule which served as reception-hall, dining-saloon, and, incidentally, as the corridor from which the *Hankow's* four small staterooms were entered, he had the chilly feeling that the darkness had eyes.

Yet he saw nothing. The cabin was dark. Three round ports glimmered greenly beyond the staircase on the cabin's forward side. The glimmer was occasioned by the refracted rays of the *Hankow's* dazzling search-light. But these were not the eyes he felt.

Gradually his own eyes became accustomed to the pulp-like darkness. He steadied his body against the gentle swaying of the steamer, and endeavored to listen above, or through, the imminent thrashing and clattering of the huge engine.

He examined the four stateroom doors anxiously. In his haste to make the experiment with the wireless machine, he had neglected to identify properly the big Mongoloid who had come aboard the last minute before sailing. He had not seen him at dinner. Where was he?

As the darkness began to dissolve slightly, Peter, still conscious that eyes were fastened upon him, made the discovery that the stateroom door adjoining his was slightly ajar. The moon favored him—Miss Vost's impersonal moon. It outlined, against the slit, between the door and the jamb, what appeared to be a large, irregular, block.

Peter decided that the irregular block was nothing more nor less than the head of a man. To prove that his surmise was correct, Peter quickly shifted the revolver from his right hand to his left, brought it even with his eyes and—struck a match.

In the startling flare of the phosphorus the evil glint of Celestial eyes was instantly revealed in the partly opened door.

With incredible softness the door was closed. Where there had been half-lidded eyes, a positive snarl, and a shock of blue-black hair was now a white-enameled panel.

Peter continued to smile along the barrel, which glistened wickedly in the dying flame of the match; but his knees, it must be confessed, were trembling, if slightly.

He pinched out the flame with his fingers, crossed the room with steps as springy and wary as a panther's, and put his ear to the closed door. There was silence, not even a rustle—that is, if the hideous clang and thump of the *Hankow's* engines were left out of consideration.

Now, it must be said here, no matter how many times it may have been remarked before, that Peter Moore was no amateur in the ways of the East.

Otherwise it would be exceedingly difficult to account for his next actions.

He gave the door no more attention. But he struck another match and ran the flickering flame up and down and across the white panel of his own stateroom door. After a while, hidden adroitly in a depression, he found a faint green chalk mark.

To Peter the upper mark was nothing but the sign of a certain band, presumably the band of the Gray Dragon. It was the lower mark, the latter closely resembling our letter "T" which aroused his interest.

That letter "T," with the little horn or knob to the left, was Chinese for death. So remarkable is the Chinese written language that if the "T" were altered in some respects it would have an entirely different meaning. For example, if the knob on the left side of the "T" were carefully and cleanly erased the symbol would mean, not death, but "I have come and gone."

By slightly moistening his little finger and wiping away the little horn, Peter very probably saved his adventurous young neck.

He unlocked the door, closed it, and shot the bolt. Switching on the electric light, he cautiously drew back the sheet, on the lookout for a certain, dark powder which would arise on slight provocation and instantly poison a man to death.

Apparently satisfied, he sniffed the air. It was nothing more than stuffy, as a stateroom that has been closed for a week or so is apt to be.

Unscrewing the fat wingbolts which clamped down the brass-bound port-glass, he let in a breath of misty river air. Simultaneously voices came into the room.

Miss Vost and Bobbie MacLaurin were conversing in clear, tense syllables. Peter could not help eavesdropping. They were seemingly standing on the deck, directly over his stateroom, only a few scant feet from his port-hole, which was situated much nearer the deck than the surging water.

Unblushingly he listened. Peter was quite as anxious to have Bobbie sell himself to Miss Vost, as Miss Vost was anxious not to have him.

"But I do—I do love you!" Bobbie was complaining in his rumbling voice. "Ever since you set foot on the old *Sunyado Maru* I've been your shadow—your slave! What more can any man say?" he added bitterly.

"Not a great deal," rejoined the lighthearted accents of Miss Vost.

She seemed to become suddenly serious. "Bobbie, I do like you. I admire you ever so much. But it happens that you are not the man for me. You don't understand me. You can never understand me. I've already told you that a half hundred times. We weren't made for each other, Bobbie. Don't you realize it? You're too sudden—too brutal—too—"

"Brutal! I've treated you like a flower. I want to shield you—"

"But I don't *need* shielding, Bobbie. I'm prudent, fearless, and—twenty-two. I don't need a watch-dog!"

"Good God, did I say anything about being a watchdog?" exclaimed Bobbie, whose patience was sorely tried. "I-I just want—"

"You just want me," completed Miss Vost. "Well, you can't have me."

"You love somebody else, then. That young pup, Peter Moore!"

Peter stifled a sharp grunt and stared sourly at the bilious moon.

"Don't you dare call him a young pup, Robert MacLaurin," retorted Miss Vost resentfully. "He is a fine, fine young man. I admire him and I respect him. I admire him and I respect him very, very much."

"He can't fool around any girl of mine!"

Peter heard Bobbie sucking the breath in between his teeth, as if he might have pricked himself with a pin. Bobbie had done worse than that.

"A girl of *yours!*" snapped Miss Vost. "You're positively insulting!"

Followed low, anxious and imploratory whispers, which Peter guessed to be a painful attempt upon Bobbie's part to patch up the *faux-pas.*

These were terminated by a long, light, and delicious laugh.

"Ha, ha, ha!" replied Miss Vost and gurgled. "Ha, ha! Bobbie, you're so *funny!*"

"I wish I was dead!" declared Bobbie despondently.

"You should go to Liauchow," suggested Miss Vost amiably.

Peter Moore pricked up his ears. Liauchow was a pleasant place. It was a manufacturing community, probably as prosperous as any city in China. He had liked the atmosphere of it.

"Why should I go to Liauchow?" grumbled the bass voice above him.

"To be happy," advised Miss Vost chirpily, "you must be born in Soochow, live in Canton, and die in Liauchow. So runs the proverb."

"But *why* should *I* go to Liauchow?" persisted Bobbie.

"Because Soochow has the handsomest people, Canton the most luxury, and Liauchow the best coffins!"

CHAPTER IX

TEMPTATION

PETER MOORE'S CURIOSITY regarding the motives which were sending Miss Amy Vost into Szechwan, most deplorable, most poverty-stricken of China's many deplorable, poverty-stricken provinces, was satisfied before the *Hankow* had put astern the great turbulent city, after which it had been named.

At Hankow the *Hankow* picked up the raft which it would tow all the way up to Chungking. Upon this raft was a long, squat cabin, in and out of which poured incessantly members of China's large and growing family.

There were stout, dirty little men, and fat, soiled little women, and quantities of fat, dirty little boys and girls. A great noise went up from the raft as the *Hankow* nosed in alongside, and hawsers were passed and made fast over the bitts.

As the big propeller thumped under them and churned the muddy water into unhealthy-looking foam, Peter Moore and Miss Vost leaned upon the rail, where it curved around the fantail, and discoursed at length, speculating upon the probable destination of that raftful of dirty humanity, and offering problematic answers to the puzzling question as to why were all these people deserting relatively prosperous Hankow for the overpopulated, overdeveloped province of Szechwan?

As the *Hankow* swung out again into mid-stream, to resume her course, the raft was dragged close in alongside until it lay flat against the bumpers. This maneuver brought within close range a number of the raft's sordid inhabitants. They were river people—that could be seen in a glance: filthy, unkempt, and pitifully arrogant of bearing.

Peter had an inkling that Miss Vost was distressed by the scene.

"Let's take a stroll forward," he suggested.

An urchin, directly below them, stood rubbing his eyes with two grimy fists. His whines were audible above the churning of the engines.

"No, no. I'm quite accustomed to this. Look—just look at that miserable little fellow!"

"He is blind," stated Peter quietly.

"Half of them are blind," replied Miss Vost. Her features were transfixed by a look of sorrow. "Wait for me. I'll return in a second."

Peter watched the graceful swing of her shoulders as she strode down the deck to the forward companionway, commenting inwardly upon the slim strength of her silk-clad ankles. She was every inch an American girl. He was proud of her.

She returned, carrying a small oblong of cardboard, upon which a photograph was pasted. She gave it to him.

Peter found himself looking into the sad, bewrinkled eyes of a gray-bearded man, a patriarchal gentleman, who stood on the hard clay at the foot of a low stone stairway. His nose, his eyes, his intellectual forehead were distinctly those of Miss Vost. A child in a freshly starched frock, with eyes opened wide in surprise and interest, was firmly clutching one of his trouser-legs.

"My father," explained Miss Vost. "That photograph was taken many, many years ago—I refuse to tell you how many! Father was stationed at Wenchow then, in charge of the Methodist mission. I have not seen him since then."

Peter remarked to himself that somehow Miss Vost did not seem to be the daughter of a missionary, nor was the costly way she dressed in key with her remark. Perhaps she divined his thoughts.

"He has money—lots of money. He has a keen, broad mind—I know he would have made a success of business. But he chose this. When he was first married he brought mother to China. He saw, and realized, China's vast problems. And he stayed. He wanted to help."

Peter gazed into her gray eyes, which seemed to take on a clear violet tinge when she was deeply moved; and in his look there was a wealth of understanding and sympathy.

"He told me to come to see him because he was growing old."

"You stopped off in Amoy," remarked Peter quietly.

"I was obedient," said Miss Vost with the ghost of a smile. "A young missionary he wanted me to meet lives there. I met him."

"Your father thought—"

"Yes," said Miss Vost decisively. "But I could not admire that young missionary. He was a—a *poseur.* He was pretending. One reason I've grown so fond of you, Mr. Moore, is because you're so sincere. He was not in sympathy with China's faults, nor her children. He was so transparent! And his 'converts' saw through him, too. They were bread-and-butter converts. They listened to him; they devoured his food—then they went to the fortune-tellers! Father could not have known Dr. Sanborn longer than a few minutes—or else he's not the father that he used to be! I inherit his love for sincerity. I-I'm sure he will like you!"

"But—but"—stammered Peter—"I don't expect to go to Wenchow. Better say he'd like—Bobbie!"

"Oh, he'd like anybody that I liked," said Miss Vost lightly. "It—it's really interesting, you know, from Chungking to Wenchow. We take bullock carts—if we can find them. Otherwise we walk. Doesn't it—appeal to you—just a little—to be all alone with me for nearly a hundred miles?"

"Very much indeed," replied Peter earnestly. "But our roads part—at Chungking. You go your way. I go directly south."

"Tibet?"

Peter made no reply.

"In search of more adventure and romance? Perhaps—perhaps a girl who is not so silly as I have been? Or—is it India—or Afghanistan?"

"Neither." Peter began to feel distressingly uncomfortable.

"A friend!"

"An old friend!" admitted Peter, sighing more easily.

"Is that why you are growing a beard to surprise—*him?*"

"Perhaps," said Peter, absently fingering the bristles which, so far, gave him the inelegant appearance of a shipwrecked sailor or a plain hobo. "Don't tell me it's unbecoming or I'll have to shave it off!"

"As if what I thought made a particle of difference!" retorted Miss Vost defiantly.

Peter gave her a thoughtful, a puzzled, stare. "If I made love to you, Miss Vost," he said slowly, "what would you do? What would you think?"

"I'd think it was quite nice—and respectful," returned Miss Vost brightly. "I'd simply let you! When shall we start?"

In light of the violet glow which suddenly came into Miss Vost's gray eyes, Peter was aware that these words were not uttered entirely in a spirit of levity. In spite of his vows, he knew that he was weakening. He could picture, with absolutely no effort, the sublime pleasure of wrapping that slender, soft body in his muscular young arms, and smothering the warm, rosebud mouth with his hot lips.

Fortunately for the peace of his oath to the other girl, he was not under the seductive influence of last night's impersonal moon. He was standing upon the unrestricted fantail of a steamboat, in the direct gaze of a number of pairs of interested and curios eyes. He was on the Whang-poo, abreast of the outskirts of Hankow; he was not in dreamland!

"There is Bobbie!" he muttered.

"Oh, rubbish!" replied Miss Vost.

"Just the same, I overheard you last night. You broke your promise. You promised to be nice to him."

"I was."

"You weren't!"

"Do you mean what I said about Liauchow?"

"That was cruel. You don't realize what you *mean* to Bobbie. My dear, dear girl—"

"I am not your dear, dear girl! You won't let me be!"

"Oh, shucks! What's the use of arguing with a woman? Why didn't you slap me in the face when I spoke to you on the bund the other night? It would have saved all this—this—heartache!"

"Does your heart ache, too, Peter?"

"Of course it does! I—I'd like to love you!"

"Then why don't you?"

"Why—why didn't I kiss you when you came aboard at Nanking—when—when I had the chance!"

"Well?"

"It wouldn't have been fair, that's why!"

"To—Bobbie?"

"Bobbie, too."

"Then there is another girl," said Miss Vost bitterly. She bit her lip. "You should have told me before."

"I thought it wouldn't be necessary."

Miss Vost dropped her eyes to Peter's hand which was resting on the rail. Her own hand moved over and nestled against it.

"Do—do you l-love her as much as th-this?" Her eyes returned to his face, deep and imploring.

"I did think I did!"

"But you're not sure—now?"

"Oh, I thought I was sure! I am sure!"

"There's little more to say, then, is there?" Her voice was small and piteous.

Suddenly she seemed to be very small and frail and helpless. Her lids were blinking rapidly as she looked down at the mob of filthy little Arabs on the flat. Her fingers plucked, trembling, at the embroidered hem of a white, wadded handkerchief. She seemed to droop all over.

"Bobbie *does* care for you so," observed Peter with unintentional cruelty.

"Oh—oh—*him!*" sobbed Miss Vost, leaving him to stare after her drooping figure as she retreated down the deck.

CHAPTER X

A CHINESE GENTLEMAN

HE WONDERED WHERE she would go for solace. Bobbie? Not likely. Perhaps she would go to her stateroom, which would be hot and stuffy at high noon. Yet she seemed on a sudden to be avoiding the entrance to the forward companionway.

He wondered why.

Miss Vost stopped, stock-still, with her hands clenched into white fists at her sides.

From the doorway, smiling suavely and wiping one hand upon the other in a gesture of solicitous meekness, emerged the tall and commanding figure of the Mongolian—or was he a Tibetan? He was attired now in the finest, the shiniest of Canton silks. His satin pants, of a gorgeous white, a courting white, were strapped about ankles which terminated in curved sandals sparkling with gold and jewels in the midday sun. His jacket, long and perfectly fitting, was of a robin's egg blue. His blue-black queue, freshly oiled, gleamed and shone like the coils of an active hill snake.

He was a picture of refined Chinese saturninity.

Miss Vost, beholding him, was properly impressed.

She stepped back, not a little appalled, maybe, and swept him from queue to sandal with a look that was not the heartiest of receptions.

Peter shortened the distance between them perceptibly.

The Mongolian, or the Tibetan, was speaking, in oiled, pleasing accents. No doubt of his being a gentleman—from the Oriental view-point.

Miss Vost would have struck him stingingly across the thin, insinuating lips, had it not been for Peter's timely intervention.

Peter placed himself between them.

"What did he say?" asked Peter.

"He simply insulted me," replied Miss Vost, composedly. "Like many fine, Chinese gentlemen, he thought, perhaps, that I might be—what do they call 'em?—a 'nice lil' 'Melican girl!' Impress him with the fact that I am not, Mr. Moore—please do that!"

She strode around the forward cabin, out of sight.

The Mongolian was regarding Peter with a cool, complacent smile. His expression was smug, uninjured.

"Looka here, Chink-a-link," advised Peter savagely; "my no savvy you; you no savvy my. My see you allatime. Allatime. You savvy, Chink-a-link?"

"I comprehend you, my friend," replied the Mongolian in slow, polished, insulting accents. "In my case, appearances to the contrary notwithstanding, pidgin is not, let me hasten to say, appropriate."

Peter shook all over. He wanted to fight. His voice trembled with rage. "Flowery talk don't go with me, Chink! Savvy me close: the next time you so much as glance in Miss Vost's direction, you're going to walk away with a pair of the dam'dest black eyes in China! Get that—you yellow weasel?"

"Unfortunately," replied the Mongolian, lifting his fine, black eyebrows only a trifle, "your suggestion—your admonitions—are, again, most inappropriate. Miss Vost—do I pronounce it correctly? Miss Vost and yourself are the victims of a gross misunderstanding."

"And you—do I pronounce it correctly? You are a damn flat-footed liar!" shouted Peter. "Take off your coat, and prove I'm wrong! I'm a better man than you are! Swallow it or—fight!"

Peter's gray tweed coat flopped in a heap upon the ironwood deck.

The Mongolian retired a few feet, with indications of anxiety.

"I-I did not intend to offend her," he retracted. His ropy throat muscles seemed to convulse. His long face flamed hotly red. He burst out, as though unable to control himself: *"Jen, jen! My sabbe allatime you so sabbe! Hua meng lang ni yao wo, pu yao!"*

"Chu hua," laughed Peter. *"Chua mao!"*

WITH the descent of twilight and the reappearance of Miss Vost's impersonal Chinese moon, Peter Moore began to itch again for the thrilling beat of the thirty thousand-meter wave in his vitrified rubber head phones.

The Mongolian, after his exhibition of unbridled rage, retired to the security of his stateroom. He even had his dinner sent to his room.

Peter dismissed the episode from his vaulting thoughts.—He became in a way an entirely different sort of person when be plumbed the vast and restless ether for its whining secrets. His discovery of the thirty thousand-meter wave aroused in him a fire not unlike the superb feeling of the artist who, with an unguarded sweep of his brush, marks upon a canvas an "accidental," a light, a vivid effect, not of his own voluntary creation.

He became nervous, exalted—slightly irritable!

Throwing in the final coil, he crouched forward in his chair, concentrating with a great, conscious effort to thrust his acute hearing through the insatiable, mad clank and thump of the *Hankow's* engines.

In broad daylight, Peter's chances for hearing the evasive signaler were remote. Sunlight casts a stifling blanket, a mysterious, unseen electric fog upon wireless waves. At night the air becomes clarified.

He watched the steel dial of the clock screwed to the white wall in front of him. Twice the sharp, black, finger swung around. Eleven o'clock. Six bells rang dull and distant in the peak.

The station was working! A piercing, unmusical note, like a veiled scream, rang in his ears. The signals, over and over, repeated the letter "K." That was wireless for "Go ahead."

From far away came the answer:

> To L.Y. L.Y. Msg for L.Y.

Peter reached noiselessly for the pad and pencil. He jotted down L.Y. The letters were repeated a number of times. Impatient, Peter drew a neat diagram of a nothing in the upper left hand corner. Who was "L.Y.," or what?

Then came the message, in signals that rose and fell like the stridulations of a cricket:

> Small. Slender. Purest-blooded Afghanistan. Brown gazel eyes. Trusting. Virtuous.

"Brown eyes! Virtuous!" grumbled Peter. "What in thunder is the lunatic driving at?"

Yet there it was in black and white before him, in the rounded compact script of the experienced operator.

The far away whispering chant ceased. Closer at hand the station that signed L.Y. squeaked a blast of undeniable O.K.'s.

What did it mean? Indisputably a chain of high-power wireless stations were working in the very heart of China. Afghanistan! Beyond the borders of China!

He shifted the handle of the tuner a few degrees, a thoroughly perplexed and exasperated young man.

This time came a lower, a graver note, faint, firm, but not so far removed as the previous one—he of the whispering chant.

L.Y. was ready. His, reply was a long string of "K's."

Peter ripped off the yellow sheet, baring a clean surface. The paper fluttered out of his fingers to the floor. But the door was closed. He would recover it later.

The low-toned fellow went directly to the heart of his business.

To L.Y.: From the Punjab. A white maiden. Skin like the dawn. Merry, brown eyes. A passion flower. Despairingly young. Desired by all men. Virtuous.

"Virtuous!" That word again! Was virtue so rare in the Punjab?

The low tone continued:

Another to L.Y.: A desert girl. Origin: Nepal. Verily a panther. Complexion defies roses. Teeth of flashing white coral. Defiant. Unwillingly a captive. Daintily tiny. Virtuous.

"Virtuous!" intoned Peter. "Is God in His heaven? Despairingly young! Unwillingly a captive! And—virtuous? Good Lord! what does all this mean?"

There was silence, jarred during split-seconds by the "O.K." of L.Y's scream. It seemed an afterthought when L.Y. added:

Answers to both of you at two o'clock. Stand by then. Good-by.

Peter sank back with a long sigh of exhaustion. His face felt wet and sticky.

What did L.Y. stand for? Who was L.Y.? Suddenly he sat up with a shudder. L.Y. were the initials of Len Yang, fountainhead, from which sprang the evil deeds of the Gray Dragon! But what—

He had gathered up the yellow slips of paper from the mahogany ledge, and when he turned to reach for the scrap which had fallen on the floor—it was not there? It was gone!

He tossed the head phones to the ledge and got down on his hands and knees. Where was that piece of paper?

The floor was bare of the electrical impedimenta usually found in a wireless room. The paper could have fluttered behind no storage batteries, no generator, no transformer case; because in the *Hankow's* wireless shack these apparatuses were disposed of on a broad shelf overhead, hanging by broad iron straps and lugs from the ceiling.

Where, then, were Peter's annotations regarding the purest-blooded Afghanistan maiden!—she of the forsworn virtue?

The paper had disappeared. He had not taken his usual precaution of locking the door. Some one had slipped in quietly when he was absorbed, had acquired the paper, had retreated with the stealth of one who was not unaccustomed to such adventures. It was incredible. Who aboard the *Hankow* could possibly place value upon a sample of his idle handwriting?

Certainly not Bobbie. Miss Vost? Peter smiled. She might have entered in a mischievous spirit, found him engaged, and stolen the paper for the fun it might give her.

He stared sullenly at the closed door. He berated his denseness. Only one living person on board the steamer was sufficiently interested in his actions to prize that scrap of yellow paper so highly.

The Mongolian!

Peter recalled the threat, uttered in a fit of rage: *"Hua meng lang ni yao, pu yao!"* A wolf can trick a wolf!

CHAPTER XI

ASSAULT AND BATTERY

HE DASHED OUT of the wireless house, and down into the throbbing vestibule. A shaded electric light was burning, throwing a circle of warm yellow upon the table full of long, keen knives and Winchesters, kept there in the event of an attack by river pirates.

Peter seized one of these rifles, and pounded with the butt upon the door of the stateroom adjoining his.

The door swung back without a sound. The Mongolian, partly undressed, stood in the entrance, wearing a look of utter gravity, of complaisance, but of lukewarm interest. His stolidity, his composure, were quite amazing, yet quite natural. He did not seem annoyed, or disturbed. His face was simply a polite, a repressed interrogation.

"Give it here—quick!" said Peter lowly and tensely; "or I'll batter your damn brains out!"

"Give you—what?" breathed the Mongolian, showing mild surprise.

"That paper—that yellow paper you stole from the floor of the wireless room. Where is it?"

"I have been here, in this room all day—since our interview," gave back the Mongolian in a constrained voice. He uttered the words in tones which might have led Peter to assume that he was a trifle aggrieved over the bluntness of that meeting.

"Out o' my way!" snarled Peter, lifting the butt of the gun.

The Mongolian stood his ground. His look of amazement continued to grow.

With an incredibly swift motion Peter swung back the gun and brought it up with a thud into the lower ribs of the Mongolian!

It knocked the wind from him! He staggered back from the doorway with a grunt like a clubbed caribou, and his fingers snatched and slid along the smooth white wall, while he grunted and gasped. He stumbled and sprawled in a heap on the floor, clutching his chest and groaning.

Peter followed him in. He snapped on the light and gave the room a quick examination.

The yellow oblong of paper, with its sharp, compact penciling which related to a maiden in Afghanistan, was lying on the white bed-cover!

The Mongolian was endeavoring to rise, gasping harshly. His long black queue flopped on the strip of green carpet like a dark rope as he struggled. He was having a desperate time of it, trying to catch his breath.

But Peter was merciless.

He stuffed the paper into his pocket, and ground the queue under his heel, which was the most insulting thing he could have done under any circumstances! He had called the Mongolian's mother a degenerate cow, he could not have wounded him more deeply.

But Peter knew exactly how far he could go with a Chinese. And Mongolians were substantially Chinese. Moreover, Peter did not believe in casting stigmas upon the ancestors of groveling beasts.

He stepped lightly over his groaning victim, tucked the Winchester under his arm, and closed the door gently after him. He replaced the rifle, paused, then went back to the door and opened it.

"Can a wolf trick a wolf, *chu mao?*" he called in with an unpleasant laugh. "Think that over, *Hua Lang!*"

A low gasp, like a sob, was the answer.

AS PETER made his way back to the wireless shack he admitted to having made a somewhat important discovery. The Mongolian had not been sent to kill him. Otherwise, he would have taken advantage of his excellent opportunity when Peter's left side the side his heart was on—was so conveniently exposed, when he had slipped in, unnoticed, and picked up the yellow blank.

Wherefore, Peter deduced, the Mongolian had been sent merely to trail him. And in Peter's eyes a trailer in the present exciting business was as dangerous as a killer.

Having his identity known to the inhabitants of Len Yang would discolor his adventure with the sheerest folly. And as long as he continued to be shadowed by the Mongolian his life was endangered.

He considered the problem and a number of not entirely convincing solutions as he returned to the wireless shack. When he clapped the rubber disks to his ears he forgot all about his Mongolian shadow.

It lacked a few minutes of one thirty when he gave up listening to the keen whine of the distant Japanese stations—in code so complicated that he had never been able to master it—and attuned his apparatus for the long waves of the Len Yang operator, and his communicants in—where—Afghanistan and the Punjab?

As the long black finger of the steel-dialed clock moved up, indicating two o'clock, the high-keyed wail of L.Y. came into the receivers.

A number of times the powerful spark gave out the "Stand by" signal in the International Code.

Then the pencil in Peter's steady fingers formed the words of an intelligible message:

> Afghanistanese girl acceptable. Usual price. Punjab white maiden acceptable. Usual price. Nepal girl not wanted.

Peter removed the nickeled head-band and placed it gently upon the ledge. He took out a cigarette and lighted it, and sank back in the deep chair with his eyes lightly closed.

The pulsing engine was in tune with the thoughts he was endeavoring to whip into shape. He puffed slowly at the cigarette, and blew smoke rings reflectively at the glittering helix coil.

"That man must be the devil himself," he muttered finally.

CHAPTER XII

THROUGH THE EYE
OF THE WOLF

ALL THAT NIGHT Peter heard evidences of restlessness upon the part of his neighbor.

He lay quietly in his bunk and listened. First an elbow or a knee would thump the thick partition. Then a scraping sound, perhaps caused by the nervous dragging of finger nails, followed.

The thumping and the scraping kept up until the faint glow of a new day crept through the port-hole of Peter's stateroom.

He could not have slept anyway. While he was reasonably sure that the signals of insomnia on the part of his next-door neighbor were caused by brooding anger, anger at his inability to avenge Peter's insults, Peter's mind focused upon the more important matter.

With little to encourage his imagination he pictured upon the room's blankness the features of an Afghanistan maiden, who was trusting, who had eyes like a scared gazel, who was— virtuous! The image of her was replaced by the face of a despairingly young girl from the Punjab, who stared back at him out of the vagueness with eyes that implored and wept. Over and over she seemed to be saying to him: "I am virtuous. Virtuous! Save me from him!"

"If I could! If I only could!" replied Peter to the lovely vision, and, writhing, cursed the rapping and the scratching on the wall at his side.

THEY came to Ichang that noon. Here some cargo was loaded upon the raft while the *Hankow* anchored in midstream.

Peter was on deck watching the somewhat hazardous procedure of transferring large cases of grass-bound tools from a tidewater steamer to the stern of the flat.

Out of the corner of his eye he saw the Mongolian emerge from the companionway and walk to the rail, forward.

Peter gave him a full stare, but the man refrained from looking in his direction.

His long, expressionless face registered no results of last night's sleeplessness. He was looking down at the muddy river, and beckoning.

Peter observed it sampan coolie give an answering wave, and the sampan sidled alongside the flat.

He could not make up his mind why the Mongolian should have business in Ichang. The next breath he recalled his uncertainty.

There was a telegraph station in Ichang, through which ran the two thin copper wires which connected the seventy millions of Szechwan Province with civilization. The telegraph extended almost as far west as the fringe of Tibet.

Would it be—possible for the Mongolian to signal his master in Len Yang and have an answer before the *Hankow* cleared Ichang?

That was the ponderable conclusion reached by Peter's resourceful mind. It seemed more than a possibility, for not until last night was the Mongolian given to know that the man he was trailing would deliberately come out into the open. After last night's violence the Mongolian could only be aware that his life was in danger.

His hands were tied by an order to watch, and report—not to kill. Now would his hands be released?

That was what Peter wanted to know.

The Mongolian returned a few minutes before the *Hankow* hauled in her anchor. His face told nothing. He retired to his stateroom and stayed there until late afternoon.

An accident on the river served to distract the moody thoughts of Peter and Miss Vost, who had taken their usual post on the fantail.

The river above Ichang was swifter, more dangerous, than in its lower course. Except for the junks and an occasional sampan, the *Hankow* had the stream to herself.

The yellow waters were tinged with red, dancing and sparkling to a fresh breeze under a fair blue sky. Great blue bills confined the swollen current. This was not the Whang-poo of yesterday. It was maddened mill-race, gorged by the mountain rains surging, rumbling. Even the gurgle under the sharp cut waters seemed to convey a menace.

Dikes were broken down. The brown waters had flowed out to right and left, forming quiet lakes where there had been fields of paddy and wheat.

The junks from up-river were having a strenuous time of it. Swarms of gibbering coolies manned the long sweeps, striving above all to keep their clumsy craft in safe mid-current.

Over the starboard counter Miss Vost glimpsed a lone junk which was being dragged up-stream by a gang of coolies ashore. Her position was perilous. The river had carved out an indentation just ahead, into which the coolies were struggling to draw her. At that spot the current swept close inshore. An up-river junk, evidently beyond control of her clustering helmsmen, bore down.

There was a moment of electric suspense. The tails of near-by sampans stopped wagging, while their coolies looked and yelled futile advice.

Miss Vost grabbed Peter's arm excitedly. He was trembling a little himself.

Everybody on board the down-coming junk shouted. The trackers ceased pulling. All eyes were on the inevitable collision; the brains behind all those eyes knew the outcome.

Miss Vost covered her eyes with her fingers, and uncovered them.

The blunt prow of the down-bound junk plunged into the side wall of the one now stationary! Smash! The sharp snapping of crushed timbers! The mad gurgling of water temporarily dammed!

The down-bound junk veered far over. Her bow was caved entirely in. She seemed to collapse!

Wreckage floated down the stream, and a few bobbing heads. Only two of the crew of twenty were observed to reach shore.

Shouts of distant laughter echoed across the water.

"That is their sympathy," remarked Peter.

Miss Vost shuddered and relinquished his arm. Her face was stone white, and her lips had become gray. Her lids fluttered, and Peter feared she was about to faint. She opened her eyes.

They were passing a long row of pyramids, green, brown and red.

But Miss Vost was staring along the deck. Peter thought for a moment her stare was an aftermath of horror.

"The Mongolian!" she muttered. "How he is grinning at you!"

The Mongolian had come upon them, apparently unintentionally. He hesitated and paused when Peter looked up. Peter saw no grin upon his lips. They were set in a firm, straight line. His long arms were folded behind his back, and his eyes were empty of mirth—or malice. They simply expressed nothing.

He looked at Peter shortly, and favored Miss Vost with a long stare.

Her eyes faltered.

Peter stepped forward.

But the Mongolian bowed, passed them at a slow, meditative walk, and was lost from their sight behind the cabin's port side.

THE IDEA grew upon Peter that the stalker had become the killer.

After dinner, during which Miss Vost became sulky—or abstracted—Peter retired to the wireless house, and tuned his instruments for the station at Len Yang. But the ether was quiet to-night.

He listened in until nearly midnight with a growing feeling of restlessness, of uneasiness. It might have been fear.

The image of a tall, lean figure skulking about in the darkness outside the wireless room with a long, sharp knife persisted in coming into Peter's mind. Several times he unlocked the door and looked out. Each time the deck was vacant.

He decided to go below.

Peter executed the action with alertness and stealth.

The light was burning over the table of weapons.

The Mongolian's door was slightly ajar. As Peter descended the stairs, the door closed.

He waited. His heart thumped, louder than the thump of the laboring engine. With a crafty smile he walked to his stateroom, opened the door, kicked the threshold, and—slammed the door!

He hastened to the table, and hid behind it. Between the table legs he had a splendid view of both doors. What would the Mongolian do?

Holding a long, straight dagger, point down, in front of him, the Mongolian slipped out of his room, tried the adjacent door-knob and entered Peter's room!

When he came out he looked perplexed and angry. He slipped the dagger into his silk blouse and looked up the stairway, listening.

His expression of rage passed away; now his look was utterly inscrutable.

Stealing across the vestibule, he approached Miss Vost's door, and rapped.

Peter ran his fingers along the edge of the table until they encountered the butt of a cutlass. He waited.

The Mongolian rapped a little louder.

There was no answer.

Again he knocked, imperatively.

Peter heard Miss Vost's sleepy voice pitched in inquiry. Her door opened an inch or two.

The Mongolian forced his way inside!

With murder in his brain Peter leaped up and darted after him!

Miss Vost uttered a short, sharp scream, which was instantly smothered.

As Peter burst into the room, the Mongolian turned with a snarl, reaching for his silk blouse.

Peter clapped his free hand to the muscled shoulder, and dragged him into the corridor.

Miss Vost, in a long, white nightgown, was framed in the doorway, staring sleepily. Her hand was clutched to her lips.

Her hair tumbled about her bare shoulders in dark, silky clusters.

Bright steel flashed in the Mongolian's hand. *"Hua mao!"* he muttered.

Peter braced himself, and thrust straight upward, striking with the fury of mania. He drove the sword through the Mongolian's right eye.

Miss Vost, a slender pillar of white, stared down at the floundering heap. She stared. She seemed to be going mad, with the green light of the electric glittering in her distended eyes.

Bobbie MacLaurin bounded down the steps.

"He tried to come into my room," said Miss Vost. "He tried to come into my room!"

"I know. I know. But it's all right," soothed Peter, panting. "You must go back to bed. You must try to sleep."

He talked to her as though he were talking to a child.

"He was a bad man. He had to—to be treated—this way!"

"You—you look like an Arab. The dark. And that beard. Where is Bobbie?"

"Right here. Right here beside you!"

"You're not hurt—either of you? You're both all right?"

"Yes. Yes. *Please* go to bed!" begged Peter.

"Please!" implored Bobbie.

To them there was something un-religious, something terrible, in the notion of Miss Vost, frightened out of her wits, standing dressed the way she was in the presence of the grim black heap in the shadow. Nor were her youth and her innocence intended to be bared before the eyes of men in this fashion.

And on this river steamer all the conventions seemed magnified, his conventions always are in savage and out-of-the-way places. Indeed, they felt that all the cruel, hard eyes of China were fixed upon her.

As if a chill river wind had struck her, she shivered—closed the door.

The men carried the limp body, which was unaccountably heavy, to the deck.

After a minute there was a splash. The *Hankow* had not even been checked. On the Whang-poo formal burial ceremonies are rarely performed.

CHAPTER XIII

DISASTER

PETER WENT TO bed at once. The *Hankow* was due at Chungking the next morning, and he felt that this would be his last civilized sleep for many months.

He tried to sleep. He counted the revolutions of the propeller. He added up a stupendous number of sheep, going through a hole in a stone wall. Every so often the sheep faded away, to be replaced by the fearful countenance of the Mongolian, who was now perhaps ten miles or more downstream.

After a while the engines were checked, turning at half speed for a number of revolutions, then ceasing as a bell rang. The only sound was the soughing gurgle of the water as it lapped along the steel plates, and the distant drone of the rapids.

He heard the splash of an anchor, accompanied by the rumble and clank of chains, forward; and a repetition of the sounds aft. Directly under him, it seemed, a loud, prolonged scraping noise took place. The fires were being drawn.

The sounds could only mean that the *Hankow* had reached the journey's end. The trip was over; the *Hankow* was abreast Chungking. She would lie in the current for a few days, before facing about and making for tidewater.

To-day would see the last of Miss Vost, a termination of that serio-humorous love affair of theirs, which, on the whole, had been one of his most delightful experiences. He wondered whether or not she would ask him to kiss her good-bye. He rather hoped she would.

On the other hand, he hoped she would do nothing of the kind. Distance was lending enchantment to Aileen Lorimer and to that hungry little sentence she had uttered when he left her on the bund.

He was sure this was not infatuation. He wanted her, wanted her for always and forever and ever and ever. She was not the first, but deep in his hungering heart he knew that she was the last, the only. He had had affairs; oh, numbers of them! But they were mere fragments of his adventurous life. They were milestones, shadowy and vague and very far away now. Dear little milestones, each of them!

Some time he would go to Aileen, and get down on his knees before her in humility, and ask her if she would condone his sins, and overlook his systematic and hardened faults! When would he do this? Frankly, he did not know.

The difficulty of getting to, and particularly *into*, that inaccessible city of Len Yang was facing him now. It lay in a southerly direction from Chungking. If a line were drawn midway between the prong of Burma and the heart of Bhatan, and if he proceeded generally along this line by caravan—provided he could find merchants so accommodating—he should be at Len Yang's walls within two weeks. A month at the outside.

Now that the Mongolian—might Confucius rest his blackened soul!—was out of his way, the possibilities of detection, if he used caution and his usual intelligence, were more remote than at any time since he had disembarked from the *Vandalia*—with Aileen clinging in his arms.

Perhaps members of the *Hankow's* small crew had been advised to watch him, to report upon him. There was certainly some likelihood of that.

There was one thing he must do as soon as he reached the merchant road which led from Chungking into India, joining the more important highway which touched the river at a lower point. He must don the clothes of a native—of a peasant, if possible. Miss Vost's phrase came back to him, and he gave it some thought. If he could fall in with peaceably inclined Afghanistan traders he might buy a costume from them. It would never do for him to enter Len Yang in his gray tweeds.

He realized that he would have to take opportunity by the halter, when a suitable opportunity presented itself. It was futile to lie awake thinking up wild schemes at this hour. He could lay down his plans after studying his problem. Afterward, a way of accomplishing his object would perhaps be clear.

He dozed off, and it seemed only an instant later when he was awakened by a persistent hoarse cry.

The port-hole was still dark. Morning was a long way off.

The cry was repeated, was joined by others, excited and fear inspiring.

Peter sat up in bed, and was instantly thrown back by a sudden lurch. Next came a dull booming and banging. The stateroom was filled with the hot, sweet smell of smoking wood, the smell that is caused by the friction of wood against wood, or wood against steel.

Another pounding and booming. Some one hammered at the door. Peter tried to turn on the electric light. There was no current. He opened the door.

Bobbie, shoeless and collarless, dressed only in pants and shirt, towered over the light of a candle which he held in one hand, a hand that shook.

"A collision! Junk rammed us! Get up quick! Don't know damage. Call Miss Vost. Get on deck! Take care of her! My hands are filled with this damn' boat!"

Peter snatched his clothes, and before he was out of his pajamas the *Hankow* began to keel over. It slid down, more and more, until the port-hole dipped into the muddy current. Water slopped in and drenched his knees and feet, and frothed and gurgled at the hole.

He yanked open the door, not stopping to lace his shoes, and called Miss Vost. She had heard the excitement, and was dressing. The floor lurched again, and he was thrown violently against a sharp-edged scantling.

Miss Vost's door was flung open, and she stumbled down the sloping floor, bracing her hands against his chest to catch herself.

"We're sinking," she said, without fear.

To Peter it was evident that Miss Vost had never been through the floundering of a ship before. He fancied he caught a thrill of eager, almost exultant, excitement in her voice. In that vestibule, he knew they were rats in a water-trap, or soon would be.

He still felt weak and limp from his fall against the scantling, and he was trying hard to regain his strength before they began their perilous ascent to the deck. He hoped his dizziness would pass quickly.

Miss Vost misunderstood his hesitancy.

"I am not afraid, not a bit!" she declared, holding with both hands the folds of his unbuttoned shirt. "I am never afraid with *you!* When I am in danger, you—you are always near by. It—it seems that you were put here to—to look after me. But there is no danger—is there?" She shook him almost playfully.

"Yes!" he gasped. "Cut out your babbling. Get to that stairway!"

He heard the breath hiss in between her teeth. But she clung to his arm obediently. They sprawled and slipped in the darkness to the stairs. Clinging to the railing, they reached the deck, which was inclined so steeply that they clung to the cabin-rail for support.

In the dark on all sides of them coolies shouted in high-pitched voices. Heavy rain was falling, drumming on the deck. The odor of wood rubbing against steel persisted. They could see nothing. The world was dark, and filled with the confusion of the unseen and the unknown.

A sharp explosion took place in the bows. Chains screamed through the air and clanged on metal and wood. One of the forward anchor-chains had parted.

The deck tilted again. Bobbie MacLaurin was not in evidence. Peter shouted for him until he was hoarse. Then he left Miss Vost and groped his way to the starboard davits. The starboard life-boat was gone!

Suddenly the rain ceased. A dull red glow smoldered on the eastern heaven.

Miss Vost was praying, praying for courage, for help. She clung to him, and sobbed. By and by her nerves seemed to steady themselves. She told Peter she was brave, and that helped to restore his own confidence.

There was nothing to do but wait for daylight—and pray that the gurgling waters might not rise any higher.

The glow in the east increased, and permitted them to see the vague outlines of a looming shape which seemed to grow out of the bows. As dawn came, Peter made out the form of a huge junk, full rigged, which had pinioned and crushed the foredeck rail under her brawny poop coaming.

Then the remaining anchor-cable snapped like a rotten thread. Dimly they saw the end of the chain whip upward and crash down. A coolie, paralyzed, stood in its way. The broken end struck him in the face. He screamed and rolled down the deck until he lodged against the rail.

Bobbie shouted their names, and scrambled and slipped down to them.

"Good! You're both safe! We're trying to get up steam. Our only chance. Both forward anchors are gone. We'll swing around with the current and lose this damn' junk. If the after anchor holds till steam's up—we're safe!" He sped aft.

The steamer shuddered, and they felt her swinging as the scattered shore lights moved from left to right. The junk was acting as a drag. The shore lights became stationary. A gang of coolies with fire bars were trying to pry up the junk's coaming. They could not budge her.

Peter was aware then that Miss Vost's arms were clinging about his neck, and that she was whimpering softly in his ear. Her nerves had let go. His own nerves were as taut as over-strained wires. Were it not for his forced responsibility he would now be shoveling coal alongside Bobbie MacLaurin.

Up-river boomed another explosion. The deck seemed to fall from under his feet. Water splashed up over his toes. In the gold-speckled dawn he could see the waters foaming and swirling, and rising higher.

He knew it was suicide to swim the Whang-poo rapids, knew the whirlpools which sucked a man down and held him down until his body was torn to shreds.

There was no alternative. And the water was now halfway to his knees.

He dragged the unresisting girl to the rail.

"Can you swim—at all?"

"A—a little," she chattered.

"Hold to my collar and swim with one hand. Only try to keep afloat."

They slipped into the racing current, were seized, and spun around and around.

Above the drone of the waters he heard the roar of a whirlpool, coming rapidly nearer—nearer!

The firm clutch of Miss Vost's hand on his collar was not loosened. Occasionally he heard her gasp and sputter as a wave washed over her face.

They were swept down—down. On they went, spinning, snatched from one eddy to another.

The roar of the whirlpool receded, became a low growl and mutter. They had escaped it!

Now they could see the churning surface covered with torn bits of wreckage. A body, bloated and discolored, spun by, and was caught and dragged under, leaving only an indescribable stench.

After a while the northern shore, a low, brown bank, crept out toward them, like a long, merciful arm. In another minute Peter's bare feet (the shoes had been torn off long ago) came in contact with slimy, yielding mud. They were in shoal water!

He picked up Miss Vost in his arms, and carried her ashore; and she clung to him, shivering, and moaning. He did not realize until afterward that she was kissing him over and over again on his wet forehead and cheeks.

COOLIES found them, and carried them to a village, and deposited them in a little red clay compound behind a building of straw. A bonfire was kindled.

The sun came up as red as blood, like a disk that might have been cut out of red tissue-paper.

A little later a tall man with shoulders that sagged with age came into the clearing with a little group of coolies who were pointing out the way. A white patriarchal beard extended nearly to his waist.

He saw Miss Vost and uttered a happy cry deep in his throat. She leaped up, and was enfolded in his arms.

Peter stared at them a moment with a look that was somewhat dazed and mystified. He picked himself up, and skulked out of the compound, in the direction of the foaming river.

His mind was not in a normal state just then, or he would not have wanted to cross to Chungking in a sampan. But he did want to cross. In the back of his brain foolish words were urging him; they seemed to have been seared into his very soul.

"You must get to Chungking. You must go on to Len Yang. Hurry! Hurry!"

He had no money. A box filled with perforated Szechwan coins now lay at the bottom of the river in what was left of the *Hankow.* Nevertheless he hailed a sampan as though his pockets were weighted down with lumps of purest silver.

The boat leaked in dozens of places. The paddle, scarred and battered, clung to the stern by means of a rotting leather thong. As Peter looked and hesitated, a long, imperative cry issued from behind him. Possibly Miss Vost wanted him to return.

The coolie stipulated his price, and Peter stepped aboard without a murmur, without looking around either. The crossing was precarious. They skirted the edge of more than one whirl; they were caught, and tossed about in waves as large as houses.

Peter kept his eye on the rotting thong, and marveled because it actually held.

Deposited on the edge of Chungking's bund, he confessed his poverty, and offered his shirt in payment. The shirt was of fine golden silk, weaved in the Chinan-Fu mills. For more than a year it had worn like iron, and it had more than an even chance of continuing to do so.

Peter stripped off the shirt before a mob of squealing children, and the *fokie* scrutinized it. He accepted it, and blessed Peter, and Peter's virtuous mother, and called upon his green-eyed gods to make the days of Peter long and filled with the rice of the land.

CHAPTER XIV

CHANG

WITH THE COMING of noon Peter sat down under a stunted cembra pinetree and contemplated the distant, rocky blue ridge of the Min-Shan with a wistful and discouraged air. He removed from his trouser-pocket two yellow loquats and devoured them.

He was dreadfully hungry. His stomach fathered a dull, persistent ache, which forced upon his attention the pains in his muscles and bones. It was their way of complaining against the abuse he had heaped upon them during the past twenty-four hours.

He was beginning to feel weak and dispirited. His was a constitution that arose to emergencies in quick, battling trim; but when the emergency was past, his vitality seemed to be drained. He was conscious, bitterly, of his weakness, and he believed that his face must be white and drawn.

He looked down the muddy brown road as he finished the second loquat (which he had stolen from a roadside farm in passing), and estimated that Chungking was all of ten miles behind him. Walking through the pasty red mud in his bare feet, with the rain streaming through his hair and down his beard and shoulders, had been tedious, trying. Several times he had stopped, with his feet sinking in the oozy, brown clay, and cursed the Whang-poo that had robbed him of his money and his clothing.

What had become of Bobbie MacLaurin? Had that noble soul been snatched down by the River of the Golden Sands?

He cursed the river anew, for Bobbie was a man after God's own heart. Never had there lived such a generous, such a fine and brave comrade. More than once they had fought back to back. More than once the mule-kick which lurked behind those big, kind, red fists had saved Peter from worse than black eyes.

He would never forget that night on the pier at Salina Cruz, when the greaser had flashed out a knife, bent on carving a hole in Peter's heart—and Bobbie had come up from behind and knocked the raving Mexican a dozen feet off the pier into the limpid Pacific!

Those days were ended now. The adventures, the excitement, the sorrows, and the fiery gladness were all well beyond recall.

Peter leaned back against the thorny trunk of the cembra pine, and sniffed the odors of drenched earth, listening to the drip and patter of the cold, gray rain, and gazed pessimistically at the blue crest of rock which lifted its granite shoulders high into the mist miles away.

Yet the Min-Shan rains were not unhealthful.

He stretched himself, groaned, and staggered on through the brown mire.

The valley was filled with the blue shades of dusk when he espied some distance beyond him what was evidently a camp, a caravan at rest. The setting sun managed at last to burrow its way through a rift of purple before sinking down behind the granite range, to leave China to the mercies of its long night.

These departing rays, striking through the purple crevice, and setting its edges smolderingly aflame with red and gold, became a narrow, dwindling spotlight, which brought out in black relief the figures of men and mules, of drooping tents and curling wisps of cook-fire smoke. The sun was swallowed up, and the camp vanished.

Peter plunged on, with one leg dragging more reluctantly than the other. But he had sensed the odor of cooking food in the quiet air.

A sentry whose head was adorned by a dark-red turban presented the point of his rifle as Peter approached. He shouted, was joined by others, both Chinese and Bengalis, and Peter, not adverse even to being in the hands of enemies as long as food was imminent, was inducted into the presence of a kingly personage, who sat upon a carved teak stool.

This creature, by all appearances a mandarin, of middle age, was garbed in a stiff, dark satin gown, heavy with gold and jewels which flashed brightly in the light of a bonfire. His severe, dark face was long, and stamped with intelligence of a high order. He wore a mustache which drooped down to form a hairy wisp on either side of his small, firm mouth.

As Peter was whisked into his presence he placed his elbow with a slow, deliberate motion upon his knee, and rested his rounded chin in his palm, bestowing upon the mud-spattered newcomer a look that searched straight into Peter's soul.

A single enormous diamond blazed upon the knuckle of his forefinger.

He put a question in a tongue that Peter did not understand. It was a deep, resonant voice, with the mellow, rounded tones of certain temple-bells, such a sound as is diffused long after the harsh stroke of the wooden boom has subsided. Vibrant with authority, it was a voice that men obey, however much they may hate its owner. He repeated the question in Mandarin, and again Peter indicated that that was not his speech.

A different voice, yet quite as impelling as the other caused Peter to look up sharply. The mandarin smiled wisely but not unkindly.

"The darkness deceived me," he said in English of a strange cast. "I mistook you for an Afghanistan beggar. You are far from the river, my friend. The bones of your steamer lie fathoms deep by now."

"She sank before dawn this morning."

"So my coolies told me. I left Chungking when the city awakened. Why are you so far from Chungking? You were stunned, perhaps?"

"I am only hungry," said Peter boldly. "My way lies into India. There I have friends."

The mandarin studied him dubiously, and clapped his hands, the great diamond cutting an oval of many colors. Coolies were given up by the night, and ran to obey his guttural, musical commands. They returned with steaming bowls of rice and meat, and a narrow lacquer table.

"Come and sit beside me. Your feet must be sore-bleeding. Your intention was to walk, unarmed, into India?"

"Yes—"

"You may call me Chang. So I am known to my British friends on the border. I have been ill, a mountain fever, perhaps. In Chungking, I had expected medicine on the river steamer."

He snapped his fingers, and whispered to a coolie whose face was gaunt and stolid in the flickering red glow of the fire.

So while Peter consumed the rice and stew, his bruised feet were bathed in warm water, rubbed with a soothing ointment, and wrapped in a downy bandage.

A blue liquor served in cups of shell silver completed the meal. The aromatic sirup, which exhaled a perfume that was indescribably celestial and exotic, sent an exhilarating fire through his veins. It seemed to clarify his thoughts and vision, to oil his aching joints, and remove their pain.

From the corner of his eye he detected the silken folds of the mandarin's lofty tent, in the murky interior of which a fat, yellow candle sputtered and dripped.

When his eyes came back to the table, the bowls and cups had been removed, and in their place was a chess-board inlaid with ivory and pearl.

Inspired by the cordial, and the queerness of this setting, Peter felt that he was the central figure of a dream. The pungent odor of remote incense, the distant tinkling of a bell, the stamping and pawing of the mules (they should have been camels), and the brooding figure in silk gold at his side, took him back across the ages to the days and nights of Scheherezade.

And the mandarin appeared to be hungry for Peter's companionship. Over the chessboard, between plays, they discoursed lengthily upon the greatness of the vast empire, once she should awake; upon the menace of the wily Japanese, upon the lands across the mountains and beyond the seas, and their peoples, of which Chang had read much but had never visited.

Wood was heaped upon the fire, which flared up and leaped after the crowding shadows.

It was the life that Peter dearly loved.

The mandarin's eyes glowed, and rested upon him for longer spaces. His words and sentences came fewer and more reluctant.

In one of these unaccountable pauses he seized Peter's hand in his. And Peter was forthwith given the meager details of a story, neither the beginning nor the end of which he would ever know. It was the cross-section of a tale of intrigue, of the plotting of one man's life against another, of cold-blooded killings that chased the thrills up and down Peter's spine; a tale of loot, of precious gems that had vanished, of ingots and kernels of gold that had leaked from iron-bound chests.

The mandarin uttered his woe in a quivering voice, shifting from a Bengal patois to Mandarin, and again to reckless English.

Peter was given to understand that in Chang's camp was a traitor, a man who eluded him, whose identity was shielded, a snake that could not be stamped out unless the lives of every one of his attendants were taken!

And out of Peter's memory crept the face of a coolie, a face that had been limned, gaunt and stolid, against the firelight. It came with accusative swiftness; it came intuitively, as one sights evil and senses it without being aware. Even now he detected the bended back of the coolie who crouched and moaned as he dreamed before the rosy embers!

In a composed voice Chang, the mandarin, was saying:

"You have walked far. You are weary. Another couch is in my tent. You shall sleep there."

THE CANDLE was guttering low in its bronze socket when Peter awoke. A cool breeze stirred the tent flaps. A queer feeling oozed in his veins.

Danger!

He lay still, breathing regularly, searching the corners with eyes that were brighter than a rat's. The low sleep-mutterings of the mandarin continued from the couch across from him.

Slowly the tent flaps were being drawn back. Peter strained his eyes until they ached. He was impelled to shout, to awaken his companion. Yet the visitor might be bent on legitimate business. He would wait. In the final analysis it was Peter's profound acquaintance with the ways of the East which sealed his lips. In China one does not strike at shadows, or shriek at sight of them. Not always.

At his side between the covers lay a strong, naked dagger. Why the mandarin had provided him with the weapon he did not know, but, in the light of his host's tale, he had his suspicions.

A gray shadow entered the tent and backed noiselessly against the front pole. Indeed, not a sound was created by his entrance, not even the rustling whisper of bare feet on dry grass. It seemed very ominous, mysterious, ghostly—startling!

The broken, bloody narrative of Chang continued to pass before his vision. Was he on the verge of witnessing a scene in this blasphemous drama?

The gray shadow floated into the candlelight, which waved and quivered a little as the still air was disturbed. Peter was conscious that his face was being acutely examined. Not a muscle of his face twitched. He continued to breathe regularly, with the heaviness of a man steeped in sleep. Tentatively he permitted his lids to raise.

The intruder's back was toward him. He was bending with slow stealth over the mandarin's face.

What was the fellow doing?

Peter caught the glint of metal, or glass. At the same time a powerful, sickening odor, resembling nothing if not opium, seemed to spread through the tent. The gray shadow was drugging the mandarin—perhaps killing him!

Peter groped for the naked dagger, bounded up from the couch with a nervous cry, and buried the steel up to its costly, jeweled hilt in the foremost shoulder.

Without a sound the man in gray turned part way round, and a shudder ran through him, causing the folds of his indiscriminate garment to flap slightly. He sank down with a sigh like wind stealing through a cavern, and his fingers clawed feebly in the leaping shadow.

Peter detected a tiny glass vial spilling out its dark, volatile fluid upon the dust.

He picked it up, but it was snatched from his hand. The dull eyes of Chang stared very close to his, with the stupefaction of sleep still extending the irises into round, dark pools. The vial was in his hand, and he was sampling its odor, waving it slowly back and forth under his wide nostrils.

He shouted, and turbaned men filed into the tent, and carried the gray figure away.

The hand of Chang rested upon Peter's shoulder, and in a voice that throbbed with the sonorousness of a Buddha temple-gong he said:

"You have rendered me a service for which I can never sufficiently repay you—for I value my life highly! Please—please ask me no questions. In the morning your mind will have forgotten, what has taken place. Try to sleep now. You will please obey—promptly!"

The candle sputtered and jumped, as if it were striving mightily to lengthen its golden life if only for another minute; and then went out.

CHAPTER XV

EYES OF THE GREEN DEATH

FROM CHOW YANG to Lung-Ling-Ting all the land could not provide costlier raiment than Peter found at his bedside when the long, high-keyed cries of the mule men opened his eyes upon another morning.

When camp was broken up, long before the sun became hot, he was given a small but able mule; and he rode down the valley toward India at Chang's side.

They moved at the head of a long, slow train, for here bandits were not feared, despite the loneliness of the land through which they were traveling. Farms became more scattered, more widely separated by patches of broken, barren rock; and, finally, all traces of the microscopic cultivation which gave Szechwan Province its fruitfulness were left behind them.

The mandarin rode for many miles in silence, occasionally changing reins, looking steadily and gloomily ahead of him, with his attention riveted, it seemed, upon the sharp and ceaseless clatter of his mule's hoofs and the twisting rock road.

Peter's mind was fixed upon the problem which crept hourly nearer. His head was cast between his shoulders as if the weight of a sorrowful world rested upon that narrow, well proportioned skull, with its covering of shining light hair.

He loved his task as a man might love a selfish and thoughtless woman, who demanded and craftily accepted all that he could give, to the last ounce of his gold and the final drop of his blood. It was a thankless task, yet it had grace.

It was well past mid-morning before Chang spoke the first word.

"A grateful dream came into my sleep last night, *chin jen* (golden youth). For years I have fought in the darkness with a man who had the heart of Satan himself. He has robbed me. Time after time he has sent into my camp his spies. Some were more adroit than others. But none so adroit as the coolie from Len Yang."

Peter repressed his surprise, and merely winked his eyes thoughtfully a number of times. Chang went on:

"In this dream last night a young man was given into my keeping whose spirit and manliness have not yet been soiled. His gratitude was immediate. In return for the acts which grew out of that gratitude, I am prepared to give him anything that is mine, or in my power, whether he desires wealth, or position, or my friendship."

"The young man of your dream," said Peter gravely, "desires neither wealth nor position. If he has been of service to the man who befriended him, that in itself is enough."

"Should he desire a favor of any kind, *chin jen*—"

"Then help him to reach his enemy, who is your enemy, who is the Gray Dragon of Len Yang!"

"In jest—"

"In all seriousness!" said Peter.

"It is death to enter Len Yang!"

"My mind is made up, Mandarin Chang!"

They had entered a narrow ravine, and on both sides of the slender trail rose up sharp elbows of hard rock. Peter's head was inclined a little to the right in an attitude he unconsciously assumed when listening for important words of man or wireless machine.

"It is the folly of adventurous youth," rang out the melodious and sincere voice of the mandarin. "It is a quest for a grail which will end in a pool of your own blood, *chin jen!* Come into India with me!"

"But I decided—long ago—mandarin!"

"Your life is your life," said the mandarin sadly.

"It is fortunate that I fell into your hands!" smiled Peter.

"It is, indeed. The City of Stolen Lives is beyond the mountain. You must be well equipped."

"I am dressed as a mandarin now. If you should permit me—"

"They are yours!" exclaimed the mandarin graciously, and lapsed for a moment into reverie. "Each city of China has a different tongue. You need not fear detection on that score! Yet you must have more than the raiment of a mandarin. Here—"

Peter watched him curiously as the great diamond flashed into the heavy blue brocade of his long satin jacket. At the end of a ruby string, spinning and twisting, hung a pair of dull-green jade ornaments, perfectly round, and carved into hideous semblance of human eyes. The hand which held them trembled slightly as Chang passed them over to Peter.

"A charm, mandarin?"

"More than a charm, *chin jen.* The eyes of the green death—"

"Ah-h!" Peter's rising intonation indicated that he was not without some knowledge of these ornaments.

"Hide them from me, *chin jen*. They have an indescribable influence upon the Chinese sight! You may test them—if you doubt me."

"Test them!"

"Yes. Dangle them before the eyes of this mule boy who follows us."

Chang drew in his mule to watch, while Peter turned in the trail and waited for the coolie to come up with him.

The coolie looked at him stupidly.

Peter opened his hand, and the green eyes dropped and dangled at the end of their crimson-beaded cord.

The boy sprang back against the mule's rump. A terrified moan issued from his lips. He drew both bands over his mouth, and sank to his knees, toppling forward until his head lay upon the rock, where he lay shaking with unholy fear!

CHAPTER XVI

TRAFFIC IN SOULS

A ROAD AS white and straight as a silver bar led directly between the black, jutting shoulders of the hills to the gates of Len Yang.

Peter, with his heart beating a wild symphony of anticipation and fear, drew rein.

The small mule panted from the long, desperate climb, his plump sides filling and caving as he drank in the sharp evening air.

Close behind the city's faded green walls towered the mountain ranges of Tibet, cold, gloomy, and vague in the purple mystery of their uncertain distance. They were like chained giants, brooding over the wrongs committed in the City of Stolen Lives, sullen in their mighty helplessness.

In the rays of the swollen sun the close-packed hovels enclosed within the moss-covered walls seemed to rest upon a blurring background of vermilion earth.

As Peter clicked his tongue and urged the tired, little animal down the slope, he recalled the fragment of a description that had once been given him of this place. Hideous people, with staring eyes, dripping the blood-red slime of the cinnabar-mines—Leprosy, filth, vermin—

His palace! It stood out above the carmine ruck, like a cube of purest ivory in a bleeding wound. Its marble outrivaled the whiteness of the Taj Mahal. It was a thing of snow-white beauty, like a dove poising for flight above a gory battle-field. And it was crowned by a dome of lapis lazuli, bluer than the South Pacific under a melting sun! But its base, Peter knew, was stained red, a blood-red which had seeped up and up from the carmine clay.

The gate to the city was down, and by the grace of his blue-satin robe Peter was permitted to enter.

And instantly he was obsessed with the flaming color of that man's unappeased passion. Red—red! The hovels were spattered with the red clay. The man, the skinny, wretched creature who begged for a moment of his gracious mercy at the gate, dripped in ruby filth. The mule sank and wallowed in vermilion mire.

Scrawny, undernourished children, naked, or in rags that afforded little more protection than nakedness, thrust their starved, red-smeared faces up at him, and gibed and bowled.

And above all this rose the white majesty of *his* palace—the throne of the Gray Dragon!

Peter urged the mule up the scarlet alley to a clearing in which he was amazed to find coolies by thousands, trudging moodily from a central orifice that continued to disgorge more and more of them. Emerging, the dreadful, reeking creatures blinked and gaped as if stupefied by the rosy light of the dying day.

Some carried lanterns of modern pattern; others bore picks
and shovels and iron buckets, and they seemed to pass on in-
terminably, to be engulfed in the lanes which ran in all direc-
tions from the clearing.

It was as though the earth were vomiting up the vilest of its
creatures. And in the same light it was consuming others of
equal vileness. Down into the red maws of the shaft an endless
chain of men and women and children were descending.

Quite suddenly the light gave way, and Peter was aware that
the night of the mountains was creeping out over the city,
blotting out its disfigurements, replacing the hideous redness
with a velvety black.

At the shaft's entrance a sharp spot of dazzling light sprang
into being. It was an electric arc light! Somehow this apparition
struck through the horror that saturated him, and he sighed as
if his mind had relinquished a clinging nightmare.

Professionally now he gave this section of Len Yang another
scrutiny. Thick cables sagged between stumpy poles like clusters
of black snakes, all converging at the mine's entrance. His acute
ears were registering a dull hum, indicating the imminence of
high-geared machinery or of dynamos.

At the further side of the red shaft, now crusted with the
night's shades, and garishly illuminated by the diamond whiteness of the frosty arc, he made out a deep, wide ditch, where
flowed slowly a ruddy current, supplied from a short, fat pipe.

Peter believed that electric pumps sucked out the red seepage
waters from the mine and lifted them to the bloody ditch.

On impulse he lifted his eyes to the darkening heavens, and
he knew now that the threads of this, his greatest adventure,
were being drawn to a meeting point; for he detected in the
sun's last refracted rays the bronze glint of aerial wires!

What lay at the base of the antenna he could guess accu-
rately, for he had heard the imperial whine of "L.Y." when a
thousand miles distant on the brown river. But who was the
man behind the key?

He hastened to the base of the nearest aerial mast—a pole reaching like a dark needle into the sky—and found there a low, dark building of varnished pine with a small door of eroded, green brass.

The rain-washed pine, the complete absence of windows, and the austerity of the massive brass door contributed to a personality of dignified and pessimistic aloofness. The building occupied a place to itself, as if its reserve were not to be tampered with, as if its dark and sullen mystery were not meant for the prying eyes of passing strangers.

Peter knocked brazenly upon the door, and it clanked shallowly, giving forth no inward echo. He waited expectantly.

It yawned open to the accompaniment of grumbled curses in a distinctly tenor whine.

A man with a white, shocked face stared at him from the threshold. The countenance was long, tapering, and it ended nowhere. Dull, mocking eyes with a burned-out look in them stared unblinkingly into Peter's face.

Peter could have shouted in recognition of the weak face, but he compressed his lips and bowed respectfully instead.

"What the hell do you want?" inquired the man on the threshold in a high-pitched, uncertain voice. He was not afraid. He was simply arrogant in the presence of an inferior being.

"May Buddha bring the thousandth blessing to the soul of your virtuous mother," said Peter in solemn, benedictive tones. "It is my pleasure to desire entrance."

"Speak English, eh?" shrilled the man. "Dammit! Then come in!" And to this invitation he added blasphemy in Peter's own tongue that made his heart turn sour. It was the useless, raving blasphemy of a weakling who cursed, simply because he could not help himself. It was the man as Peter had known him of old. But a little worse.

He still wore what remained of his Marconi uniform, tattered, grease-stained coat and trousers, with the ragged white and blue emblems of the steamship line by which he had been employed before he had disappeared. His bony hands trembled incessantly, and his face had the chalky pastiness inevitable in the opium fiend.

Peter, reflecting upon the honor which that uniform had always meant for him, felt like knocking this chattering, wild-eyed creature down and trampling upon him.

But Peter bowed respectfully, and entered. The door clanged behind him, and his eye absorbed in an instant the details of the ponderously high-powered, electrical apparatus.

"Speak God's language, oh?" whined the man. "Sit down and don't stare so. Sit down. Sit down."

"A mandarin never seats himself, O high one until thrice invited."

"Thrice, four, five times, I tell you to sit down." he babbled. "Men, even rat-eaters like you, who speak my language, are too rare to let go by. Mandarin?"

He stepped back and eyed his guest with stupid humor.

"I say, men who speak my language are rare. Nights I listen to fools on this machine, and tell them what I please. What is the news from outside? What is the news from home?"

"From where?"

"From America." He stumbled over the words, and took in his breath with a long, trembling hiss between his yellow teeth.

"It is many years since I visited that strange land, O great one. It is many, many years, indeed, since I studied for the craft which you now perform so honorably."

"You—what was that?"

"I, too, studied to your honorable craft, my son. But it was denied me. Buddha decreed that I should preach his doctrines. It is my life to bring a little hope, a little gladness into the hearts—"

"You stand there and tell me that you know the code?" cried the white-faced man shrilly.

"Such was my good fortune," replied Peter slowly and gravely.

"Well, I believe you're a damn' liar, you Chink!" scoffed the other, who was swinging in nervousness or irritation from side to side.

Peter shrugged his shoulders, and permitted his gaze to fondle the monstrous transmission coil.

"I'll show you!" railed the man. "I'll give you a free chance, I will! Now, listen to me. Tell me what I say." He pursed his lips and whistled a series of staccato dots and dashes.

"What you have said," replied Peter in a deep voice, "is untrue, O high one."

"What did I say?"

"You said, 'China, it is the hell-hole of the world.' Do I speak the truth?"

Peter thought that this crazy man whose name had formerly been Harrison was preparing to leap at him. But Harrison only sprang to his side and seized his hands in a clammy, excited grip. Tears of an exultant origin glittered in the man's eyes, now luminous.

"You stay with me, do you hear?" he babbled. "You stay here. I'll make it worth your while! I'll see you have money. I'll see—"

"But I have no need of money, O high one," interrupted Peter in a somewhat resentful tone, striving to mask his eagerness.

"You stay!" cried Harrison.

"Lotus eater!" said Peter, knowing his ground perfectly.

"What if I am?" demanded Harrison defiantly. "So are you! So are we all! So is everybody who lives in this rotten country!"

"To the sick, all are sick," quoted Peter sorrowfully.

"Rot! As long as I must have opium, there's nothing more to be said. Now, I pry my eyes open with matches to stay awake. With you here—"

His thin voice trailed off. He had confessed what Peter already knew. It was the blurted confession, and the blurted plea, of a mind that was half consumed by drugs. A diseased mind which spoke the naked truth, which caught at no deception, which was tormented by its own gnawings and cravings to such an extent that it had lost the function of suspecting. Suspicion of a low, distorted sort might come later; but at its present ebb this mind was far too greedy to gain its own small ends to grope beyond.

The lids of Harrison's smoldering eyes drew down, and they were blue, a sickly, pallid blue. With their descent his face became a death-mask. But Peter knew from many an observation that such signs were deceptive; knew that opium was a powerful and sustaining drug; knew that Harrison, while weak and stupid and raving, was very much alive!

"There is little work to be done," went on the thin voice. "Only at night. Say you will stay with me!" he pleaded.

Peter permitted himself to frown, as if he had reached a negative decision.

Harrison, torn by fitful desire, flung himself down on his ragged knees, and sobbed on Peter's hand. Peter pushed him away loathfully.

"What is my task?"

Harrison sank back on his heels, oblivious of the wet streak which ran down from his eyes on either side of his thin, sharp nose, and delved nervously into his pocket. He withdrew a lump of black gum, about the size of a black walnut, broke off a fragment with his finger-nails, and masticated it slowly. He smirked sagely.

"He won't care. Why should he care?"

"Who, my son?"

"That man—that man who owns Len Yang, and me, and these rat-eaters. All *he* wants is results."

"Ah, yes. He owns other mines?"

"What does *he* care about the mines? Of course he directs the other mines by wireless. He owns a sixth of the world. *He* does. He is rich. Rich! You and I are poor fools. He gives me opium"—Harrison glared and gulped—"and he does not ask questions."

"Wise men learn without asking questions, my son," said Peter gravely.

"Certainly they do! He knows everything, and he never asks a question. Not a one! He answers them, *he* does!"

"You have asked him questions?"

"I? Humph! What an innocent fool you are, in spite of that gold on your collar! Have I seen him to ask questions?"

"That is what I meant."

"Not I! He is no fool. You may be the Gray Dragon for all of me. No one in Len Yang sees him. No one dares! It is death to see that man! Didn't I try? But only once!"

"You did try?"

"That was enough. I got as far as the first step of the ivory palace. Some one clubbed me! I was sick. I thought I was going to die! There is a scar on my neck. It never seems to heal."

The senile whine trailed off into a thin, abusive whimper. His bony jaws moved slowly and meditatively. He went on:

"He is crazy, too. Women! There is no harem like his in all the world. There never was! Beautiful women for the mines! Men—men—men everywhere know the price he will pay. In pure silver!"

"He pays well, my son?"

"A thousand taels, if he is satisfied. That is where this hole got its name. You know the name—the City of Stolen Lives? It should be the City of Lost Virtue. None enters here that is not virtuous. And none ever leave, virtue or not. The ivory palace swallows them up. What becomes of them?"

"Ah! What does become of the stolen lives?"

The sunken eyes stared playfully at him. "What is a thousand taels to him? He is rich, I tell you! They say his cellar is filled with gold—pure gold; that his rooms and halls run and drip with gold, just as his rat-eaters run and drip with the cinnabar poison. And the wireless—*he* has stations, and this is the best. Mine is the best. I say to that, let me tell you!"

"To be sure!"

"These hunters, these men who know his price for beautiful women—virtuous women—he will have none other—and who are paid a thousand taels—"

"Where did you say these stations are?"

"In all parts. There is a station in Afghanistan, between Kabul and Jalalabad, and one in Bengal, in the Khasi Hills, and another in northern Szechwan Province, and one in Siam, on the Bang Pakong River—"

"A station on the Bang Pakong?"

"Yes, I tell you. All over. These hunters find a woman, a lovely virgin; and they must describe their prize in few words. He is sly! The fewer the better. If the words appeal to him, he has me tell them to come. Lucky devils! A thousand taels to the lucky devils! Some day I myself may become a hunter."

"It is tempting," agreed Peter.

"Tonight I will listen. You can watch me. Then you can see how simple it is. It is time."

Peter was aware that the door had opened and closed behind his back, and now he heard the faint scraping of a sandaled foot, heavy with the red slime. A Chinese, in the severe black of an attendant, stood looking down at him suspiciously or distrustfully. His eyebrows were shaved, and a mustache drooped down to his sharp, flat chin like seaweed.

He asked Harrison a sharp question in a dialect that smacked of the guttural Tibetan.

"He wants to know where you came from," translated Harrison irritably.

"From Wenchow. A mandarin. He should know."

The man in severe black bowed respectfully, and Peter looked at him frigidly.

Harrison slipped the Murdock receivers over his ears, and his voice went on in a weak, garrulous and meaningless whimper.

"Static—static—static. It is horrible to-night. I cannot hear these fellows. Ah! Afghanistan has nothing, nor Bengal. Hey, you fool, I cannot hear this fellow in Szechwan. He has a message. Hey, you, I cannot hear him. Not a word! He is faint, like a bad whisper. They will beat me again if I cannot hear!"

He tried again, forcing the rubber knobs against his ears until they seemed to sink into his head.

"Have you good hearing?"

"I will try," said Peter.

"Then sit here. You must hear him, or we will both be beaten. This fellow goes straight to *him.*"

Peter slipped into the vacated chair and strapped down the receivers. A long, faint whisper, as indistinguishable as the lisp of leaves on a distant hill, trickled into his ears. Ordinarily he would have given up such a station in disgust, and waited for the air to clear. Now he wanted to establish his ability, to demonstrate the acuteness of hearing for which he was famous.

Behind him the black-garbed attendant muttered, and Peter scowled at him to be silent.

With deftness that might have surprised that wretch, Harrison, had his wits been more alert, he raised and closed switches for transmission, and rapped out a quick, professional, "O.K."

He cocked his head to one side, as he always did when listening to faraway signals, and a pad and pencil were slid under his hand.

The world and its noises and the tense, eager figures behind him, retreated and became nothing. In all eternity there was but one thing—the message from the whispering Szechwan station.

His pencil trailed lightly, without a sound, across the smooth paper:

A message for L.Y. A message for L.Y. An American girl. Brown hair. Eyes with the moon's mystery. Lips like a new-born rose. Enchantingly young. Virtuous.

The blood boiled into Peter's brain, and the pencil slipped from fingers that were like ice. There was only one girl in the world who answered to that description. Aileen Lorimer! She had been captured again, and brought back to China! How could he forestall this monstrous proceeding.

He grabbed for the paper. It was gone. Gone, too, was the black-garbed attendant, hastening to his master.

Harrison was pawing his shoulder with a skinny, white hand, and making emotional noises in his throat.

"You lucky fool! He'll give you *cumshaw*. God, you have sharp ears! Only one man I ever knew had such sharp ears. He always gives *cumshaw*. You must divide with me. That is only fair. But what difference? Here you can enter, but you can never leave. You have no use for silver. I have."

The face of Aileen Lorimer swam out of Peter's crazed mind. Miss Vost, that lovely, innocent-eyed creature, fitted the same description!

Peter stared stupidly at the massive transmission key, and disdained a reply. Miss Vost—and the Gray Dragon! He shuddered.

Harrison was whining again at his ear.

"He says yes. Yes! Tell that fellow yes, and be quick. The Gray Dragon will give him an extra thousand taels for haste. Oh, the lucky fool! Two thousand taels! Tell him, or shall I?"

How could Peter say no? The ghastly white face was staring at him suspiciously now.

While he hesitated Harrison pushed him aside, and his fingers flew up and down on the black rubber knob. "Yes—yes—yes. Send her in a hurry. A thousand taels bonus. The lucky devil!"

Out of Peter's anguish came but one solution,—and that vague and indecisive. He must wait and watch for Miss Vost, and take what drastic measures he could devise to recapture her when the time came.

The pallid lips trembled again at his ear.

"Here! You must divide with me. A bag of silver. A bag of it! Listen to the chink of it!"

Peter seized the yellow pouch and thrust it under his silken blouse.

He was beginning to realize that he had been exceptionally lucky in catching the signals of the Szechwan station. He was vastly more important now than this wretch who plucked at his arm.

"Give me my half!" whined Harrison stubbornly, angrily. Peter doubled his fist.

"Give me my half!" Harrison clung to his arm and shook him irritably.

Peter hit him squarely in the mouth.

CHAPTER XVII

THE JAWS OF THE DRAGON

AS NIGHT MELTED into day and day was swallowed up by night, the problem which confronted Peter took on more serious and baffling proportions. His hope of entering the ivory palace was dismissed. It was imperative for him to give up the idea of entering, of piercing the lines of armed guards and reaching the room where the master of the City of Stolen Lives held forth.

That had been his earlier ambition, but the necessity of discarding the original plan became hourly more important with the drawing near of the girl captive.

If he could deliver Miss Vost from this dreadful city, that would be more than an ample reward for his long, adventurous quest.

He could not sleep. Perched on an ancient leather stool upon the roof of the wireless building, he kept a nightly and a daily watch with his eyes fixed upon the drawbridge. A week went by. Food was carried up to him, and he scarcely touched it. The rims of his eyes became scarlet from sleeplessness, and he muttered constantly, like a man on the verge of insanity, as his eyes wandered back and forth over the red filth, from the shadowy bridge to the shining white of the palace.

Drearily, like souls lost and wandering in a half world, the prisoners of Len Yang trudged to the scarlet maws of the mine and were engulfed for long, pitiless hours, and were disgorged, staggering and blinking, in Tibet's angry evening sun.

The woeful sight would madden any man, and yet each day new souls were born to the grim red light of Len Yang's day, and clinging remorsefully to the hell which was their lot, other bleeding souls departed, and their shrunken bodies fed to the scarlet trough, where they were washed into oblivion in some sightless cavern below.

IT WAS a bitterly cold night, with the wind blowing hard from the ice and snow on the Tibetan peaks, when Peter's long vigilance was rewarded. A booming, at the gate, followed by querulous shouts, aroused him from his lethargy.

He looked out over the crenelated wall, but the cold moonlight revealed a vacant street.

The booming and shouting persisted, and Peter was sure that Miss Vost had come, for in cities of China only an extraordinary event causes drawbridges to be let down.

He slipped down the creaking ladder into the wireless-room. Harrison was in a torpor, muttering inanely and pleadingly as his long, white fingers opened and closed, perhaps upon imagined gold.

Peter opened the heavy brass door, and let himself into the deserted street. The jeweled sandals with which Chang, the mandarin, had provided him sank deep into the red mire, and remained there.

He sped on, until he reached the black shadow of the great green wall. Suddenly the bridge gave way with many creakings; and groanings, and Peter saw the moonlight upon the silvery white road beyond.

A group of figures, mounted on mules, with many pack-mules in attendance, made a grotesque blot of shadow. Then a shrill scream, the scream of a soul in the torture of fear and agony, rang out.

Hoofs trampled hollowly upon the loose, rattling boards, and the cavalcade marched in.

A slim figure in a long, gray cloak rode on the foremost mule. Peter, aided by the black shadow, crept to her side.

"Miss Vost! Miss Vost!" he called softly. "It is Peter. Peter Moore!"

He heard her gasp in surprise, and her moan went into his heart like a ragged knife.

Peter tried to keep abreast, but the red clay dragged him back. Behind him some one shouted. They would emerge into the sharp moonlight in another second.

"Help me! Oh, help me!" she sobbed. "He is following; but he is too late."

She was carried out into the moonlight. At the same time, countless figures seemed to arise from the ground—from nowhere—and in every direction Peter was blocked. The stench of Len Yang's miserable inhabitants crept from these figures, and the chill night air was befouled.

Naked, unclean shoulders brushed him; moist, slimy hands pressed him back. But he was not harmed; he was simply pushed backward and backward until his bare foot encountered the first board of the bridge which was still lowered.

His heart throbbed with the pain of his helplessness. And each moment the mules were drawing nearer to the steps of the forbidden palace! He would have given his life then for the revolver which lay now in the wreckage of the *Hankow*.

Behind him an order was hissed. He placed his back to the surging shadows. Coils of heavy rope were unfolding. The drawbridge was being raised.

Down the white road, veering drunkenly from one side to the other, came a leaping, black dot.

The drawbridge creaked, the ropes became taut, and the far end lifted an inch at a time.

Peter shouted, but no one heeded him. His breath pumped in and out of his lungs in short, anguished pants. He leaped out upon the bridge, and shouted again. The creaking ceased; the span became stationary. The rope-pullers and their foreman crept out to him, crouching and shadowy. He beckoned to them, and they followed into the moonlight.

The drunken dot leaped into the form of a giant upon a galloping mule which swept upon them in a confusion of dust.

Peter tugged at his blouse, his shaking fingers closed over the charm of the mandarin, Chang, and he dragged out into the light the two carved eyes of green jade.

He dangled them before their eyes, and he heard their low grunts and growls as they clustered to see what he held. All at once they seemed to glimpse the hideous ornaments, and as one man they groveled at his muddy red feet.

Hoofs pounded on the bridge; the giant on the mule drew rein, and to Peter it was given to look upon the face of the man he thought dead. The raging eyes of Bobbie MacLaurin swept from his face to his muddy feet.

"Bobbie MacLaurin!" he cried.

"Peter, where have they taken her?" ripped out the giant on the mule.

"Dismount and follow me. To the white palace! Are you armed?"

"And ready to shoot every damn yellow snake in all of China!"

He jumped heavily to the boards, and Peter caught the gleam of steel-tipped bullets in the narrow strap which was slung from shoulder to waist.

The foreman of the rope-pullers dared to raise his head, and Bobbie kicked him with his heavy-shod foot in the stomach, and the coolie bounded up and backward, and lay draped limply over the side.

As they ran under the broad, dark arch into the street, he gave Peter in one hand the thick butt of an army automatic, and in the other a half-dozen loaded clips.

And they began blazing their way to the palace steps. Weird figures sprang up from the muck, and were shot back to the earth, for the army automatic is the most powerful of all hand weapons.

They reached the hilltop, and the green moon of Tibet scored the roof of the white palace.

A handful of guards, with rifles and swords, rushed down the broad, low flight.

The two men flung themselves upon the clay, while high-powered bullets plunked on either side of them or soughed overhead.

The two automatics blazed in shattering chorus. The guards parted, backed up, some ran away, others fell, and Peter felt the sudden burn of screaming lead across his shoulder. He slipped another clip of cartridges into the steel butt; they leaped up and raced to the white steps. A rifle spurted and roared in the black shadow. Bobbie groaned, staggered, and climbed on. Now they were guided by a woman's sharp screams issuing from an areaway. And they stopped in amazement before a majestic white-marble portal.

With two coolies struggling to pinion her arms, the girl was kicking, scratching, biting with the fire of a wildcat, dragging them toward the broad, white veranda.

Bobbie shot the foremost of them through the brain, and the other, gibbering terribly, vanished into the shadow.

Peter caught Miss Vost by one hand and raced down the steps. Bobbie, holding his head in a grotesque gesture, ran and staggered behind them.

Peter waited, but Bobbie waved his free arm savagely.

"Don't wait for me! Get her out of this place! Don't take your eyes from her till you reach Wenchow!"

He wheeled and shot three times at a figure, which had slunk up behind him. The figure spun about and seemed to melt into a hole in the earth.

Peter wrapped his arm about Bobbie's waist and dragged him down the hill. Miss Vost, as he realized after that demonstration in the areaway, could handle herself.

The bridge was up. Lights glowed from hovel ways like evil red eyes. Peter released the rope and the bridge sprang down to the road with a boom that shook the solid walls. Bobbie's mule nosed toward them, and Peter all but shot the friendly little animal!

Between Peter and Miss Vost, who was chattering and weeping as if her heart was breaking, their wounded companion was lifted into the saddle.

They crossed the bridge, and the bridge was whipped up behind them.

Not until they attained the brow of the hill did they look back upon the gloomy walls of Len Yang, now black and peaceful under the high clear moon. And it was not until then that Peter marveled upon their easy escape, upon the snatching up of the bridge as they left. Why had no shots been fired at them as they climbed the silver road? Could the green jade eyes have anything to do with the phenomenon? He wondered!

They trusted to no providence other than flight. All night long they hastened toward the highway which led to Chungking—and India. And they had no breath to spare for mere words. At any moment the long arm of the Gray Dragon might reach out and pluck them back.

Only once they paused, while Peter ripped out the satin lining of his mandarin coat and bound up the wound in Bobbie's dazed head.

Miss Vost sat down upon a moss-covered rock and wept. It had been a frightful experience for her, and her poor nerves were in tatters. She made no effort to help him, but stared and wiped her eyes with her hands.

A misty, rosy dawn found them above the valley in which ran the connecting road between Chungking and India.

Miss Vost was the first to see the campfires of a caravan. She laughed, then cried, and she tottered toward Peter, who stood there, a lean, weird figure in his tattered blue robe and his tangled beard.

He knew then, with all the fervor of his nature, that he could never, never love Miss Vost. He was sorry that she felt the way she did about him.

She extended her arms slightly as she approached, and her gray eyes were luminous with a soft and gentle fire.

Bobbie staggered away from the mules heaving sides, with one hand fumbling weakly at the satin bandage, and in his eyes, too, was the look that rarely comes into the eyes of men.

In a single glance Peter could see to the very depths of that man's unselfish, magnificent soul. It was like glancing into the light of a golden autumn morning.

Miss Vost lifted both of Peter's hands, and one was still blue from the back-fire of the automatic. She lifted them to her lips and kissed them solemnly.

With a little fluttering sigh she looked up at Bobbie, standing beside her and towering above her like a strong hill.

They looked long at one another, and Peter felt for a moment curiously negligible.

He had cause to feel that his presence was absolutely unessential when, with a happy, soft little laugh, Miss Vost sprang up and was crushed in the cradle of Bobbies great, long arms.

Peter looked down into the green valley with tears standing in his grave, blue eyes. The caravan was slowly winding out upon the trail. In three weeks it would enter the pass into India.

Peter felt exceedingly happy as he hastened down the hillside to catch that caravan.

III

THE BITTER FOUNTAIN

CHAPTER I

THE LONG ARM

She bends over her work once more:
"I will wave a fragment of verse among the flowers of his
robe,
and perhaps its words will tell him to return."
—Li-Tai-Pe

PETER MOORE, NEWLY arrived wireless operator of the Java, China, and Japan liner, *Persian Gulf*, deposited his elbows upon the promenade deck-rail, and cast a sidelong glance at the Chinese coolie who had taken up a similar position about a bumboat's length aft. And the coolie returned his deliberate stare with a look of dreamy interest, then quickly shifted his glance to the city which smoldered and vibrated across Batavia's glinting, steel-blue harbor.

Without turning his head the wireless man continued to watch sharply the casual movements of this Chinese, quite as he had been observing him since they had left the Tanjong Priok in the company's launch and come out to the *Persian Gulf* together.

He had suspected the fellow from the very first, and he was prepared, on the defensive; yet he was willing and eager to take the offensive should this son of the yellow empire so much as show the haft of his dagger, or whisper a word of counsel in his ear. The latter he feared quite as much as the former, for it would mean many things.

As the fellow sidled a little closer, Peter was aware that the man was milking queer signals with his slanting eyes for the purpose of attracting his attention, without arousing the curiosity or interest of any persons who might be observing the two.

Whereupon Peter turned on his left heel, walked to the other's side and gave him a stare of deliberate hostility.

The coolie moved backward a few inches by flexing his body; his feet remained as they were. And as Peter ran his eye from the black crown hat to the faded blue jacket, the black-sateen pants, which were clipped about the ankles, giving them a mild pantaloon effect, and to the black slippers with their thick buck-soles, the coolie smiled.

It was a smile of arrogance, of self-satisfaction. Indeed, it was the smile of a hunter who has winged his prey, and smiles an instant to watch it squirm before administering the death-shot.

"You wanchee my?" inquired Peter succinctly.

"You allatime go Hong Kong way?" replied the coolie, his smile becoming a little more civil, while he measured Peter's length, breadth, and seemed to estimate his brawn.

It was a foolish question, for the *Persian Gulf,* as everybody in Batavia knew quite well, made a no-stop run from the Javanese port to Hong Kong. Peter indicated this fact impatiently.

"No go Hong Kong way?" persisted the coolie, not relaxing that devilish grin. *"Maskee* Hong Kong."

The wheezy old whistle of the *Persian Gulf* told the world in unmistakable accents that sailing time was nigh. The *Persian Gulf* was not a new boat or a fast boat, and she sailed in the intermediate service south of Java. Yet she was stout, and typhoons meant very little to her as yet.

"Why not?" demanded Peter in the tones of an interlocutor.

The coolie simply lifted the flap of his blue tunic, and Peter was given the singular glimpse of a bone-hafted knife, the blade of which he could guess lay flat against the man's paunch.

Still the Chinese smiled, without avarice. Plainly he was stating the case as it was known to him, reciting a lesson, as it were, which had been taught him by one skilled in the ways of killing and of espionage.

The facts of this case were that Peter Moore should immediately postpone or give up entirely his trip to Hong Kong for reasons best known to the powers arrayed against him. And strangely enough, Hong Kong was one of the two cities in China where Peter had pressing business.

It made him furious, this knowledge that the man of Len Yang had picked up the trail again.

So Peter glanced up and down the deck to see if there would be any witnesses to his act, and there was only one, a passenger. The Chinese was still smiling, but by degrees that smile was becoming more evil and sour. He was perplexed at the wireless operator's furtive examination of the promenade deck. Yet he was not kept in the dark regarding Peter's intentions much longer than it would have taken him to utter the Chinese equivalent of Jack Robinson.

With an energetic swoop, Peter seized him by the nearest arm and leg, and in the next breath the coolie was shooting through an awful void, tumbling head over heels like a bag of loose rice, straight for the oily bosom of Batavia's harbor!

So much for Peter's slight knowledge of jiu-jitsu.

He was angrily at a loss to account for the appearance of this trailer, for he had been watchful every moment since escaping from the green walls of that blood-tinted city in the mountains of Tibet, and he was positive that he had shaken off pursuit. Yet somewhere along that trail, which ran from Len Yang to Rangoon, from Rangoon to Penang, and around the horn of Malacca, his escape had been betrayed.

But where and by whom? He had left the caravan at Mandalay, had made no friends, had traveled for the most part at night. He had refrained from shaving his long, blond beard, after having dyed it red with henna, until reaching Singapore.

Here he had spent an entire week in hiding, had crossed back his trail by visiting Penang and immediately facing south again.

He had gone aboard a Blue Funnel steamer at night, had entered his name on the ship's register as Oliver Fenwick, and had secreted himself in his stateroom until the steamer was a day at sea.

Where had the trail been picked up? It would be hard to say.

Arriving in Batavia, he had made another energetic attempt to throw off pursuers, should any have tracked him this far, by journeying on horseback into the mountains and returning after night had fallen.

The spies of Len Yang's master must have possessed divining rods which plumbed the very secrets of Peter's soul.

In Batavia Peter attended to a task long deferred. He despatched a cablegram to Aileen Lorimer in Pasadena, California, advising her that he was still on top, very much alive, and would some day, he hoped, pay her a visit.

He wondered what that gray-eyed little creature would say, what she would do, upon receipt of the message from far-away Java. It had been many long months since their parting on the rain-soaked bund at Shanghai. That scene was quite clear in his mind when he turned from the Batavia cable office to negotiate his plan with the wireless man of the *Persian Gulf*.

Peter found the man willing, if not positively eager, to negotiate—a circumstance that Peter forecasted in his mind as soon as his eyes had dwelt a fleeting moment upon the pudgy white face with its greedy, small, black eyes. The man was quite willing to lose himself in the mountains behind Batavia until the *Persian Gulf* was hull down on the deep-blue horizon, upon a consideration of gold.

The price was named, the deal was consummated, and Peter presented himself to the fat, jovial captain of the *Persian Gulf*. As his ticket was good and his record clean, the good-natured master signed him on with a willingness that spoke not too highly for the popularity of the wireless cabin's latest incumbent, who was concealed now in the blue hills near Salak.

Peter could have paid his passage to Hong Kong, and achieved his ends quite as handily as in his present role of wireless operator. But his fingers had begun to itch again for the heavy brass transmission key, and his ears were yearning for the drone of radio voices across the ethereal void.

It was on sailing morning that he was given definite evidence in the person of the Chinese coolie that his zigzagged trail had been picked up again by those alert spies of Len Yang's monarch.

He steamed out to the high black side of the steamer in the company's passenger launch, gazing back at the drowsy city, quite sure that the pursuit was off, when he felt the glinting black eyes of the coolie boring into him from the tiny cabin doorway.

His suspicions kindled slowly, and he admitted them reluctantly. It was the privilege of any Chinese coolie to stare at him, quite as it was the privilege of a cat to stare at a king. But the seed of mistrust was sown, and it was sown in fertile soil.

Peter ignored the stare, however, until the launch puffed up alongside the Jacob's ladder, then he gave the coolie a glance pregnant with hostility and understanding.

Taking the swaying steps three at a time, Peter hastened to his stateroom, emerging about five minutes later in a white uniform, the uniform of the J.C. & J. service, with a little gold at the collar, bands of gold about the cuffs, and gold emblems of shooting sparks, indicative of his cast, upon either arm.

He looked for the coolie and found him on the starboard side of the promenade deck. The subsequent events have already been partly narrated.

CHAPTER II

TWO WOMEN

THE COOLIE PLUNGED into the water with a weltering splash which sent a small spiral of spray almost to the deck. For a moment the man in the water pedaled and flailed, vastly frightened, and gasping, above the clang of the engine-room telegraph, for a rope. The black side of the *Persian Gulf* started to slide away from him.

"You better make for shore," shouted Peter between megaphonic hands.

Several boatmen were poling in the coolie's direction, but all of them refrained from slipping within reach of the thrashing hands. A Javanese boatman can find more amusing and enjoyable scenes than an angry Chinese coolie flailing about in the water; but he must travel many miles to find them.

"Swim to the Priok," shouted Peter again. He knew there were sharks in that emerald pond.

His attention then was diverted by a flutter of white at his elbow. He turned his head. The lonely passenger, a girl, was smiling mischievously into his face. But in her very dark eyes there was a blunt question.

"Why did you do that?" she asked in a voice that rang with a low musical quality. Her voice and her beauty were of the tropics, as were the features which, molded together, gave form to that beauty; because her hair and eyes were of a color, dark like walnut, and her skin fair olive, was like silk under silk, with the rosy color of her youth and fire showing underneath.

She was rather startling, especially her deep, dark and restless eyes. It was by sense rather than by anything his eyes could base conclusions upon that Peter realized her spirited personality, knew instinctively that radiant and destructive fires burned behind the somber, questioning eyes. The full, red lips might have told him this much.

And now these lips were forming a smile in which was a little humor and a great deal of tenderness.

Why there should be any element of tenderness in the stranger's smile was a point that Peter was not prepared to analyze. He had been subjected to the tender smiles of women, alas, on more than one occasion; and it was part of Peter's nature to take these gifts unquestioningly. He was not one to look a gift smile in the mouth! Yet, if Peter had looked back upon his experience, he would have admitted that such a smile was slightly premature, that it smacked of sweet mystery.

And it is whispered that richly clad young women do not ordinarily smile with tenderness upon young ruffians who throw apparently peaceful citizens from the decks of steamers into waters guarded by sharks.

To carry this argument a step farther, it has always seemed an unfair dispensation of nature that women should fall in love so desperately, so suddenly, so unapologetically and in such numbers with Peter the Brazen.

The phenomenon cannot be explained in a breath, or in a paragraph, if at all. While he was good to look upon, neither was Peter a god. While he was at all times chivalrous, yet he was not painstakingly thoughtful in the small matters which are supposed to advance the cause of love at a high pace. Nor was he guided by a set of fixed rules such as men are wont to employ at roulette and upon women.

Peter did not understand women, yet he had a perfectly good working basis, for he took all of them seriously, with gravity, and he gave their opinions a willing ear and considerable deference.

The rest is a mystery. Peter was neither particularly glib nor witty. Instinctively he knew the values of the full moon, the stars, and he had the look of a young man who has drunk at the fountain of life on more than one occasion, finding the waters thereof bitter, with a trace of sweetness and a decided tinge of novelty.

Life was simply a great, big adventure to Peter the Brazen; and he had been shot, stabbed, and beaten into insensibility on many occasions, and he was not unwilling for more. He dearly loved a fight, he dearly loved a dark mystery, and he had a certain reluctant fondness for a woman's bright, deceptive eyes.

As from a great distance he heard the jeers of the Javanese boatmen and the flounderings of the coolie as he looked now into the dark, deep eyes of this pretty, smiling stranger.

"Why did you do that?" she repeated softly.

"Because I wanted to," returned Peter with his winning smile.

"But there are sharks in there." This in a voice of gentle reproof.

"I hope they eat him alive," said Peter, unabashed.

"You threw him overboard just because you wanted to. And if you want to, I'll go next, I suppose."

"You might," laughed Peter. "When I have these spells I simply grab the nearest person, and over he goes. It is a terrible habit, isn't it?"

"Perhaps he insulted you."

"Or threatened me."

"Ah!" Her sigh expressed that she understood everything. "May I ask: Who are you?"

"I? Peter Moore."

"I mean, your uniform. You are one of the ship's officers, are you not?"

"The wireless operator. Shall we consider ourselves properly introduced?"

"My name is Romola Borria. I presume you are an American—or British."

"American," informed Peter. "And you? Spanish—*señorita?*"

"I have no nationality," she replied easily. "I am what we call in China, a 'B.I.C.'"

"Born in China!"

"Born in Canton, China. Father: Portuguese; mother: Australian. Answer: What am I?" She laughed deliciously, and Peter was moved.

They lingered long enough to see the coolie drag himself up on the shore unassisted, and then separated, the girl to make ready for lunch and to request the steward to assign them to adjoining seats at the same table, and Peter to take a look at the register, the crew, and what passengers might be on deck.

The passengers, lounging in steamer chairs awaiting the call to tiffin, and the deck crew, strapping down the forward cargo booms and battening the forward hatch, Peter gave a careful inspection, retaining their images in an eye that was rapidly being trained along photographic lines.

It was a comparatively simple matter, Peter found, to remember peoples' faces; the important point being to select some striking feature of the countenance, and then persistently drive this feature home in his memory. He knew that the human memory is a perverse organ, much preferring to forget and lose than to retain.

So he looked over the crew and found them to be quite Dutch and quite self-satisfied, with no more than a slight but polite interest in him and his presence. Wireless operators, as a rule, are self-effacing individuals who inhabit dark cabins and have very little to say.

He called at the purser's office and helped himself to the register, finding the name of Romola Borria in full, impulsive handwriting, giving her address as Hong Kong, Victoria; and a long list of Dutch names, representing quite likely nothing more harmful than sugar and coffee men, with perhaps a sprinkling of copra and pearl buyers.

Peter then investigated the wireless cabin, which was situated aft on the turn of the promenade deck, and commanding a not entirely inspiring view of the cargo well and the steerage.

Assuring himself that the wireless machine was in good working order, Peter hooked back the door, turned on the electric fan to air the place out, and with his elbows on the rail gave the steerage passengers a looking over.

He did not look far before his gaze stopped its traveling.

Directly below him, sitting cross-legged on a hatch-cover, was a Chinese or Eurasian girl whose face was colorless, whose lips were red, and whose eyes, half-lidded, because of the dazzling sunlight, were of an unusual blue-green shade.

Had Peter wished to make inquiries regarding this maiden, he would have found that she was from the Chinese settlement in Macassar, and on her way to Canton, to pay a visit to a grandmother she had never seen. But it was Peter's nature to spin little dreams of his own whenever he contemplated exotic young women, to place them in settings of his own manufacture.

Her blue-black hair was parted in a white line that might have been centered by the tip of her tiny nose and an unseen point on the nape of her pretty neck.

Peter could not know, as he studied her, how this innocent maid from Macassar was destined to play an important and significant part in his life, entering and leaving it like a gentle and caressing afternoon monsoon. His guess, as he looked away, was that she was a woman of no caste, from her garb; probably a river girl; more than likely, worse. Yet there was an undeniable air of innocence and youth in her narrow shoulders as she slowly rocked. Peter could see the tips of bright-red sandals peeping from under each knee, and he guessed her to be about eighteen.

She caught sight of Peter, who had folded his arms and was resting their elbows idly upon the teak rail, and their eyes met and lingered. A light, indescribably sad and appealing, shone in the blue-green eyes, which seemed to open larger and larger, until they became round pools of darting, mysterious reflection. It was a moment in which Peter was suspended in space.

"I am afraid that wireless operators are not always discreet," purred a low, sweet voice at his side.

Peter smiled his grave smile, and vouchsafed nothing. The girl in the steerage had returned to her sewing and was apparently quite oblivious of his presence, And still that look of demure, wistful appeal stood out in his memory.

Romola Borria was murmuring something, the context of which was not quite clear to him.

"Eh? I beg pardon?"

"It is quite dreadful, this traveling all alone," she remarked.

"Yes," he admitted. "Sometimes I bore myself into a state of agony."

"And it breeds such strange, such unexplainable desires and caprices," the girl went on in her cultivated, honeyed tones. "Strangers sometimes are so—so cold. For instance, yourself."

"I?" exclaimed Peter, supporting himself on the stanchion. "Why, I'm the friendliest man in the world!"

Romola Borria pursed her lips and studied him analytically.

"I wonder—" she began, and stopped, fretting her lip. "I should like to ask you a very blunt and a very bold question." Her expression was darkly puzzled.

"Go right ahead," urged Peter amiably, "don't mind me."

"Why I speak in this way," she explained, "is that since I ran away from Hong Kong—"

"Oh, you ran away from Hong Kong!"

"Of course!" She said it in a way that indicated a certain lack of understanding on his part. "Since I ran away from Hong Kong I have been looking, looking for such—for such a man as you appear to be, to—to confide in."

"Don't you suppose a woman would do almost as well?" spoke Peter, who, through experience, had grown to dislike the father-confessor rôle.

"If you don't *care* to listen—" she began, as though he had hurt her.

"I am all ears," stated Peter, with his most convincing of smiles.

"And I have changed my mind," said Romola Borria with a disdainful toss of her pretty head. "Besides, I think the Herr Captain would have a word with you."

The fat and happy captain of the *Persian Gulf* occupied the breadth if not the height of the doorway, wearing his boyish grin, and Peter hastened to his side with a murmured apology to the girl as he left her.

He merely desired to have transmitted an unimportant clearance message to the Batavia office, to state that all was well and that the thrust-bearing, repaired, was now performing "smoot'ly." Dropping the hard rubber headphones over his ears, Peter listened to the air, and in a moment the silver crash of the white spark came from the doorway.

Romola Borria stared long and venomously at the little Chinese maiden, who was sewing very industriously as she rocked to and fro on the hatch. Immersed in her own thoughts the girl, removing her quick eyes from the flying needle, glanced up at the deep, blue sky and, smiling, shivered in a sort of ecstasy.

CHAPTER III

"DRAGONS"

AT DINNER PETER met the notables. It seemed the fat and handsome captain had taken a fancy to him. And it was as Peter had deduced earlier. These passengers were stodgy Dutchmen, each with a little world of his own, and forming the sole orbit of that little world. For the most part they were plantation owners escaping the seasonal heat for the cool breezes of a vacation in Japan, boastful of their possessions, smug in their Dutch self-complacency, and somewhat gluttonous in their manner of eating.

The fat captain beamed. The fat plantation owners gorged themselves and jabbered. The three-piece orchestra played light opera that the world had forgotten. The company became light-hearted as more frosty bottles of that exotic drink, arracka, were disgorged by the *Persian Gulfs* excellent ice-box. And all the while, speaking in light, soothing tones, Romola Borria gazed alluringly into the watchful eyes of Peter Moore.

At length chairs were pushed back, and Peter, with this fairy-like creature in a dinner-gown of most fetching pink gossamer clinging to his arm, took to the deck for an after-dinner Abdul-lah.

They chatted in low, confiding tones of the people in the dining-room. They whispered in awe of the Southern Cross, which sparkled like frost on the low horizon. She confessed that at night the moon was her god, and Peter, feeling exalted under the influence of her exquisite charm, the touch of the light fingers upon his arm which tingled and burned under the subtle pressure, became bold and recited that verse of "Mandalay" wherein "I kissed her where she stood."

It was quite thrilling, quite delicious, and altogether quite too fine to last.

After a while, when they were passing the door of the wire-less cabin, Romola squeezed his arm lightly and expressed a desire to have him send a message, a message she had quite forgotten. When Peter replied that such a message would be costly, involving an expensive retransmission by cable from Manila to Hong Kong, she only laughed.

Peter snapped on the green-shaded light and handed her pad and pencil. Dropping lightly to the couch which ran the length of the opposite wall, she nibbled at the pencil's rubber, and her smooth brow was darkened by a frown of perplexity.

Peter, lowering the aerial switch, sent out an inquiring call for the Manila station. The air was still as death. A dreary bush filled the black receivers, and then, through this gloomy silence trickled a far-away silver voice, the brisk, clear signals of Manila.

He swivelled half around, and the girl nervously extended the pad of radio blanks.

The message was directed to Emiguel Borria, the Peak, Hong Kong, and it contained the information that she would reach the Hong Kong anchorage on the following Tuesday morning. The last sentence; "Do not meet me."

Peter inclined his eyebrows slightly, but not impertinently, counted the words, and flashed them to the operator at Manila.

This one shot back the following greeting:

"Who are you? Only one man on the whole Pacific has a fist like that."

Peter changed the manner of his sending, resorting to a long and painful "drawl."

"I am a little Chinese waif," Peter spelled out slowly; and smiled, adding: "Good hunting to you, Smith!" He signed off.

The silvery spark of Smith was quick in reply.

"If you are Peter Moore, the Marconi people axe scouring the earth trying to find you. Are you Peter Moore?"

"In China," replied Peter breezily, changing back to the inimitably crisp sending for which he was famous, "we bite off people's noses who are inquisitive. Good night, old-timer!"

The voice of Manila screamed back in faint reprisal, but Peter dropped the nickeled band to the ledge, and pivoted quickly, to face the girl.

It was startling, the look she was giving him. Perhaps he had completed the transmission before she was aware. At all events, when Peter turned with a smile, her eyes bored straight into his with a distorted look, a look that seemed cruel as if it might have sprung from a well of hate; and hard and glinting and black as polished jade.

All of this vanished when she caught Peter's eyes, and it was as the passage of a vision, unreal. In its place was an expression of demureness, of gentle, almost fondling meekness. Had she been staring, not at him, but beyond him, over the miles to a detestable scene, a view of horror? It seemed more than likely.

Then he observed that the door of the wireless room was closed. He made as if to open it, but she interrupted him midway with a commanding gesture of her white, small hand.

"Lock it, and sit down here beside me."

Somewhat dazed and greatly flabbergasted, Peter obeyed.

He locked the door, then sat down beside her. She moved closer, took his hand, wrapped both of hers tightly around it, and leaned toward him until the breath from her painted lips was upon his throat, moist and warm, and her eyes were great shining balls of limpid mystery and dancing excitement, so close to his that he momentarily expected their eyelashes to mingle.

She caught her breath, and then, for those dramatic circumstances, made a most ridiculous remark. She realized that herself, for she whipped out:

"It is a foolish question. But, Mr. Moore, do you believe in love at first sight?"

Peter's tense look dissolved into a smile of giddy relief. He was expecting something quite frightful, and the clear wit of him found a ready answer.

"Foolish?" he chuckled. "Why, I'm the most devout worshiper at the shrine! The shrine brags about me! It says to unbelievers: Now, if you don't believe in love at first sight, just cast your orbs upon Peter Moore, our most shining example. Allah, by Allah! The old philanderer is assuredly of the faith!"

"I am quite serious, Mr. Moore."

"As I was afraid, Miss Borria. Seriously, then, I *do* believe in love at first sight. If you must know it, then here goes: As soon as I saw you I was mad about you! Call it infatuation, call it a rush of blood to my foolish young head, call it anything you like—"

"Why don't you stop all this?" she broke him off.

"All what?" he inquired innocently.

"This—this life you are leading. This indolence. This constant toying with danger. This empty life. This sham of adventure-love that you affect. It will get you nothing. I know! I, too, thought it was a great lark at first, and I played with fire; and you know just what happens to the children who play with fire.

"At first you skirt the surface, and then you go a little deeper, and finally you can do nothing but struggle. It is a terrible feeling, to find that your wonderful toy is killing you. Certain people in China, Mr. Moore, are conducting practises that you of the western world frown down upon. And blundering upon these practises, as perhaps you have, you believe you are very bold and very daring, and you are thrilled as you rub elbows with death, in tracing the dragons to their dens."

"Dragons!" The syllables cracked from Peter's lips, and his wits, which were wandering in channels of their own while this lecture progressed, suddenly were bundled together, and he was alert and keenly attentive.

"Or call them what you will," went on the girl in a low-pitched monotone. "I call them dragons, because the dragon is a filthy, wretched symbol."

"You have some knowledge of my encounters with—dragons?" put in Peter as casually as he was able.

"I profess to know nothing of your encounters with anybody," replied the girl quietly and patiently. "I base my conclusions only on what I have seen. This morning I saw you throw a Chinese coolie into the harbor at Batavia. It happens that I have seen that coolie before, and it also happens that I know a little—do not ask me what I know, for I will never tell you—a little about the company that coolie keeps."

"I guess you are getting a little beyond my depth," stated Peter uncomfortably. "Would you mind sort of summing up what you've just said?"

"I mean, I want to try to persuade you that the life you have been living is wrong. At the same time, I want you to help me, as only you can help me, in putting a life of wretchedness behind me. It is asking a great deal, a very great deal, but in return I will give you more than you will ever realize, more than you can realize, for you cannot realize the danger that surrounds your every movement, and will continue to surround you until they—*they*—are assured that you have decided to forget them."

"What—what are you driving at?" stammered Peter.

"Do I look wicked?" Miss Borria wanted to know.

She squeezed his hand.

Peter shook his head, forgetting to wonder what an officer might think upon finding the door locked. Would the jovial little captain be quite so jovial viewing these incriminating circumstances? Not likely. But Peter had dismissed the fat captain from his mind, together with all other alien thoughts, as he concentrated upon the amazing words of this exceedingly amazing and beautiful girl. She was looking down at the chevron of gold sparks on his sleeve.

"I can tell you but one more thing of consequence," she continued. "It is this: Together we can stand; divided we will fall, just as surely as the sun follows its track in the heavens. I have a plan that will offend you—perhaps offend you terribly—but there is no other way. When *they* know that we have decided to forget them, we can breathe easily. Our secrets, grown stale, are not harmful to them."

"I am always open to any reasonable inducement," said Peter dryly.

The eyes meeting his were quite wild.

"How would you like to go to some lovely little place, to have money, to live comfortably, even luxuriously, with a woman of whom you could be justly proud, and who would bend every power with the sole view of making you happy"—she was blushing hotly—"and all this woman would demand in return would be your loyalty, your respect—and later your love, if that were possible."

"But this—this is—astounding!" exclaimed Peter.

"I expected you to say that. But let me assure you, I have thought this over. I have given it every possible consideration, and now I know there is no other way. I want to leave China. I want to go away forever and ever. I must leave."

Her shoulders jerked nervously.

"My life has been miserable—so miserable. And I am not brave enough to go through with it alone. I am afraid, terribly afraid. And afraid of myself, and of my weakness. I must be encouraged, must have some one to make me strong and brave, and afterward to take the good in me and bring it out, and kill the bad."

She relinquished Peter's hand and thumped her chest with small fists.

"There *is* good in me; but it has never been given a chance.

"I want a man who will bring that good out, a man who will make me fine and true and honorable. For such a man I would give everything—my life!" She lowered her voice. "I would give my best—my love. When I saw you lift the coolie, after he showed you his knife, I thought you were such a man; and when I looked into your face I believed I had found such a man. The rest—remains—for you to say."

"Where do you want me to t-take you?" demanded Peter.

"Ah! That is of so little importance! To Nara—Nagoya—to Australia—America."

She shrugged, as if to say, "And little I care."

"Now I am offering you only two rewards for that sacrifice— your safety against *them*—and money. You can name your price. I feel that you will come to love me; but that can come, if it cares, any time. When you want me—I will be waiting. I want you to consider this now. Now! Will you? Tell me that you will!"

"I-I don't know what to say!" stammered Peter in a husky voice. "Are—you are not joking, are you, Miss Borria? You can't be! But this is so serious! Shocking! Why, you never saw me before! Why should you pick me for such a thing when you never saw me? You don't know me. You don't know what a brute I might be. Why, I might be married for all you know—"

"I am reasonably sure," said the girl with some of her former serenity.

"But this—this is unbelievable!" cried Peter. "You never saw me before to-day. Why, you're a nice girl. You're not the kind of girl who runs away with a man at first sight. You're not in love with me at all. Not at all. Miss Borria—"

A flame of hot suspicion shot athwart Peter's mind. He seized her hands, glared into her eyes, dragged her to her feet.

"Now, listen!" he clamored. "Now, listen. You tell me what you really want. What's your game, eh? You're a wise little bird, you are. I may look stupid, I may not see all the way through this talk you've been giving me, but I can see something, You're holding back. What is it? Come on! Out with it!"

She was not disturbed in the least at his harshness, nor did she seemingly disapprove of the rough way he handled her.

"I am married," she said simply.

CHAPTER IV

THE SIREN STRAIN

TO PETER THIS revelation was like the addition of a single grain to a bucket brimming with sand.

"Well, what of it?" he barked.

"To a man who is fat and untidy, a man old enough to be my father, who treats me as if I were a thief, or a dog. I loathe him. And he detests me. You see,"—she smiled ironically—"we are not very happy. I ran away from him a month ago, from Hong Kong. I ran as far as Singaraja, and now I have to go back because I have not the courage to stay away. A stronger will would make me give him up. Would make me go away, and stay. And I grabbed at you."

"As a drowning man would grab at a straw."

"Not at all! Perhaps, let us say, I had pictured such a man as you. And then you came. He will beat me when I return."

"No!"

"Yes!" She pressed down the gauzy stuff which came up almost to her throat in the form of a high "V." And across the rounded white curve of her chest were four angry red stripes, the marks of a whip.

He shuddered. "This is terrible."

"Will you help me—now?"

"What can I do? What can I do?" He was striving to adjust himself to this exceedingly difficult situation. "But I don't understand how you can place all this confidence in me."

"Because when I saw you I knew you were a man who stopped at nothing."

"But why—why does he beat you? It—it's incomprehensible!"

He stared at the beautiful face, the long, white appealing face, and the deep, dark eyes with their fringe of long lashes. If ever a girl was meant to be loved and protected it was this one.

"I know I am asking a great deal, far more than I have any right, and not taking you into consideration at all. But you will help me. You must. Have I talked to you in vain? Do you think I would make you unhappy?"

"That's not the question, not the question at all. But you don't know me. We are perfect strangers!"

That is what Peter had been trying to get out of his system all of this time. Had he been thinking connectedly at this trying moment, not for the life of him would he have uttered those words. He had convinced himself that he was above and beyond all shallow conventions. And in an unguarded moment this thought, which had been in and out of his mind, popped out like a ghost from a closet. We are perfect strangers!

"So is every man a stranger to his wife, What difference does time make? Very little, I think. A day—a week—a month—a year—twenty!—you and I would still be strangers, for that matter. Who can see into any man's heart?"

She stopped talking, and kneaded her hands as if in anguish.

"And think! Do think of me!"

"I am thinking of you," said Peter constrainedly.

"We can go to Nara, if you like, to the little inn near the deer-path, and be so happy—you and I. Think of Nara—in cherry-blossom time!"

"I can't see the picture at all," said Peter dryly. "But since you've elected me to be your—your Sir Galahad, I'll tell you what I will do."

Nervously the girl was fumbling at her throat, where, suspended by a fine gold chain, hung a cameo, a delicately carved rose, as red as her lips, and as lifelike. She nodded, quite as though her life hung by that gold thread and depended at the high end upon his decision.

"Where do you live?" he asked abruptly.

"On the Peak, Hong Kong."

"Your husband's nationality?"

"He is a Portuguese gentleman, my father's cousin."

"It would be possible for me, perhaps, to aid a lady in distress by punishing the cause of it."

"You mean—"

"I will gladly undertake to thrash the gentleman, if it would do any good."

"No, no! That would not do."

"Then there's no choice for me. Either I must accept or decline your invitation."

"I pray you will! I have told you frankly and quickly, because time is valuable. We have none to lose. A steamer leaves for Formosa and Moji the morning after we arrive—at daybreak. We would scarcely have time to complete our plans, and embark."

Peter raised his eyebrows. "Complete our plans?" he intoned.

"Yes. We must raise money. You see, there is money, thousands of dollars, always in that house. It would be necessary to—to take whatever of it we needed. That is why I will need you, too."

"I think," declared Peter with decision, "that we had better call this a misdeal, and play another game for a while. In the first place, I will not run away with you, because it is against my principles to run away with a strange young woman. In the second place, stealing for pleasure is one of the seven deadly sins that I conscientiously avoid.

"When something good, something worth while, is to be gained by thieving, I admit frankly I stoop to it, like Robin Hood practised banditry. Now that I have aired my views, now that I have proved to you I'm not as fine and brave as you hoped me to be, let's shake hands and part the best of friends, or the best of enemies."

The girl rose from the chair into which she had dropped when Peter began his say. Alternately she was biting her upper and lower lips in nervousness or irritation. She put her back to the door and braced her hands against the white enameled panels. Her breast was heaving. She was desperately pale, and little dots of perspiration shone on her white forehead. And she was limp, as though his last remark had drained the final drop of vitality from her.

"I-I won't give you up," she said in a small, husky voice. "Besides, you are wrong, wrong in saying and believing that stealing his money would not be for a good cause. He is a brute, a monster, and worse than a thief. I cannot tell you how he gets his money. I would not dare to whisper it. You will be doing a fine and splendid thing in taking his money. You will be freeing me! Does that sound like heroics? I don't care if it does! But with that money you can buy my soul out of bondage. You can make me happy. Won't you? Won't you do—that—for me?"

Peter stood there like a block of ice—melting rapidly! But he said nothing. His thoughts were beyond the expression of clumsy words.

Her dumb hand found the key, turned it. The door opened, and a sweet breath of the cool sea air crept into the small room.

For a moment her white, distraught face hung down on her breast like that of a child who has been scolded without understanding why. Then she darted out of the room.

CHAPTER V

THE GIFT

WHEN PETER SNAPPED off the switch he found that he was trembling, trembling from his knees to his neck. With a feeling akin to guilt he wiped the sweat from his face and walked unsteadily to the rail which overhung the cargo-well.

He lighted an Abdullah, and watched the little smoke pool, which the wind snatched and tossed up into the booms and darkness.

It must have been a nightmare, this scene just past. What an incredible, a preposterous request for a woman to make! And the more thought he fed to the enigma the more incredible and unreal it became.

It was too big and complex a thought to hold all together in his tired brain now. In the morning he would tackle it with some zest, with an inner eye washed clean by a long sleep, just now he felt the need of relaxation, and as he smoked, his thoughts flitted afar, to come back now and then, irresistibly drawn by the vivid picture painted in his mind by Romola Borria.

His eyes, commanders of his thoughts, traveled out over the stern, which rose and sank with a ponderous, wallowing sound in the heaving ground swells, and he made out the weaving and coiling, the lustrous but dim windings of the phosphorescent wake.

As he became more accustomed to the shadowy, pointed darkness of the steerage cabins, he became aware of a small figure crouching on the hatch-cover near the starboard rail. He studied this intently, and at length he made out the long, black

queue of the Chinese girl who had stared at him in such be-
witching fashion a little earlier in the day.

And his mind was carried back at the thought of this small
maiden to the grim and red Tibetan city, whose memories now
were scarcely more than a confused and hideous dream. He
pictured again the splendors of the blue-domed white palace
which reposed like a beast of prey atop the red filth disgorged
by the cinnabar mine.

Out of an adventurous impulse he had broken into that place
to meet and to undo its master, the monarch of Len Yang,
sometimes called the Gray Dragon. He had hoped to do away
with the Gray Dragon as he would have done away with a
man-eating python. He had wanted to stop for once and all
the hideous traffic in which that beast indulged.

Even now, while others slept, Peter knew that hunters of the
Gray Dragon were searching eagerly for such maidens as this
one who was crouched on the canvas cover below him; hunters
who were paid, as he knew, fabulous prices for the wretched
ones acceptable to the beast whose lust was responsible for this
traffic.

Peter's heart thumped in youthful resentment as the thought
of that evil spirit came to him now. When would he meet the
Gray Dragon face to face? When would he again penetrate the
stronghold of that unhappy red city? Who could say? Probably
never.

The small Chinese girl on the hatch-cover had found him
staring at her, and with a little shiver of surprise Peter made
the discovery that she was smiling archly at him; and she inclined her head. She was beckoning to him? It seemed so,
indeed.

Because Peter was a youth of deep and subtle understandings,
he did no more than nod slightly, and forthwith descended the
companion-ladder to the well, and crossed the well to her side.

Her eyes were given a queer little twinkle by the near-by
electric which burned dimly over the door of the engine-room

galley, and she motioned him to be seated. He squatted, Chinese fashion, and she took a deep, sighing breath, holding out her hands with a quick gesture.

Across her wrists and drooping to her knees and beyond them into the shadow was a strip of heavy, deep-blue silk. All down its length were stitched small, round dots of dark red. Peter knew this for a sarong, an ornamental waist-sash, affected by most Javanese gentlemen and many Australians and New Zealanders.

While he hesitated, she laid this in his lap with a shy impulsiveness.

"It is yours, sar," she informed Peter in English of a very strange mold. She spoke in a rather high-pitched, bell-like voice, pure and soft, and tinkling with queer little cadences. "It is yours, sar. I made it for you."

Indubitably the girl was Eurasian. Asiatic features predominated, with the exception of her eyes, which were more round than oblique, from which circumstance Peter could surmise that her Aryan blood, provided she was a half-caste, came from her mother's side; the predominance of the Mongoloid in her features being due to an Asiatic father, a Chinese.

The colorless fare, relieved by the bright color of her lips, the slightly oblique eyes, told him that; yet her accents were those of a Javanese, a Malay from the south.

"You made this—for me?" replied Peter, surprised.

"Oh, yes, sar," said the tinkling little voice.

"Well, that is fine. It is beautiful," he said, feeling his way with prudence. "And how much do I owe you, small one?"

She shook her head indignantly.

"It is a geeft," she informed him. "I am no longer poor, my lord. I can now give geefts. I like you. I give this to you."

Peter was moved momentarily beyond speech.

"You are very fine, *busar satu*," went on the tiny, musical voice. "So is this sarong. You will wear it, great one, around thy middle?"

"Around my middle, to be sure, small one," laughed Peter; "until my middle is clay, or until the sarong is no more than a thread."

"Ho! It is said, *busar satu!*" The girl giggled, bobbing her small head in happy approval. "It is twice blessed: with my love and with my foolish blood; for I pricked my finger on the wicked needle. But I covered that spot with a red *mata-ari* (sun). You can never, never tell."

"Assuredly not!" cried Peter gaily.

"Let the sarong be wound about thy middle," commanded the Chinese maiden. "Arise, sar, and wind it about thy middle."

And Peter did rise, winding the sarong about his lean waist twice, allowing one end to dangle down on his left side in a debonair and striking fashion. It was very becoming. It set off his slim figure in a rather bizarre way, lending to him a touch of the exotic, or romance.

"It's bully!" he exclaimed, pirouetting with one hand on his head after the style of the matador.

"It is bully!" she echoed, in such quaint reflection of his exclamation that Peter laughed outright. "Now, sit down again, sar," she invited. And when Peter had again disposed himself at the side of this light-hearted young person, she went on:

"I am coming a long, long way to visit my aged grandmother (may the green-eyed gods grant her the twelve desires!) who lives Canton-way. My dear father sells opium. He has grown rich in that trade, even though the stupid eyes of the Dutch *babis* are on him all the while. When I have seen my ancient grandmother, and given her geefts, I will go home, to the south, Macassar-way."

"Now, where, oh where, do I fit in this scheme?" was what Peter thought. "What have I that this maiden desires?"

"Ah, *busar satu!*" the maiden was saying, deftly and unaffectedly patting the sarong. "It is bully! And now—"

"And now—" intoned Peter calmly, for even as a life pays for a life, and an eye for an eye, and a tooth for a tooth, so does a gift pay for a gift.

"And now," went on the maid from Macassar, whose father had grown rich in the opium-trade under the very eyes of the Dutch, "tell me but one thing, my lord—is Hong Kong safe for such as I?"

"When one is young and virtuous," spake Peter in the drone of an ancient fortune-teller, "one keeps her eyes pinned on the front. One hears nothing; and one becomes as discreet of tongue as the little blue sphinx at Chow-Fen-Chu."

"Those are the words of Confucius, the wise one," retorted the little bell-like voice with a tinkling laugh. "I need no guide, then? I have heard that China is unsafe. That is why I asked."

"Small one," replied Peter, with a smile of gravity and with much candor in his blue eyes, "in China, such a one as you are as safe as a Javanese starling in a nest of hungry yellow snakes. You will travel by daylight, or not at all. You will go from Kowloon to your venerable grandmother by train. You will carry a knife, and you will use it without hesitation. Have you such a knife?"

The small head bowed vehemently.

"In Hong Kong you will go aboard a sampan and be rowed Kowloon-way, from whence the train runs by the great river to Canton."

"That will be safe, that sampan?"

"I will make it safe, small one. For I will go with you as far as Kowloon, if that is what you wish."

"And does the brave one admire my sarong?" the small voice wavered.

"It shames my ugly body," said Peter. "Now run along to bed—*kalak!*" And he clapped his hands as the small figure bobbed out of sight, with her long, black pigtail flopping this way and that, and disappeared in the companionway of the woman's steerage.

CHAPTER VI

THE ROSE CAMEO

IT CAME TO Peter as he climbed up the iron-fretted steps
to the lonely promenade-deck that life had begun to take on
its old golden glow, the luster of the uncertain, the charm of
women who found in him something not undesirable.

At this he smiled a little bit. He had never known, as far back
as the span of his adventures extended, a woman who deemed
his companionship as quite so valuable a thing as the mysterious and alluring Romola Borria, the husband-beaten, incredible, and altogether dangerous young woman who passion-
ately besought him to accompany her on a pilgrimage of
forgetfulness into the flowery heart of dear old Japan.

Ascending the ladder to the unoccupied deck, he was conscious of the sweet drone of the monsoon, which blew off the
shores of Annam over the restless bosom of the China Sea,
setting up a tuneful chant in the *Persian Gulf's* sober rigging,
and kissing his cheeks with the ardor of a despairing maiden.

Peter the Brazen decided to take a turn or two round deck
before going to his bunk, to drink in a potion of this intoxicat-
ing, winelike night. The wheel of fortune might whirl many
times before he was again sailing this most seductive of oceans.

And he was a little intoxicated, too, with the wine of his
youth. His lips, immersed in the fountain, found very little
bitterness there. Life was earnest and grave, as the wiseacres
said; but life was, on the whole, sublime and poignantly sweet.
A little bitterness, a little dreary sadness, a pang at the heart
now and again, served only to interrupt the smooth regularity,
the monotony, to add zest to the nectar.

When he had finished the cigarette, he flung the butt over
the rail into the gushing water, which swam south in its phos-

phorescent welter, descended between decks, to the stateroom that had been assigned to him, and fitted the key to the lock.

He felt decidedly young and foolishly exalted as he closed the door after him and heard the lock click, for to few men is it given to have two lovely young women in distress seek aid, all in the span of a few hours. Perhaps these rosy events had served merely to feed oil to the fires of his conceit; but Peter's was not a conceit that rankled anybody. And there were always volunteers, hardened by the buffets of this life, to cast water upon that same fire.

So, humming a gay little tune, Peter snapped on the light, bathing the milk-white room in a liquid mellowness, opened the port-hole, wound his watch, hung it on the curtain-bar which ran lengthwise with his berth, pushed the flowered curtains at either end as far back as they would go, in order to have all the fresh air possible, and—

Peter gasped. He declared it was absolutely impossible. Such things did not happen, even in this world of strange happenings and of stranger stirrings below the surface of actual happenings. His self-complacencies came shattering down about his ears like mountains of senseless glitter and he stooped to recover the object was lying upon, almost ready to tumble from, the rounded, neat edge of the white berth.

A rose of cameo! The hot breath from his lips, which drooped in astonishment and chagrin, seemed to stir the delicate petals of the exquisitely carved red rose which reposed in its mounting of soft gold in the palm of his trembling hand. The fine gold chain, like a rope of gold sand, trickled between his fingers and dangled, swinging from side to side.

The impossible thought pounded at the door of his brain and demanded recognition. Romola Borria had been a visitor to his room. But why? He had no secrets to conceal from the prying ears of any one, not now, at all events, for he had destroyed all evidences depending upon the excursion he had made from Shanghai to Len Yang, and from Len Yang to Mandalay, to Rangoon, to Penang, Singapore, and Batavia.

Naturally, his first impulsive thought was that Romola Borria was somehow entangled with those who ruled the destinies of the hideous mountain city, which crouched amidst the frosty emerald peaks on the fringe of Tibet. He had felt the weight of that ominous hand on other occasions, and its movements were ever the same. Night stealth, warnings chalked on doors, the deliberate and cunning penetration of his secrets; all of these were the typical machinations of the Gray Dragon, and of those who reported back to the Gray Dragon.

And this act was symbolic of those who actually and actively represented his enemy, the man he had never seen. This was based upon literal past experience.

No one would break into his stateroom who was not the tool of Len Yan's unknown king. Thus the finger of accusation was brought to bear unwaveringly upon Romola Borria.

Yet he struggled now, reluctant to reconcile this theory with his conception of Romola Borria, with the anguished sincerity of her plea, with the look of genuine terror that had glowed in her dark eyes.

Yes, it was incredible that this girl, with those scarlet stripes across her breast, could in any way be complicated with the wanton designs of the beast in Len Yang. Yet here was evidence, damning her, if not as a wilful tool of the cinnabar king, then at least as a room-breaker. Why had she come into his room? And how?

He searched the room, then dragged his suit-case from under the bunk to the middle of the blue carpet, and spilled its contents angrily upon the floor. It took him less than ten seconds to discover what was missing; not his money, nor the few jewels he had collected in his peregrinations, for they were untouched in the small leather bag.

Peter looked again, carefully shaking each garment, hoping, and refusing to hope, that the revolver would make its appearance. It was an American revolver, an automatic, which he had purchased at much pains and considerable cost in a pawnbroker's shop in Singapore. And now this excellent weapon was missing.

He felt that eyes were upon him, that ears were listening slyly to his stertorous breathing, that lips were rusting in bated whispered comments upon the fury with which he took this important loss.

Snapping off the light, he plunged down the murky corridor, with the guilty rose cameo clutched in his sweating hand, and came at length to the purser's office. This dignitary was absent, at midnight lunch probably; so Peter rifled the upper drawer in the desk, and brought out the passenger register, finding the name and room number he sought after an instant of search.

Carefully he replaced the ledger in its original position, closed the drawer, and darted back up the corridor.

In front of a room not far from his own he paused and rapped. His knock, sharp and insistent, was one of practise, a summons which would not be mistaken by the occupants of adjoining staterooms, nor was it likely to disturb them.

After a moment, light showed at the opened transom. Some one rustled about within, and in another instant the door opened far enough to admit a head from which dark masses of hair floated, framing a face that was white and inquisitive.

At sight of her midnight visitor Romola Borria opened the door wide and smiled a little sleepily. She had paused long enough in arising to slip into a negligee, a kimono of blackest satin, revealing at the baglike sleeves and the fold which fell back from her throat a lining of blood-red silk.

One hand was caught up to her throat in a gesture of surprise, and the other was concealed behind her, catching, as Peter surmised, nothing if not his own automatic revolver, which had been loaded, ready for instant use, immediately the safety-catch was released.

She stared at him softly, with eyes still mirroring the depths of the sleep from which he had so rudely aroused her, her delicate red lips forming a curious smile. And she continued to smile more gently, more tenderly, as she became quite conscious of his presence.

"You have come to tell me that you will go to Japan with me," she stated.

Peter shook his head slowly, and with equal deliberateness lifted up the small object in his hand until the light from the ceiling-lamp fell directly upon it.

"My cameo!" she exclaimed with a start of surprise. "Where did you find it?" She reached impulsively for the ornament, but Peter closed his fingers upon it firmly.

"You have something to give me in return, I think," he said sternly.

She was staring at the closed hand with something of despair and fright, as if reluctant to believe this truth, while her fingers groped at her throat to verify a loss apparently not before detected.

She stepped back into the room and said:

"Close the door. Come inside."

He thought: If she had wanted to shoot me, she had plenty of chance before. A shot in this room, a murder, would fasten evidence upon her, and besides, it would instantly arouse the occupants of the adjoining staterooms, if not one of the deck crew on watch.

So he entered and closed the door, presenting a full view of his broad, white-uniformed back, and the gaudy-blue sarong about his waist. He took more time than was necessary in closing the door and sliding the bolt, to give her every opportunity to arrange this scene she desired.

But the girl was only drawing the curtains over the porthole, to keep out prying eyes, when he turned about.

She sat down on the edge of her berth, with her small white feet almost touching the floor, and the huge blue automatic resting upon her knees. It was unlikely that she did not appreciate fully the seductive charm of the red and black gown which adapted itself in whatever pose to the youthful carves of her body; and she permitted Peter to sit down on the narrow couch opposite and to examine her and perhaps to speculate for a number of seconds before she seemed to find her speech.

Meekly her dark eyes encountered his.

"I was afraid," she explained in a voice, low but free in her remarkable self-possession. "I knew you would not care, and I hoped that you would have a revolver in your room. So I went there. How did I get in? I borrowed a pass-key from the purser on the plea that I had left mine in my room. I hoped you would not miss it until we reached Hong Kong, and I intended to return it then and explain to you.

"My life," she added deprecatingly, "is in some slight danger, and, like the small fool that I am—even though I am fully aware that no one in the whole world cares whether I am living or dead—well, Mr. Moore, for some reason I still persist in clinging to the small hope."

She smiled wanly and earnestly, so Peter thought. A dozen impulses militated against his believing a word of this glib explanation; his common sense told him that he should seek further, that the explanation was only half made; and yet it cannot be denied that she had gone unerringly to his greatest weakness, perhaps his worst fault, his belief in the sincerity of a woman in trouble.

"Why didn't you ask me?" he demanded in his most apologetic voice, as though he had wronged her beyond repair. "Why didn't you tell me you were in danger? I'd have loaned you the revolver willingly—willingly!"

"I did try to find you," she replied; "but the wireless room was dark. You were no place on deck."

Peter was aware that for some reason Romola Borria did not prefer to share the secret of her real or fancied danger with him. He felt a little dissatisfied, cheated, as though the straightforward answer for which he had come had been turned into the counterfeit of evasion.

The situation as it now had shaped itself demanded some sort of decision. Without the whole truth he was reluctant to leave, and it was imprudent to remain any longer.

Romola, in this constrained pause in their conversation, feeling perhaps the reason for his silence, lowered her dark lashes and drew up her feet until they were concealed by the red folds of the kimono, and she drew the satin more closely about her soft, pink throat.

"You have decided nothing, then?" she parried.

"What decision I might have formed," he said, a trifle coolly, "has been put off by this. You see, I must admit it, this—this rather complicates things for me. I'm in the dark altogether now, you see. I wanted to help you, however I could. And then— then I find this cameo."

She nodded absently, fingering the groove in the automatic's handle.

"I'm afraid I took too much for granted," she said in a low voice. "Don't you suppose my curiosity was aroused when you threw the coolie overboard? I said nothing; rather, I asked you no questions; and I thought that a man who was self-poised enough to meet his enemies in that way would be—what shall I say?—charitable enough to overlook such a discrepancy as I have committed.

"When I confessed that you and I are facing a common enemy, that the same hands are eager to do away with both of us, I thought that bond was sufficient, was strong enough, to justify what might shock an ordinary man. I mean—"

"I think I understand," Peter took her up in contrite tones. "I'll ask nothing more. In the morning we will talk the other matter over. I must have a little time. For the present, I want you to keep the revolver, and—here is the cameo. For I for being so unreasonable, so—so selfish."

He leaned over. She seemed uncertain a moment, then caught the gold chain lightly from his hand.

"And—your revolver," she said. "Those are the terms of the agreement, I believe."

"No, no," he protested. "I have no use for it; none whatever. You keep it."

But quite as resolutely Romola Borria shook her head and extended the automatic, butt foremost, to him. "I insist," she said.

"But you say you're in danger," he argued.

"No. Not now. I have something else that will do quite as well. If it is written that I am to die, why give Death cause to be angry? I am a fatalist, you see. And I want you to take back your revolver, with my apologies, and quite without any more explanation than I have given you, please."

"But—" began Peter.

"Look," she said.

In the small space of the stateroom he could not avoid bending so low as to sense the warmth of her skin, in order to study the object toward which she was directing his gaze. A sense of hot confusion permeated him as her fingers lightly caressed his hand; her physical nearness obsessed him.

She had drawn back the fluffy pillow, and on the white sheet he glimpsed a long, bright, and exceedingly dangerous-looking dagger, with a jewel-incrusted hilt.

The singular thing about this knife was the shape of the blade, which was thin and with three sides, like a machinist's file. It would be a good dagger to throw away after a killing because of the triangular hole it would leave as a wound, a bit of evidence decidedly incriminating.

Peter straightened up, round-eyed, accepted the automatic, and slipped it into his pocket, smoothing his coat and the sarong over the lump, and approached the door.

For a moment his heart beat in a wild desire, a desire to take her in his arms as she stood so close and so quiet beside him,

smiling wistfully and a little sadly; and unaccountably she
seemed to droop and become small and limp and pitifully helpless in the face of him and of all mankind.

"Good night, Mr. Moore, and thank you so—much," she
murmured. "And I do—hope you will forgive me for being a—a
thief."

He thought that she was on the point of kissing him, and
his eyes swam and became of a slightly deeper and more silky
blue than a moment before. But she faltered back, while the
faintest suggestion of a sigh came from her lips.

In the next instant, as the door closed quietly behind him,
Peter was mightily glad that neither he nor she had yielded to
impulse. He was not, in the light of the literal version, the owner
of a wholly untarnished record, for he had given in to weakness,
as most men do give in to weakness.

But he was above temptation now, not because temptation
was put behind him, but because he had had the strength to
resist; and it was his full, deep desire to hold himself until that
girl, far across the Pacific, who inspired the finest and best in
him, should bear the name he bore.

It was a splendid thing, that feeling. It gave him courage and
confidence, and took him quite light-heartedly, with head erect
and shoulders back, out of the dreariest of his moments.

So, quick in a new and buoyant mood, Peter joggled, the key
in the lock of his stateroom door, slipped in, and was before
long dreaming of a cottage built for two, of springtime in
California, albeit snoring almost loud enough to drown out the
throb of the *Persian Gulf's* old but still useful engines.

CHAPTER VII

ENIGMA

BECAUSE OF THE fatigue which possessed his every muscle,
fatigue springing from the arduous, the trying hours now past,

Peter the Brazen was sleeping the slumber of the worthy, when, at a somewhat later hour in the night, some time before dawn crept out of the China Sea, a figure, lean and gray, flitted past his stateroom on the narrow orlop deck, peered in the darkened port-hole, and passed on.

Awakened by an instinct developed to a remarkable degree by his training of the past few months, Peter established himself upon one elbow and looked and listened, wondering what sounds might be abroad other than the peaceful chum of the engine.

Quite as intuitively he slipped his hand under the pillow and encountered the reassuring chill of the blued steel. Half withdrawing this excellent weapon, he shifted his eyes alternately from the door to the port-hole, conscious of an imminent danger, a little stupefied by his recent plunge into the depths of sleep, but growing more widely awake, more alert and watchful, with the passage of each instant.

The port-hole loomed gray and empty, one edge of it licked by the yellow light of some riot far distant deck-lamp. With his eye fastened upon this scimitar of golden light, Peter was soon to witness an unusual eclipse, a phenomenon which sent a shiver, an icy shiver, of genuine consternation up and down his backbone.

As he watched, a square of the yellow reflected light was blotted out, as though a bar of some nature had cast its shadow athwart that metallic gleam. This shadow then proceeded to slide first up and then down the brass setting of the port-hole, and the shadow dwindled.

As Peter sat up on the edge of his cot, gripping the square butt of the automatic in his hand and tentatively fingering the trigger, the origin of the shadow moved slowly, ever so slowly, into the range of his perplexed and anxious vision.

What appeared at first glance to be a cat-o'-nine-tails on a rather thick stem, Peter made out to be, as he built some hasty comparisons, the Maxim silencer attached either at the end of a revolver or of a rifle; for the black cylinder on the muzzle was circumscribed at regular intervals with small, sharp depressions, the clinch-marks of the silencing chambers.

As this specter crept up and over the edge of the port, Peter, with a deliberate and cold smile, raised the automatic revolver, slipped out of the berth with the stealth and litheness of a cat, crept into the corner where the stateroom door was hinged, and leveled the weapon until his eye ran along the dark obstruction of the barrel.

Slowly and more slowly the silencer moved inward until the blunt end of it was registered precisely upon a point where Peter's head would lie if he were sleeping in a normal attitude.

This amused him and perplexed him. All Peter wanted to see was the head or even the eye of this early morning assassin, whereupon he would take immediate steps to receive him with a warm cordiality that might forestall future visitations of a kindred sort.

In the space between heart-beats Peter stopped to inquire of himself who his visitor might be. And even as he stopped to inquire, a bright, angry, red flame spurted straight out from the mouth of the silencer, and Peter would have willingly gambled his bottom dollar that the bullet found its way into his pillow, a wager, as he later verified, upon which he would have collected all of the money he was eager to stake.

The lance of yellow-red flame had occasioned no disturbance other than a slight smack, comparable with the sharp clapping of a man's hands.

In the second leaping flame Peter was far more interested. Having delivered himself of one shot, the assassin could be depended upon to make casual inquiries, and to drop at least one more bullet into the darkness between the upper and lower berths, to make a clean job of it.

And it was on the appearance of the inquiring head that Peter relied to repay the intruder in his own metal, that metal taking the form of a wingless messenger of nickel-sheathed lead.

But the visitor was cautious, waiting, no doubt, for sounds of the death struggle, provided the shot had not gone directly home, its home being, as Peter shuddered to think, his own exceedingly useful brain.

He waited a little longer before his guest apparently decided that the time was come for his investigation; and thereupon a small, square head with the black-tasseled hat of a Chinese coolie set upon it at a rakish angle was framed by the port-hole.

Smirking nervously, Peter released the safety catch and brought pressure to bear slowly and firmly upon the trigger.

Click! That was all. But it told a terrible story. The weapon was out of commission, either unloaded or tampered with. And Peter's panic-stricken thoughts leaped, even as the square head leaped away from the window, to the Borria woman, to the cause of his desperate helplessness.

Romola Borria, then, had tampered with this revolver. Romola Borria had plotted, that was sure, with the coolie outside the port-hole for his assassination. That explained the visit to his room. That explained her perturbation over his discovery of her visit, of her sly and cool evasions and dissimulations.

It was with these thoughts hammering in his brain that Peter dropped out of range of the deadly port-hole and squirmed, inching his way into the doubtful shelter provided by the closet. At any instant he expected another red tongue to burn the now still darkness above his head, to experience the hot plunge of a bullet in some part of his slightly clad anatomy. And then— death? An end of the glorious adventures whose trail he had followed now for well upon ten years?

And still the death bullet was withheld. Groping about in the darkness with one hand as he loosened the magazine clip on the butt, and finding that the clip of cartridges had been removed, he finally discovered the whereabouts of the suitcase, and dragged it slowly toward him, with his eyes pinned upon the vacant port.

Fumbling among the numerous objects contained in the suitcase, his fingers encountered at length a cartridge clip. He slipped this into the magazine, and indulged in a silent grunt of relief as the clip moved up into place. He drew back the rejecting mechanism, and heard the soft, reassuring *snick* of the cartridge as it slid from the magazine into the chamber.

Then sounds without demanded his attention, the sounds of a tussle, of oaths spoken in a high, feminine tongue, in a language not his own.

Peter would have shouted, but he had long ago learned the inadvisability of shouting when such grim business as to-night's was being negotiated.

Slipping on his bath-robe, he opened the door and tentatively peered out into the half-light of the orlop deck from the cross corridor vestibule-way, for indications of a shambles.

They were gone. The deck was deserted. But he caught his breath sharply as he made out a long, dark shape which lay, with the inertness of death, under his porthole, blending with the shadows.

Who his benefactor had been was a problem. He rolled the man over upon his back, and dragged him by the heels under the deck-light, and, dragging him, a dark trail spread out upon the boards, and even as Peter examined the cold face, the spot broadened and a trickle broke from it and crept down toward the gutter.

Stabbed? More than likely. Pausing only long enough to reassure himself that this one was the assassin whose square head had been framed by the port, Peter looked for a wound, and shortly he found the wound, and Peter was not greatly astounded at the proportions thereof.

It was a small wound, running entirely through the neck from a point below the left ear to one slightly below and to the right of the locked jaw.

Keeping constantly before him some of the facts of this night, Peter was not surprised, I repeat, when upon close scrutiny the death wound proved to be small and thorough, and of a triangular pattern.

Just why he had expected to find that triangular wound Peter was unable to explain even to himself, but he was quite as sure that Romola Borria's hand was in this latest development as he had been sure a moment before that her steady, small hand had deliberately removed the clip of cartridges from the butt of the automatic, to render him helpless in the face of his enemies.

Silently contemplating the stiffening victim of Romola Borria's triangular dagger, Peter heard the rustle of silk garments and looked up in time to observe the slender person of Romola Borria herself, attired exactly as he had left her a few hours previous, detach itself from the corridor vestibule-way which led to his stateroom. She approached him.

A thousand questions and accusations swam to his lips, but she was speaking in low, impassioned tones.

"I knocked at your door. God! I thought he had killed you! I was afraid. For a moment I thought you were dead."

"You stabbed him," said Peter in an expressionless voice, as if he were making a statement in reference to the weather.

She nodded, and drew a long, sobbing breath.

"Yes. He tried to shoot you. I saw him pass my window. I was waiting. I watched. I knew he would try. Oh, I'm so glad—"

"You knew? You knew that?"

"Yes, yes. He was the—the mate of the coolie you threw overboard in Batavia. You know, they always travel in pairs. You didn't know that?"

"No; I did not know. But I could have defended myself easily enough if it had not been for—"

"Your clip of cartridges? Can you forgive me? Can you ever forgive me for taking them out? I took them out, Oh, Mr. Moore, believe me, I am concealing nothing! I did remove the clip, and in my carelessness I forgot to give them back to you when you left my room."

"I see. Have you them?"

"Yes."

"Please give them to me. You have not by any chance, in another of those careless moods of yours, happened to tamper with the bullets, have you?"

"Mr. Moore—" she gasped, clutching her white hands to her breast in indignation.

"You *are* clever," said Peter sarcastically. "You're altogether too damn clever. What your game is, poor little husband—beaten wretch, I'm not going to take the trouble to ask. You—you—"

"Oh, Mr. Moore!" She caught his arm.

He cast it away.

"Didn't tamper with the bullets, eh?" he went on in a deep, sullen voice. "Well, Miss Borria, here is what I think of your word. Here is how much I trust you."

And with a single motion Peter whipped all seven cartridges from the clip and tossed them into the sea. He snarled again:

"You *are* clever, damn clever; but not quite clever enough even for me, poor fool that I am. Poor, poor little thing! Still want to go to Japan with me, my dear?"

"I do," stated the girl, whose eyes were dry and burning.

"Sure! That's the stuff," railed Peter bitingly; "whatever you do, stick to your story."

He grabbed her wrist, and she looked at him with a look that should have softened granite.

"For example," he sniffed; "that neat little cock-and-bull story you made up about your cruel, brutal husband. Expect me to believe that, too, eh?"

"Not if you don't care to," said the girl faintly.

Peter knocked away her hand, the hand which seemed always to fumble at her throat in moments of strain. He pulled down the black kimono and dragged her under the light, forcing her back against the white cabin. He looked.

The white, soft curve of her chest was devoid of all marks. It was as white as that portion of a woman's body is said to be, by the singing poets, as white as alabaster, and devoid of angry stripes.

Peter seized both limp wrists in one of his hands.

"By God, you *are* clever!" he scoffed. "Now, Miss Enigma, you spurt out your story, and the true story, or, by Heaven, I'll call the skipper! I'll have you put in irons—for murder!"

She hung her head, then flung it back and eyed him with the sullen fire of a cornered animal.

"You forget I saved your life," she said.

As if they were red hot, Peter dropped her hands, and they fell at her sides like limp rags.

"I-I—" he stammered, and backed away a step. "Good God!" he exploded. "Then explain this; explain why you took the clip from my automatic. Explain why you put up that story of a brutal husband, and showed me scars on your breast to prove it—then washed them off. And why—why you killed this man who would have murdered me."

"I will explain what I am able to," she said in a small, tired voice. "I took the clips from the revolver because—because I didn't want you to shoot me. I know *their* methods far better than you seem to; and I knew I could handle this coolie myself far better than you could; and I wanted to run no risk of being shot myself in attending to him.

"As for the 'brutal-husband story,' every word of that is the truth. If you must know, I used rouge for the scars. Since you are so outspoken, I will pay you back in the same cloth. There are scars on my body, on my back and my legs."

Her face was as red as a poppy.

"And I killed this man because—well," she snapped, "perhaps because I hate you."

Had she cut him with a whip, Peter could not have felt more hurt, more humiliated, more ashamed, for gratitude was far from being a stranger to him.

He half extended his arms in mute apology, and, surprised, he found her lips caressing his, her warm arms about his neck. He kissed her—once—and put her away from him; and he could thank that guiding star of his in California that Romola Borria's embrace was rather more forgiving than insinuating or compelling.

"We must get rid of this coolie," she said, brushing the clusters of dark hair from her face. "I will help you, if you like. But over he goes!"

"But the blood."

"Call a deck-boy. Tell him as little as you need. You are one of the ship's officers. He will not question you."

He hesitated.

"Can you forgive me for this—way I have acted, my—my ingratitude?"

"Forgiveness seems to be a woman's principle role in life," she said with a tired smile. "Yes. I am sorry, too, that we misunderstood. Good night, my dear."

And Peter was all alone, although his aloneness was modified to a certain extent by the corpse at his feet. The dead weight he lifted with some difficulty to the railing, pushed hard, and heard the muffled splash. Quickly he got into his uniform, slipped his naked feet into looped sandals, and sought the forecastle.

The occupants of this odorous place were sawing wood in an unsynchronous chorus. No one seemed to be about, so he seized a pail half filled with sujee, a block of holystone, and a stiff broom.

With these implements he occupied himself for fully a half-hour, until the spots on the deck had faded to a satisfactory whiteness. The revolver with Maxim silencer attached he discovered, after a long search, some distance away in the deck-gutter.

He meditated at length upon the advisability of consigning this grim trophy to the China Sea. Yet it is a sad commentary upon his native shrewdness that Peter had not yet recovered from his boyish enthusiasm for collecting souvenirs.

At last he decided to retain it, and he dropped it through the port-hole upon the couch, thereupon forgetting all about it until the weapon was called to his attention on the ensuing morning.

With all evidences of the crime removed, he returned the pail, the stone, and the broom to the forecastle locker, and sneaked back to his stateroom. He locked the door, barricaded the port-hole with the pink-flowered curtains—those symbols which had reminded him earlier of springtime in California—and examined his pillow.

It had been an exceedingly neat shot. The bullet had bored clean through the pillow, had struck the metal L-beam of the bunk, and rebounded into a pile of bedclothes. Dented and scorched, Peter examined this little pellet of lead, balancing it in the palm of his hand.

"Every bullet has its billet," he quoted, and he was glad indeed that the billet in this case had not been his vulnerable cerebrum.

Snapping off the light, he drew the sheet up to his neck and lay there pondering, listening to the whine of the ventilator-fan.

The haggard, distressed face of Romola Borria swam upon the screen of his imagination. This woman commanded his admiration and respect. Despite all dissemblings, all evasions, all actual and evident signs of the double-cross, he confided to his other self that he was glad he had kissed her. What can be so deliciously harmless, as a kiss? he asked himself.

And wiser men than Peter have answered: What can be so harmful?

CHAPTER VIII

A WIZARD OF THE WIRELESS

NIGHT BRINGS COUNSEL, say the French. Only in sleep does one mine the gold of truth, said Confucius.

When Peter was aroused by the golden dawn streaming through the swinging port-glass upon his eyes the cobwebs were gone from his brain, his eyes were clear and of a bright sea-blue, and he was bubbling with enthusiasm for the newborn day.

His ablutions were simple: a brisk scrubbing of his gleaming, white teeth, a dousing of his hands and face in bracing, cold water, with a subsequent soaping and rinsing of same; followed by a hoeing process at the mercy of a not-too-keen Japanese imitation of an American safety-razor.

Assured that the deck below his porthole was spotless, be ventured to the dining-room, half filled and buzzing with a noticeable excitement.

He was given to understand by a dozen gesticulating passengers that some time in the course of the night a deck-passenger, a Chinese coolie, from Buitenzorg to Hong Kong, or Macao, had fallen overboard, leaving no trace.

It was whispered that the helpless one had been done away with by foul means. And Peter became conscious during the meal that his fat and jovial little captain was looking at him and through him with a glance that could not be denied or for long avoided.

Wondering what his Herr Captain might know of the particulars of last night's doings, Peter sucked a mangosteen slowly, arranging his thoughts, card-indexing, his alibis, and making cool preparations for an official cross questioning. Clever lying out of his difficulty was the order, or the alternative for Peter was the irons.

When the fat fingers of Mynheer the Captain at length dabbled in the lacquered finger-bowl, after rounding out his fourth pomelo, Peter got up slowly and walked thoughtfully to the foot of the staircase. Here the captain caught up with him, touched his elbow lightly, and together they proceeded to the promenade-deck, which was shining redly in places where the wetness of the washing down had not yet been evaporated by the warm, fresh wind.

Mynheer the Captain fell into pace at Peter's side, gripped his fat Javanese cigar between his teeth, and caught his fat wrists together stolidly behind his back, and his low, wide brow slowly beetled.

"*Mynheer,*" he began in a somewhat constrained voice, low and richly guttural, "it iss known to you vat took place on der ship some dam during der nacht? Ja?"

"I overheard the passengers talking about a coolie falling overboard last night, sir," replied Peter guardedly. As long as no direct accusation came, he felt safer. He was reasonably sure, basing his opinion of skippers on many past encounters, that this one would go typically to his subject. In his growing cock-sureness, Peter expected no rapier-play. It would be a case, he felt sure, of all the cards on the table at once; a slam-bang, as it were.

"You know nodding of dot bissness, young man?"

"Nothing at all, Myn Captain."

"Dot iss strange. Dot iss strange," muttered the captain as they rounded the forward cabin and made their way in slow, measured strides down the port side. "I haf seen you come aboard yesterday, *mynheer,* und I haf seen you t'row over der side a coolie, a coolie who wass wit' der coolie who dis'ppeared last nacht. Why did you t'row him over der side, eh?"

"He threatened me with his knife," replied Peter without an instant's hesitation. "*Mynheer,* he was a bad Chink, a killer."

"*Ja. Tot ver vlomme!* All of 'em are bad Chinks."

"Why should he stab me?" intoned Peter. "I never saw him before. I am a peaceful citizen. The only interest I have on this ship, Mynheer Captain, is the wireless apparatus."

"*Ja?* Dot iss gude to hear, young man. I haf liked you—how does one say it?—immensely. Der oder man wass no gude. He is gude rittance. You intend to stay wit' us. *Ja?*"

"I hope so," said Peter heartily and with vast relief.

"You like dis ship, eh?"

"Very much, indeed."

"And I vant you to stay, young man. I vant you to stay joost as long as you feel like staying. But I vant to ask you one t'ing, joost one t'ing."

"I'll do anything you say, sir."

The fat, jovial skipper of the *Persian Gulf* eyed Peter with beady, cunning eyes, and Peter was suddenly conscious of a sinking sensation.

"Joost one t'ing. Better, first I should say, ven you vrow overboard der coolies you dislike, it vould be best not to keep—vat are dey called?—der soufenirs. Sooch t'ings as peestols."

"But, *mynheer*—"

The fat hand waved him to silence.

"Bot' of dem vas bad Chinks. I know. I know hot' of dose coolies a long, long time. T'ieves and blood men. *Tot ver vlomme.* It iss gude rittance, as you say. Young man, I haf nodding but one more t'ing to tell you. I say, I like you—immensely. I vant you very much to stay. But der next time coolies are to be t'rown over der side, I will be pleased to haf you ask my permission."

Peter stared hard at the fat little man, with a quick glaze of gratitude over his eyes. The skipper had left him, doubling back in the direction of the wheel-house. And something in the unsteadiness of the broad, plump shoulders gave to Peter in his perplexity the not inaccurate notion that the fat little man had enjoyed his joke and was giggling to such an extent that it almost interfered with his dignified strut.

Before buckling down to the day's business he made sure of one thing. Gone from his stateroom was the revolver with its Maxim silencer.

Because the wireless room at sea is a sort of lounging-room for those passengers who are bored from reading, or poker, or promenading, or simply are incompetent to amuse themselves without external assistance, Peter ignored the dozen pair of curious and interested eyes which were focused on his white uniform as he passed, with those telltale chevrons of golden sparks at the sleeves, strode into the wireless cabin, hastily closed the door, locked it, and thereupon gave his attention to the void.

He was not surprised to hear the shrill yap of the Manila station dinning in the receivers, and having no desire to allow his fair name to be besmirched by what might be professional inattention to duty, he gave Manila a crackling response, and told him to shoot and shoot fast, as he had a stack of business on hand, which was the truth.

Steamship and commercial messages were awaiting his nimble fingers, a half-dozen of them, in a neat little pile where the purser had left them to attract his attention as soon as he came on duty.

Manila's first message, with a Hong Kong date-line, and via the Philippine cable, was a service message, directed to Peter Moore, "probably aboard the steamer *Persian Gulf,* at sea." The context of this greeting was that Peter should report directly upon arrival in Hong Kong to J.B. Whalen, representative of the Marconi Company of America, residence, Peak Hotel.

Following this transmission, the Manila operator was anxious to know whether or not this was Peter Moore at the key; that he had been given instructions by the night man, who claimed to be a bosom companion of Peter Moore's, to make inquiries regarding Peter Moore's whereabouts during the past few months.

He further expressed a profane desire to know, provided the man at the key was Peter Moore, how in Hades he was, where in Tophet he had been keeping himself, and *why* in Gehenna he had so mysteriously vanished from the face of this glorious earth.

"But why all the hubbub about Peter Moore?" flashed back Peter to the inquisitive Manila operator, who was only about two hundred miles distant by now and rather faint with the coming up of the sun.

"Are—you—Peter—Moore?" came the faint scream.

"No, no, no!" shrieked the voluptuous white spark of the *Persian Gulf.*

"Is—he—on—board?"

"No, no, no!" rapped Peter making no effort to disguise that inimitable sending of his.

"You—are—a—double-barreled liar!" said the Manila spark with vehement emphasis. "No operator on the Pacific has that fist. You might as well try to disguise the color of your eyes!"

Manila tapped his key, making a long series of thoughtful little double dots, the operator's way of letting his listener know he is still on the job, and thinking. Then:

"Why did you leave the *Vandalia* at Shanghai?"

"I never left the *Vandalia* anywhere," retorted Peter. "I've just come up from Singapore and Singaraja way. I am taking the YZZ (YZZ were the *Persian Gulf's* call letters) to Hong Kong, and back to Batavia."

"No—you're—not," stated Manila's high-toned spark. "You're going to be pinched as soon as you land in Hong Kong for deserting your ship at Shanghai. That's a secret, for old friend-ship's sake."

It was now Peter's turn to tap off a singularly long row of little double dots.

"It may be a secret, but only a thousand stations are listening in," he said at length. "But, thanks, old-timer, just the same. If they pinch Peter Moore in Hong Kong, they will have to ex-tradite him from Kowloon. In other words, they will have to go some. Besides, what Peter does in Shanghai cannot be laid against him in Hong Kong. The law's the law."

A savage tenor whine here broke in upon Manila's laughing answer, the Hi! Hi! Hi! of the amused radio man; and Peter listened in some annoyance to the peremptory summons of a United States gunboat, probably nosing around somewhere south of Mindanao.

"YZZ-YZZ—Stand by, Manila," shrilled this one. "YZZ—YZZ—message for YZZ." He broke off with a nimble signature.

"Good morning, little stranger," roared Peter's stridulent machine. "You're pretty far from home. Won't you get your feet wet? The ocean's pretty dewy this morning. Well, what do you want? Shoot it, and shoot fast. Peter Moore's at the key, and the faster you shoot them the better Peter likes them."

The gunboat stuttered angrily.

"A message for Peter Moore, operator in charge, steamer *Persian Gulf,* at sea. Report immediately upon arrival in Hong Kong to American consul for orders. (Signed) B.P. Eckles, commanding officer, U.S.S. *Buffalo.*"

To which Peter composed the following pertinent reply:

"To Commander Eckles, U.S.S. *Buffalo*, somewhere south of Mindanao. What for? (Signed) Peter Moore."

The promptness of the reply to this indicated that the recrudescence of Peter Moore, dead or alive, was of sufficient interest to command the presence of the gunboat's commander in the wireless house. In effect, Peter now realized that his confession had got him into considerable hot water.

Back came the *Buffalo's* nervous answer: "To Peter Moore, operator in charge, steamer *Persian Gulf,* at sea. Orders. Obey them. (Signed) B.P. Eckles."

Peter cut out the formalities. "Please ask the commander what's the trouble."

And out of the void cracked the retort: "He says, ask the American consul at Hong Kong."

There seemed nothing much to do aside from attending to the accumulated business on hand. In Hong Kong he had only the alternative of making a choice between which of the two he would honor first, the Marconi supervisor or the American consul; for in strange lands one falls into the custom of complying with the requests of his countrymen.

But Peter was beginning to feel a little of the old-time thrill. It was fine to have the fellows recognize that lightning fist of his; fine to have their homage. For the stumbling signals of both Manilla and the Buffalo were homage of the most straightforward sort.

For Peter Moore as a wireless operator was swift of the swiftest; he despatched with a lightning lilt, and the keenness of his ears, for which he was famous on more than one ocean, made it possible for him to receive signals with rarely ever the necessity for a repeat.

Manila, obeying orders, was standing by, and Peter, tightening a screw to bring the silver contacts of the massive transmission key in better alinement, despatched his string at the highest speed of which he was capable. As long as his listeners knew he was Peter Moore, he might as well give them, he decided, a sample of the celebrated Peter Moore sending.

For five minutes the little wireless cabin roared with the undiminishing rat-tat-tat of his spark explosions, and Manila, a navy man of the old school, rattled back a series of proud O.K.'s.

Proud? Because Peter Moore, of the old *Vandalia,* of the *Sierra,* the *Mongolia,* and a dozen other ships, was at the key. And an operator who said. "O.K." at the termination of one of Peter's inspired lightning transmissions had every right to be proud, as any wireless operator—who has ever copied thirty-three words a minute will bear me witness.

CHAPTER IX

TENTACLES OF FEAR

WHEN PETER EMERGED from the wireless room, having completed his business for the morning, he found Romola Borria with elbows on the rail gazing thoughtfully at a small Chinese girl who sat cross-legged on the hatch cover immersed in her sewing.

And Peter marveled at the freshness of Romola Borria's appearance, at the clarity of her sparkling brown eyes, the sweet pinkness of her complexion, and the ease and radiance of her tender smile.

"You look troubled," she said, as her smile was replaced by a look of tender concern. "What is it?" She lowered her voice to a confidential undertone. "Last night's affair, *desu ka?*"

Peter shook his head with a grave smile.

"I am discovered, Miss Borria. That is to say, I have just given myself away to the Manila navy station, not to speak of the commander of a gunboat, not far from us, off the coast of Mindanao. It seems"—he made a wry face—"Peter Moore is not popular with the authorities for deserting a certain ship in Shanghai."

"The *Vandalia?*" said the girl, and suddenly bit her lip, as though she would have liked to retract the statement.

Peter sank down on his elbows beside her, until his face was very close to hers, and his expression was shrewd and cunning.

"Miss Borria," he remarked stiffly; "I told you last night you're clever; and now you've given me just one more reason to stick to my guns; one more reason to believe that you know more than you're supposed to know. Now, let's be perfectly frank—for once. Let's not erase any more rouge stripes, so to speak. Won't you please tell me just what you do know about my activities in this neighborhood?"

His outflung gesture indicated the whole of Asia.

"In other words, I'm calling your bluff."

The girl pursed her lips and a hard twinkle, like that of a frosty arc-light upon diamonds, came into her eyes. "Yes, Mr. Moore," she said vigorously, "I will. But you must promise— promise faithfully—to ask no questions. Will you do that?"

Peter nodded with a willingness that was far from assumed.

Romola Borria placed the tips of her slender, white fingers together and looked down at them pensively. "Well," she said, looking up and raising her voice slightly, "you escaped from the liner *Vandalia* in the middle of the Whang-poo River, at night, in a deep fog, in a sampan, with a young woman named Aileen Lorimer in your arms. This occurred after you had delivered her from the hands of certain men, whom I prefer to call, perhaps mysteriously, by the plain word *them*.

"You sent this young lady home on the *Manchuria*, or the *Mongolia*, I forget just which. That night on the bund near the bridge near the French legation, you met, quite by accident, another young lady who found your companionship quite desirable. It is believed by them that you mistook her at first for the young woman then sailing eastward on the Pacific Mail steamer. Her name was Miss Amy Vost, a bright little thing."

"You don't happen to know," put in Peter ironically, "what Miss Lorimer had for breakfast morning, by any chance?"

"At last accounts she was studying for a doctor's degree in the university at Palo Alto, Mr. Moore."

"Indeed!" It was on the tip of Peter's tongue to tell this astounding Romola Borria that she was nothing short of a mind reader. Instead, he nodded his head for her to continue.

"As I was saying, you met Miss Vost, quite by accident, and danced with her at a fancy dress ball at the Astor House. You wore the costume of a Japanese merchant, I believe, thinking, a little fatuously, if you will permit me, that those garments were a disguise. A little later, in the bar at the Palace Hotel, after you left Miss Vost, you met a sea captain, ex-first mate of the Toyo Kisen Kaisba steamer, the *Sunyado Maru*. He was an old friend.

"With Captain MacLaurin and Miss Vost you made a trip on the Whang-poo in a little river steamer, the *Hankow*, which foundered in the rapids just below Chung-king. This occurred after you had stabbed and killed one of their most trusted spies."

"H-m," grunted Peter, at the thought of that wild night.

"When the *Hankow* sank, you followed what now appears to be your professional habit, your habit of a trustworthy gallant, by taking a lady in distress into your arms, and swam the whirl-pools to the little village across the river from Chungking. Then Miss Vost was met by her father, an incurable missionary from Wenchow, and by devious routes, well known to them, you joined a caravan, owned by a garrulous old thief who calls himself a mandarin, the Mandarin Chang, who told you many lies, to amuse himself—"

"Lies?" snapped Peter.

"Of course they were lies, Mr. Moore. Chang is one of *his* most trusted henchmen. He even permitted you to kill one of his coolies. The coolie would have died anyway; he was begin-ning to learn too much. But it tickled Chang, and him, to let you have this chance, to see how far you would go. And Chang had orders to help you reach Len Yang. It gave you confidence in yourself, did it not?"

"I don't believe a word," declared Peter in a daze. He refused to believe that Chang, kindly old Chang, was in league with that man, too.

"And the funny little green jade eyes that the Mandarin Chang gave you for—for saving his life! The eyes of the green death. Oh, they were real! The Chinese are frightfully afraid of those nauseating green eyes. Didn't the drawbridge tenders at Len Yang turn green when you showed them the eyes in the moonlight! Didn't they, though!

"Then you entered Len Yang, the city of stolen lives, and *he* watched you, and when you heard a difficult wireless message on the instruments at the mine, he gave you a present of money—five hundred taels, wasn't it—hoping, perhaps, that you would 'give up your foolishness,' as he expressed it, and settle down to take the place of the opium-befuddled wireless man you fooled so cleverly. *He* valued you, Mr. Moore, you see, and he was not in the least afraid of you!

"A dozen times, yes, a hundred times he could have killed you. But he preferred to sit back and stroke those long, yellow, mandarin mustaches of his, and watch you, as a cat watches a foolish mouse. I can see him laughing now. Yes! I have seen him, and I have heard him laugh. It is a hideous, cackling laugh. Quite unearthly! How he did laugh at you when you rescued Miss Vost, dear little clinging Miss Vost, from the jaws of his white palace!

"But he let you go; and he and his thousand sharpshooters who lined the great, green walls, when you and Captain MacLaurin and Miss Vost galloped bravely out, with one poor little mule! A thousand rifles, I say, were leveled upon you in that bright moonlight, Mr. Moore. But *he* said—*no!*"

Peter looked up at the stolid rigging of the *Persian Gulf,* at the sunlight dancing brightly on the blue waves, which foamed at their crests like fresh, boiling milk; at the passengers sleeping or reading in their deck chairs; and he refused to believe that this was not a dream. But the level voice of Romola Borria purred on:

"Then you joined a caravan for India, and, for a little while, they thought your trail was lost. But you reappeared in Mandalay, attired as a street fakir; and you limped all the way to Rangoon. Why did you limp, Mr. Moore?"

"A mule stamped on my foot, coming through the merchant's pass into Bengal."

"It healed rapidly, no doubt, for you were very active from that time on. You took passage to Penang, to Singapore, doubling back to Penang, and again to Singapore, and caught a blue-funnel steamer for Buitenzorg, and a little sailing-boat to Batavia."

"But, Miss Borria," writhed Peter, "why, with all this knowledge, hasn't he done away with me? You know. He knows. You've had your chance. You could have killed me in your stateroom last night. Please—" And Peter cast the golden robe of the adventurer temporarily but completely from him, becoming for the moment nothing more than a terribly earnest, terribly concerned young man.

"I gave you an inkling last night," replied Romola Borria composedly. "Until you left Batavia he believed that you had given up your nonsense. The coolie you threw overboard in Batavia was there, not to stab you, but to warn you away from China. Those warning, of which you have had many, are now things of the past. You have thrown down the glove to him once too often. He is through toying.

"It was great fun for him, and he enjoyed it. He treats his enemies that way—for a while. You have now entered upon the second stage of enmity with him. Last night was a sample of what you may expect from now on. Only the sheerest luck saved you from the coolie's bullet—and my almost-too-tardy intervention."

Peter gave her a hard, a thoughtful, and thoroughly respectful stare.

"I take it," he said, "that you are a special emissary, a sort of minister plenipotentiary, from the Gray Dragon. As a matter of fact, you are here simply to persuade me to correct my erring ways; to persuade me to give you my promise for *him* that I will put China and Len Yang forever and a day out of my plans."

"Express it any way you please, Mr. Moore. I have told you about all that I am able. I know this game, if you will permit me, a little, just a little better than you do, Mr. Moore. I know when fun stops and downright danger begins. The moment you put your foot in China, you are putting your foot in a trap from which you can never, never so long as you are permitted to live extricate yourself. And, believe me, seriously, that will not be for long. A day? Perhaps. An hour? Very likely not any longer than that.

"Call me a special emissary if you choose. Perhaps I am. Perhaps I am only a friend, who desires above everything else to help you avoid a most certain and a most unpleasant death. I have given you your opportunity. From my heart I gave you, and I still do give you, the chance to leave—with me. Yes; I mean that. Your promise, backed by your word of honor, is a passport to safety for both of us. Your refusal, I might as well confess, means to me—death! Won't you stop and consider? Won't you say—yes?"

Peter's head had snapped back during this epilogue; his white-clad shoulders were squared, and his blue eyes were lighted by a fire that might have made a crusader envious.

"You may report to him," said he, "that I have listened to his proposal; that I have considered it calmly; and that, as long as the gauntlet is down—it is—*down!* I want but one thing: a man's chance at that beast, the beast which has dragged its trail, like slime, across the smile of Asia. You can tell him just that from me, Miss Borria, and anything else that occurs to you. I am sorry. I refuse your offer!"

He turned his broad back squarely upon her!

She seemed on the point of uttering a final word, a word that might have been of the greatest importance to Peter the Brazen; but the word never got beyond her lips.

Into her eyes crept a look of despair, of mute horror, awful beyond the ken of man. She half raised her hand; withdrew it. Her shoulders sagged. She staggered to a deck chair, and sank into it, with her head back, her eyes closed, her long, dark lashes lying upon cheeks that had become as white as cold marble.

Standing there with his eyes glued to the blue of the sea, Peter the Brazen felt the confidence oozing from him as water oozes out of a leaky pail. He felt himself in the presence of a relentless power which was slowly settling down upon him, crushing him, and overpowering him.

It occurred to him, as his thoughts raced willy-nilly, to flash a call of help to the gunboat which prowled south of Luzon, a call which would have met with a response both swift and energetic.

Yet that impulse smacked of the blunderer. It would put an end forever to his high plan, now boiling more strongly than ever before, in the back of his racked brain: to meet and some day put down the beast in Len Yang.

A bright, waving hand distracted his attention from the sea. The maid from Macassar was endeavoring to attract him. He looked down with a pale, haggard smile.

"You have not forgotten—Kowloon, *busar satu?*" said her tinkling little voice.

"Not I, small one!" Peter called back in accents that entirely lacked their accustomed gaiety.

CHAPTER X

THE ASSIGNATION

DURING THE REMAINDER of the voyage Romola Borria did not once, so far as Peter was aware, leave her stateroom. Her meals were sent there, and there she remained sending out words in response to his inquiries that she was ill, could see no one—not that Peter, after that latest astounding interview, cared particularly to renew the friendship. He was simply thoughtful.

Yet he felt a little angry at his demonstration of frank selfishness, and not a little uneasy at the uncanny precision of her recital of his recent history, an uneasiness which grew, until he found himself waiting with growing concern for the rock-bound shore-line of Hong Kong to thrust its black-and-green shoulders above the horizon.

The *Persian Gulf* anchored outside at night, and in the morning steamed slowly in amidst the maze of masts, of sampans and junks, which latter lay with their sterns pointing grotesquely upward, resembling nothing so closely as great brown hawks which had flown down from a Brobdingnagian heaven, to select with greater convenience and fastidiousness what prey might fan within reach of their talons.

Peter was aware that many of these junks were pirate ships, audacious enough to pole into Victoria Harbor under the very guns of the forts, under the noses of battleships of every nation. Not with a keen sense of pride did Peter's eye seek out the low white hull of the U.S.S. *Maryland,* which stood at her anchorage, sans boilers, as she had stood there for goodness knows how many years, the laughing-stock of this severely naval and military community.

When the launch from quarantine swung alongside, Peter went below and changed from the uniform to a light, fresh suit of Shantung silk, a soft collar, a soft Bangkok hat, and comfortable, low walking shoes, not neglecting to know about his waist the blue sarong.

The steerage passengers were lined up when he came above a little later, sticking out their tongues for the eagle-eyed doctors, and giggling at a proceeding serious enough, had they known it, to send every mother's son and daughter of them back to the land whence they came, if they displayed so much as a slight blemish, for Hong Kong was then in the throes of her latest cholera scare.

Satisfied at length that the eyes and tongues of the steerage and deck passengers gave satisfactorily robust testimony, the doctors came up to the first-class passengers, who stood in line on the promenade deck; and Peter saw the change that had come over Romola Borria.

Her face bore the pallor of the grave. Her large, lustrous eyes were sunken, and lines seemed to have been engraved in a face that had previously been as smooth and fair as a rose in bloom.

He felt panic-stricken as she recognized him with an almost imperceptible nod, and he stared at her a trifle longer than was necessary, with his lips slightly ajar, his nails biting into his palms, and he sensed rather than saw, that her beauty had been transformed into one of gray melancholy.

At that juncture a small, tinkling voice shrilled up at him from the after cargo-well, and Peter turned to see his small charge, the maid from Macassar, smiling as she waited for him beside a small pile of silken bundles of the rainbow's own colors. He had not forgotten the Eurasian girl, but he desired to have a parting word with Romola Borria.

He called over the rail, and instructed her of the black pigtail to wait for him in a sampan, and he yelled down to one of the dozens of struggling and babbling coolies, whose sampans swarmed like a horde of cockroaches at the ladder's lower extremity.

Romola Borria, alone, was awaiting him, adjusting her gloves, at the doorway of the wireless cabin when he made his way back to that quarter of the ship. She greeted him with a slow, grave smile; and by that smile Peter was given to know how she had suffered.

Her face again became a mask, a mask of death, indeed, as her lids fluttered down and then raised; and her eyes were tired, inexpressibly tired.

He extended his hand, trying to inject some of his accustomed cheerfulness into the gesture and into the smile which somehow would not form naturally on his lips.

"This—is *adieu*—or *au revoir?*" he said solemnly.

"I hope—*au revoir*," she replied dully. "So, after all, you refuse to take my counsel, my advise, seriously?"

Peter shrugged.

"I'm rather afraid I can't," he said. "You see, I'm young. And you can say to yourself, or out loud without fear of hurting my feelings, that I am foolish. I guess it is one of the hardships of being young—this having to be foolish. It will pass away, I suppose, one of these days before I grow old and feeble."

He laughed, but without humor.

"Ten years from now I would take your advice. I would act upon it, very probably without a whimper. I would scurry back home, and behave. Yet, as you have already informed me, there may be no such date as ten years from to-day, in my life. Wasn't it to-day that I was to become immortal, with a knife through my floating ribs, or a bullet in my heart?

"As I grow older I will become more serious, with balance. Perish the thought! But in the end—shucks! Confucius, wasn't it—that dear old philosopher who could never find a king to try out his theories on—who said:

"The great mountain must crumble.
The strong beam must break.
The wise man must wither away like a plant."

She nodded.

"I am afraid you will never become serious, Mr. Moore. And perhaps that is one of the reasons why I've grown so—so fond of you in this short while. If I could take life—and death—as stoically, as happily, as you—oh, God!"

She shut her eyes. Tears were in their rims when she opened them again.

"Mr. Moore, I'll make a foolish confession, too, now. It is—I love you. And in return—"

"I think you're the bravest girl in the world," said Peter, taking her hands with a movement of quick penitence. "You—you're a brick."

"I guess I am," she sighed, looking moodily away. "A brick of clay! Perhaps it is best to walk into the arms of your enemies the way you do, with your head back and eyes shining and a smile of contempt on your lips. If I only could!"

"Why speak of death on a day like this?" said Peter lightly. "Life is so beautiful. See those red-and-yellow blossoms on the hill, near the governor's place, and the poor little brats on that sampan, thinking they're the happiest kids in the world. What hurts them, hurts them; what pleases them, pleases them. They're happy because they don't bother to anticipate. And think of life, beautiful old life, brimming over with excitement and the mystery of the very next moment!"

"If I could only see that next moment!"

"Ugh! What a dreary monotony life would become!"

"But we could be sure. We could prepare for—for—well—" She threw up her head defiantly. "For death, I'll say."

"But please don't let's talk of death. Let's talk of the fine time you and I are going to have when we see each other again."

"Will there be another time, Peter?"

"Why, of course! You name that time; any time, any place. We'll eat and drink and chatter like a couple of parrots. And you will forget all this—this that is behind us."

Her teeth clicked.

"To-night," she said quickly. "I'll meet you. Let me see. On the Desveaux Road side of the Hong Kong Hotel balcony, the restaurant, up-stairs, you know."

"Right!" agreed Peter with enthusiasm. "Will we let husband go along?"

Her face suddenly darkened. She shook her head.

"I will be alone. So will you, at seven o'clock. You'll be there, without fail?"

A coolie guarded her luggage near by impatiently. They could hear the sobbing of the J.C.J. passenger launch as it rounded the starboard counter.

"I forget," said Peter, with his flashing smile. "I'll be dead in an hour. The steel trap of China, you know."

"Please don't jest."

"I'll tell you what I will do. I'll put a tag on my lapel, saying, deliver this corpse to the Desveaux Road balcony of the Hong

Kong Hotel restaurant at seven sharp to-night! Without fail!
C.Q.D."

These last words were addressed to the empty wireless cabin
doorway. The white skirt of Romola Borria flashed like a taunt-
ing signal as she hastened out of his sight with the boy who
carried her grips.

CHAPTER XI

THE RED-FACED MAN

WEARING A SLIGHT frown, Peter made his way through
piles of indiscriminate luggage to the port ladder, where his
sampan and the maid from Macassar were waiting.

As he descended this contrivance he scanned the other
sampans warily, and in one of these he saw a head which pro-
truded from a low cabin. The sampan was a little larger than
the others, and it darted in and out on the edge of the waiting
ones.

The head vanished the instant Peter detected it, but it made
a sharp image in his memory, a face he would have difficulty
in forgetting. It was a long, chalk-white face, topped by a black
fedora hat—a face garnished at the thin gray lips by a mustache,
black and spikelike, resembling nothing more closely than the
coal-black mustache affected by the old-time melodrama villains.

An hour of life? Did this man have concealed under his black
coat the knife which had been directed by the beast in Len
Yang to seek out his heart, to snuff out his existence, the existence of a trifling enemy?

As Peter reached the shelving at the foot of the ladder the
thought grew and blossomed, and the picture was not a pleasant one. The man in the sampan, as Peter could judge by his
face, would probably prove to be a tall and muscular individual, such a man as would handicap him in a long fight.

And then Peter caught sight of another face, but the owner of it remained above-board. This man was stout and gray, with a face more subtly malignant. It was a red face, cut deep at the eyes and in the region of the large purple nose, with lines of weather or dissipation. Blue eyes burned out of the red face, faded blue eyes, that were, despite their lack of luster, sharp and cunning.

The hand of its owner beckoned imperiously for Peter, and he shouted his name; and Peter was assured that in the other hand was concealed the knife or the pistol of his doom.

With these not altogether pleasant ideas commanding his brain he jumped into the sampan in which the maid from Macassar was smilingly waiting.

Peter saw that his coolie was big and broad, with muscles which stood out like ropes on his thick, sunburned arms and legs. He gave the coolie his instructions, as the sampan occupied by the red-faced man was all the while endeavoring to wiggle closer. Again the man called Peter by name, peremptorily, but Peter paid no heed.

"To Kowloon. Man! Man!" shouted Peter. "*Cumshaw.* Sabbe?" He displayed in his palm three silver dollars, and the coolie bent his back to the sweep, the sampan heeling out from the black ironside like a thing alive.

Behind them, as this maneuver was executed, Peter saw the two duly accredited agents of the Gray Dragon fall in line. But Peter had selected with wisdom. The coolie verified with the passage of every moment the power his ropy muscles implied. Inch by inch, and yard by yard, they drew away from the pursuing sampans.

Then something resembling the scream of an enraged parrot sang over their heads, and he instinctively ducked, turning to see from which of the sampans this greeting had come.

A faint puff of light-blue smoke sailed down the wind between the two. Which one? It was difficult to say.

They were beginning to leave the pursuit decidedly in the lurch now. Peter's coolie, with his long legs braced far apart on the running-boards, bent his back, swaying like a mighty metronome from port to starboard, from starboard to port, whipping the water into an angry, milky foam.

The pursuers crept up and fell back by fits and starts; slowly the distance widened.

The girl crouched down in the cabin, and Peter, with his automatic in his hand, waited for another telltale puff of blue smoke.

Finally this puff occurred, low on the deck of the larger craft. The bullet plunked into the water not two feet from the sweep, and the coolie, inspired by the knowledge that he, too, was inextricably wrapped up in this race of life and death, sweated, and shouted in the savage "Hi! Ho! Hay! Ho!" of the coolie who dearly loves his work.

Satisfied as to the origin of both bullets, Peter took careful aim at the yellow sampan and emptied his magazine, slipping another clip of cartridges into the oblong hole as he watched for the result.

The yellow sampan veered far from her course, and a sweep floated on the surface some few yards aft. Then the sampan lay as if dead. But the other plunged on after.

This exciting race and the blast of Peter's automatic now attracted the earnest attention of a gray little river gunboat, just down from up-stream, and inured to such incidents as this.

A one-pound shell snarled overhead, struck the water a hundred yards further on, near the Kowloon shore, and sent up a foaming white pillar.

The pier at Kowloon loomed close and more close. It was unlikely that the gunboat would follow up the shot with another, and in this guess, Peter, as the French say, "had reason."

The fires under the gunboat's boilers were drawn, and there was no time for the launching of a cutter.

A great contentment settled down upon Peter's heart when he saw that the on-coming sampan could not reach the pier until he and his charge were out of sight, or out of reach, at least.

He examined his watch. The gods were with him. It lacked three minutes of train-time.

It was only a hope that he and the girl would be safe on board the Canton train before the red-faced man could catch up.

The sampan rubbed the green timbers of the Kowloon landing stage. Peter tossed up the girl's luggage in one large armful, lifted her by the armpits to the floor of the pier, and relieved himself hastily of four dollars (Mexican), by which the grunting coolie was gratefully, and for some few hours, richer.

They dashed to the first-class compartment, and Peter dragged the girl in beside him.

"To Canton, too?" she inquired in surprise.

Peter nodded. He slammed the door. A whistle screamed, and the station of Kowloon, together with the glittering waters of the blue bay, and the white city of Hong Kong, across the bay, all began moving, first slowly, then with acceleration, as the morning express for Canton slid out on the best-laid pair of rails in southern China.

Had his red-faced pursuer caught up in time? Peter prayed not. He was tingling with the thrill of the chase; and he turned his attention to the small maiden who sat cuddled close to his side, with hands folded demurely before her, imprisoning between them the overlap of his flaunting blue sarong.

"We are safe, brave one?" she was desirous of knowing.

He patted her hand reassuringly, and she caught at it, lowering her green-blue eyes to the dusty floor, and sighing.

Peter might have paused in his rapid meditations long enough to be aware that, here he was, dropped—plump—into the center of another ring of romance; nothing having separated him from his last love but two misdirected revolver shots, the warning boom of a gunboat's bow cannon, and a mad chase across Victoria Bay.

Holding hands breaks no known law; yet Peter was not entirely aware that he was committing this act, as his eyes, set and hard, stared out of the window at the passing pagodas with their funny, turned-up roofs.

His mind was working on other matters. Perhaps for the first time since the *Persian Gulf* had dropped anchor to the white sand of Victoria Harbor's bottom, he began to realize the grim seriousness of Romola Borria's warning. He was hemmed in. He was helpless.

An hour to live! An hour alive! But he was willing to make the very best of that hour.

Absently, then by degrees not so absently, be alternately squeezed and loosened the small, cool hands of the maid from Macassar. And she returned the pressure with a timid confidence that made him stop and consider for a moment something that had entirely slipped his mind during the past few days.

Was he playing quite squarely with Aileen Lorimer? Had he been observing perhaps the word but not the letter of his self-assumed oath? On the other hand, mightn't it be possible that Aileen Lorimer had ceased to care for him? With time and the miles stretching between them, wasn't it quite possible that she had shaken herself, recognized her interest in him as one only of passing infatuation; and, perhaps already, had given her love to some other?

A silly little rime of years ago occurred to him:

Love me close! Love me tight! *But*
Love me when I'm out of sight!

And perhaps because Peter had fallen into one of his reasoning moods, he asked himself whether it was fair to carry the flirtation any further with the girl snuggled beside him. He knew that the hearts of Oriental girls open somewhat more widely to the touch of affection than their Western sisters. And it was not in the nature of women of the East to indulge extensively in the Western form of idle flirtation. The lowering of eyelids, the flickering of a smile, had meaning and depth in this land.

Was this girl flirting with him, or was hers a deeper interest? That was the question! He took the latter view.

And because he knew, from his own experience, that the hearts of lovers sometimes break at parting, he finally relinquished the cool, small hands and thrust his own deep into his pockets.

There was no good reason, apart from his own selfishness, why he should give a pang of any form to the trustful young heart which fluttered so close at his side.

"Where does your aged grandmother live, small one?" be asked her briskly, in the most unsentimental tones imaginable.

"I have the address here, *birahi*," she replied, diving into her satin blouse and producing a slip of rice paper upon which was scrawled a number of dead-black symbols of the Chinese written language.

"A rickshaw man can find the place, of course," he said. "Now, look into my eyes, small one, and listen to what I say."

"I listen closely, *birahi*," said the small one.

"I want you to stop calling me *birahi*. I am not your love, can never be your love, nor can you ever be mine."

"But why, *bi*—my brave one?"

"Because—because, I am a wicked one, an *orang gila*, a destroyer of good, a man of no heart, or worse, a black one."

"Oh, Allah, what lies!" giggled the maid.

"Yes, and a liar, too," declared Peter venomously, permitting his fair features to darken with the blackest of looks. Was she flirting with him? "A man who never told the truth in his life. A bad, bad man," he finished lamely.

"But why are you telling such things to me, my brave one?" came the provocative answer.

She *was* flirting with him.

Nevertheless, it was a very appropriate question, indeed, and one for which Peter could find no immediate or satisfying response.

He merely grunted and relapsed again into the form of meditative lethargy which of late had grown habitual if not popular with him.

A little before noon the train thundered into the narrow, dirty streets of China's most flourishing city, geographically, the New Orleans of the Celestial empire; namely, Canton, on the West River.

As Peter and his somewhat amused young charge alighted from the train he cast a furtive glance up and down the station platform, and he was dumfounded to glimpse, not two yards away, alighting from another compartment, the man with the red, deeply marked face. His blue eyes were ablaze, and he advanced upon Peter threateningly.

It was a situation demanding decisive, direct action. Peter, hastily instructing the girl to hold two rickshaws, leaped at his pursuer with doubled fists, even as the man delved significantly into his hip pocket.

Peter let him have it squarely on the blunt nub of his red jaw, aiming as he sprang.

His antagonist went down in a cursing heap, sprawling back with the look in his washed-out eyes of a steer which has been hit squarely in the center of the brow.

He fell back on his hands and lay still, dazed, muttering, and struggling to regain the use of his members, which were temporarily out of commission.

Before he could recover Peter was up and away, springing lightly into the rickshaw, and spinning with haste down a narrow, muddy lane, banked on either side with dingy shops and hovels.

They turned and darted up one narrow, dirty alley into a narrower and dirtier one, the two coolies shouting in blasphemous chorus to clear the way as they advanced.

After a quarter of an hour of twisting and splashing and turning, the coolies stopped in front of a shop of clay-blue stone.

Paying off the coolies, Peter entered, holding the door for the girl, and sliding the bolt as he closed it after her.

He found himself in the presence of a very old, very yellow, and very wrinkled Chinese woman, who smiled upon the two of them perplexedly, nodding and smirking, as her frizzled white pigtail flopped and fluttered about in the clutter on the shelves behind her.

It was a shop for an antique collector to discover, gorged with objects of bronze, of carved sandalwood, of teak, grotesque and very old, of shining red and blue and yellow beads, of old gold, and old silver.

On the low, narrow counter she had placed a shallow red tray filled with pearls; imitations, no doubt, but exquisite, perfect, of all shapes; bulbular, pear, button, and of most enticing colors.

But the small girl was babbling, and a look of the most profound surprise came slowly into the old woman's face. A little pearl-like tear sparkled in either of her old eyes, and she gathered this cherished granddaughter from far away Macassar into her thin arms.

At that sight Peter felt himself out of place, an intruder, an interloper. The scene was not meant for his eyes. He was an alien in a strange land, and he did not belong.

As he hesitated, conjuring up words of parting with his little friend, he gasped. Peering through the thick window-pane in the door was the red-faced man, and his look sent a curdle of fear into Peter's brave heart. Would he shoot through the pane?

The girl, too, saw. She chattered a long moment to her wrinkled grandmother, and this latter leaped to the door and shot a second strong bolt. She pointed excitedly to a rear door, low and green, set deep in the blue stone.

Peter leaped toward it. Half opening this, he saw a tiny garden surrounded by low, gray walls. He paused. The maid from Macassar was behind him. She followed him out and closed the door.

"*Birahi,*" she said in her tinkling voice, and with gravity far in advance of her summers, "we must part now—forever?"

He nodded, as he searched the wall for a likely place to jump. "It is the penalty of friendship, *birahi*. You do not mind if I call you *birahi* in our last moment together?"

"No. No."

"I am curious, so curious, my brave one, about the red-faced man, and the one with the black coat. But we women are meant for silence. *Birahi,* I have played no part—I have been like a dead lily—a burden. Perhaps, if you are in great danger—"

"I am in great danger, small one. The red toad wants my life, and you must detain him."

"I will talk to him! But the others, the black-coated one— what of them? They would like the feel of your blood on their hands, too!"

Peter nodded anxiously. He was thinking of Romola Borria.

"I will do anything," declared the maid from Macassar patiently.

"Has your grandmother a sampan, a trustworthy *fokie?*"

"Aie, *birahi!* She is rich!"

"Then have that *fokie* be at the Hong Kong landing stage with his sampan at midnight. Have him wait until morning. If I do not come by dawn he will return immediately to Canton. By dawn, if I am not there, it will mean—"

"Death?" The small voice was tremulous.

Peter nodded.

"If the *fokie* returns with that message, you will write a short note—"

"To one you love?"

"To one I love. In America. The name is Aileen Lorimer; the address, Pasadena, California. You will sky simply, 'Peter Moore is dead.'"

"Ah! I must not say that. It will break her heart! But you must go now, my brave one. I will talk to the red toad!"

The green door closed softly; and Peter was left to work out the problem of his escape, which he did in an exceedingly short space of time. Even as he took the fence in a single bound he fancied he could hear the panting of the red-faced man at his heels.

He found himself in a crooked alleyway, which forked out of sight at a near-by bend. Speeding to this point, he came out upon a somewhat broader thoroughfare. He looked hastily for a rickshaw, but none was in sight.

So he ran blindly on, resorting at intervals to his old trick of doubling back, to confuse his pursuers. He did this so well that before long he had almost lost his sense of direction, the sun having gone from the sight of man behind a mass of dark and portentous clouds.

At length he came to the City of the Dead, and sped on past the ivy-covered wall, circling, doubling back, and giving what pursuit there might have been a most tortuous trail to follow.

He was hooted at and jeered at by coolies and shrieking children, but he ran on, putting the miles behind him, and finally dropped into a slow trot, breathing like a spent racehorse.

The afternoon advanced. At the pottery field he found a rickshaw, estimated that he still had time to spare to make the Hong Kong train, and was driven to the station. Dead or alive, he had promised to deliver himself to Romola Borria at the Hong Kong Hotel at seven.

Peter was decanted at the station, and, upon finding he had an hour on his hands before the train for the bay was made up, be discreetly hid himself behind a towering pile of silk bales consigned to Cairo, and pondered upon the probable use of

Chinese silk in Egypt for the long hour until the train was made up.

Visions of the malignant face of his red-featured enemy were constantly in his mind.

But he breathed more easily as the train chugged out of the grim, gray station. He sank back in the seat, letting his thoughts wander where they would, and beginning to feel, as the miles were unspun, that he was at least one jump ahead of the red death which had threatened him since his departure from the friendly shelter of the *Persian Gulf.*

CHAPTER XII

THE LONG ARM AGAIN

THE SHADOWS WERE lengthening, the sky was of a deeper and vaster blue, when the train came to a creaking stop in the Kowloon Station.

Peter emerged, scanning the passengers warily, but catching not a glimpse of his red-faced enemy. What did that one have in store for him now? This chase was becoming a game of hide-and-seek. But in Hong Kong he would feel safer. Hong Kong was a haunt of civilized men, and of able Sikh policemen, who detested the yellow men of China.

He took the ferry-boat across the bay to the city, which rose tier upon tier of white from the deep-blue surface; and he made his way afoot to the American consulate.

With auspicious celerity the sad-eyed clerk bowed him into the presence of an elderly gentleman with white side whiskers and an inveterate habit of stroking a long and angular nose.

This personage permitted his shrewd, grave eyes to take in Peter from his blond hair to his tan walking shoes, and with a respectful mien Peter prepared his wits for a sharp and digging cross-examination.

"I have been advised," began the American consul, giving to Peter's blue eyes a look of curiosity in which was mingled not a little unconcealed admiration, as he might have looked upon the person of Pancho Villa, had that other miscreant stepped into his gloomy and somewhat ponderous-furnished office—"I have been advised," he repeated importantly, "by the commander of the auxiliary cruiser *Buffalo* that you contemplated a visit to Hong Kong."

He sank back and stared, and it took Peter several moments to become aware that the context of the remark was not nearly so important as its pronunciation. The remark was somewhat obvious. The American consul desired Peter to make the opening.

Peter inclined his head as he slowly digested the statement.

"I was told by Commander Eckles to report to you," he replied respectfully, "for orders."

The American consul laid his hands firmly upon the edge of the mahogany desk.

"My orders, Mr. Moore, are that you leave China immediately. I trust—"

"Why?" said Peter in a dry voice.

"That is a matter which, unfortunately, I cannot discuss with you. The order comes, I am permitted to inform you, from the highest of diplomatic quarters. To be exact, from Peking, and from the American Ambassador, to be more specific."

It was crystal clear to Peter that the American consul was not cognizant of what might be behind those orders from the American Ambassador; yet his face, for all of its diplomatic masking, told Peter plainly that the American consul was not entirely averse to learning.

"Have I been interfering with the lawful pursuit of the Chinese Empire?" he inquired ironically.

The American consul stroked his long nose pensively.

"Well—perhaps," he said. "On the whole, that is something you can best explain yourself, Mr. Moore. If you should care to give me your side of the question, ah—"

"I haven't a thing to say," rejoined Peter. "If the United States government chooses to believe that my presence is inimical to its interests in China—"

"Pressure might have been brought to bear from another quarter."

"Quite so," admitted Peter.

"Now, if you should desire to make me acquainted with your pursuits during the past—ah—few months, let us say, it is within the bounds of possibility that I might somehow rescind this drastic—ah—order. Suffice it to say, that I shall be glad to put my every power at your aid. As you are an American, it is my duty and my pleasure, sir, if you will permit me, to do all within my power, my somewhat restricted power, if I may qualify that statement, to reinstate you in the good graces of those—ah—good gentlemen in Peking."

It was all too evident that, back and beyond the friendly intentions of this official, was a hungry desire for information regarding this young man whose dark activities had been recognized by the high powers to an extent sufficient to set in motion the complicated and bulky wheels of diplomacy.

Peter shook his head respectfully, and the consul permitted his reluctantly admiring and inquisitive gaze to travel up and down the romantic and now international figure.

"I am able to say nothing," he expressed himself quietly. "If the American Ambassador has decreed that I ought to go home—home I go! I'll confess right now that I did not intend to go home when I stepped into this office, but I do respect, and I will respect, the authority of that order."   .

"If the President, for example, should request you to continue—ah—what you have been doing, for the good, let us say, of humanity, you would continue without hesitation, Mr. Moore?"

Peter gave the long, pale face a sharp scrutiny. Did this innocent-faced man know more than he intimated, or was he merely applying the soft, velvet screws of diplomacy, endeavoring to squeeze out a little information?

"I certainly would."

The consul rose, with a bland smile, and extended his hand.

"It has been gratifying to know one who has become such a singular, and permit me to add, such a trying figure, in diplomatic circles, during the past week. Good day, sir!"

Peter walked down Desveaux Road in a state of mental detachment. A week! Only a week had passed since he had sailed from Batavia, a week since he had thrown overboard the emissary of the Gray Dragon. He concluded that in more than one way could his presence be dismissed from this land of darkness and distrust.

How had the Gray Dragon brought pressure upon the American Ambassador, a man of the highest repute, of sterling and patriotic qualities? The answer seemed to be, that the coils of the Gray Dragon extended everywhere, like an inky fluid which had leaked into every crevice and crack of all Asia.

He was still under orders to pay a visit to J.B. Whalen, the Marconi supervisor. That cross-examination he was glad to post-pone.

He called at the office of the Pacific Mail, and found that the *King of Asia* was due to leave for the United States the following morning at dawn. He made a deposit on a reservation.

CHAPTER XIII

HER LAST CARD

THE HOUR LACKED a few minutes of seven when Peter ascended in the lift to the second floor of the Hong Kong Hotel and made his way between the closely packed tables to the Desveaux Road balcony.

Romola Borria was not yet in evidence.

He selected a table which commanded a view of the entrance, toyed with the menu card, absentmindedly ordered a Scotch highball, and slowly examined the occupants of the tables in his neighborhood. He felt vaguely annoyed, slightly uneasy, without being able to sift out the cause.

For a moment he regretted his audacity in encountering the curious eyes of Hong Kong society, a society in which there would inevitably be present a number of his enemies. It cannot be denied that a number of eyes scrutinized him leisurely and at some pains, over tea cups, wine-glasses, and fans.

But these were for the larger part women, and Peter was more or less immune to the curious, bright-eyed glances of this sex.

His attire was somewhat rakish for the occasion; and it appeared that sarongs were not being sported by the more refined class of male diners, who affected as a mass the somber black of dinner jackets. At all Hong Kong hotels the custom is evening dress for dinner, and Peter felt shabby and shoddy in his silk suit, his low shoes, his soft collar.

An orchestra of noble proportions struggled effectively in the moist, warm atmosphere somewhere in its concealment behind a distant palm arbor with "Un Peu d'Amour," and also out of Peter's sight, an impassioned and metallic tenor was sobbing:

"Jaw-s-s-st a lee-e-e-edle lof-f-f-ff—
A le-e-e-edle ke-e-e-e-s—"

And Peter in his perturbation wished that both blatant orchestra and impassioned tenor were concealed behind a soundproof stone wall.

He was tossing off the dregs of the highball when there occurred a low-voiced murmur at his side, and he arose to confront the pale, worn face of Romola. She gave him her hand limply, and settled down across from him, her eyes darting from table to table, and occasionally nodding rather stiffly and altogether impersonally as she recognized some one.

"You see,"—he smiled at her, as she settled back and fostered upon him a look of brooding tenderness,—"you see, my dear, I am here, untagged, Nearly twelve hours have passed since you sounded that note of ominous warning. I have yet to feel the thrill, just before I die, of that dagger sliding between my ribs."

She accepted this with a nod almost indifferent.

"Simply because I have persuaded them to extend your parole to one o'clock. If you linger in China, you have—and need I say that, the same applies to me six more hours in which to jest, to laugh, to love—to live!"

"For which I am, as always in the face of favors, duly grateful," said Peter in high humor. "None the less I have this day, since we parted this morning, indulged in one pistol duel between sampans, with one of your admirable confrères—"

"Yes, I heard of that. But it stopped there. You winged his sampan coolie."

"And at the Canton station, if I may be pardoned for contradicting, I encountered the red-faced one. To tell you what you may already know, I punched him in the jaw, doggone him!"

She seemed to be distressed.

"You must be mistaken."

Peter shook his head forcibly.

"A choleric gentleman in a brown suit, born with the habit of reaching for his hip pocket," he amplified.

She studied him with wide, speculative eyes.

"He must be from the north. Some of them I do not know. But all of them have been informed."

"To permit me to live and love until one to-morrow morning?"

She nodded.

The aspiring and perspiring orchestra and the impassioned tenor had again reached the chorus of "Un Peu d'Amour."

"I could ge-e-e-eve you all my life for the-e-e-e-s—"

"Badly sung, but appropriate," commented Romola Borria.
Peter's countenance became a question mark.

"It may mean that I am giving you all my life for—this," she
explained.

"For these few minutes, when we were to chatter, and make
love, and be happy?" demanded Peter indignantly. "My dear—"
He reached out for her hand, and she let him fondle it, not
reluctantly. "I'd give all my life, too, for these few minutes with
you. Do you know—you're perfectly adorable to-night! There's
something—something irresistible about you—to me!"

"To you?"

"Yes," he said in a deep voice, and sincerely. "I'd come all the
way 'round the world, and lay my life at your feet—thus." And
he placed his knuckles on the white cloth, as if they were knees.

"Ah! But you don't mean that!"

"When I'm in love, I mean everything!"

"I know. You are fickle. Miss Lorimer—Miss Vost—
Romola—they come, they love, they are gone, quite as fate-
fully and synchronously as life follows death, and death follows
life."

"I *do* wish you wouldn't talk about death in that flippant
manner," he gibed, wondering how under the sun he might get
her out of this gloomy mood.

"But death is in my mind always—Peter. When you have
gone through—"

"Romola, I refuse to be lectured."

"Very well; I refuse to talk of anything but love and death."

"Excellent, my own love! Tell me now how it feels when you
are in the heavenly condition."

"Most hopeless, Peter; because death, you see, is so close
upon the heels of my love."

"Meaning—me?"

"No—my heart. The death of love and the death of life follow
my love. Now I want to pick up the threads of a moment ago.

Peter, don't hold my hand. That woman is—staring. You said—you said, you would come away around the world to see me, to help me, possibly, if I were in trouble. You weren't serious."

"Cross my heart!"

"On the *Persian Gulf* that day—that day I told you something of your recent adventures and your apparently miraculous escapes, I intended to ask you—"

"Seeress, I am all ears—"

"I intended asking a favor, a most important one, an alternative—"

"The trip to Nara?"

"Yes; an alternative to that. Tell me truly how much at heart you hate the man at Len Yang. Wait. Don't answer me yet. At heart, do you really hate him, as you pretend, or are you simply bowing down to your vanity, to the pride you seem to take in these quixotic deeds, such as attacking the devil's own stronghold, storming a fortress that no nation cares to tamper with?

"For one thing, there is very little money in what you are doing. If you should approach these adventures a little differently, perhaps, you might put yourself in a position to be rewarded for the troubles you take, the dangers you risk. I mean that."

"I admit I'm not a money hater," frowned Peter, striving without much success to feel her trend.

"It would be so easy for you to make all the money you need in only a few years by—how shall I say it?—by 'being nice.' Wait! I have not finished. You said I was a special emissary from him. You hit the mark more squarely than you thought. Oh, I admit it! I was sent to Batavia to meet you, to intercept you, and, to be quite frank, to ask you your terms."

"From *him?*"

"Yes. He has observed you. He can use you, and oh!—how badly he wants you and your boldness and that unconquerable fire of yours! He needs you! He wants you, more than any man he has known! And he will pay you! Name your price! A half million gold a year? Bah! It is a drop to him!"

"Don't," begged Peter in a whisper. "Please—don't—go on."

His face had become almost as white as the table-cloth, and his lips were trembling, ashen.

"God! I put my confidence in you, time after time, and each time you show me treachery, deeper, more hideous, than before. Please don't continue. I'm trying, trying hard, as hard as I know how, to appreciate your position in that wretched mess—and trying to find some excuse for it. For you! And it's hard. Damned, brutally hard. Let's part! Let's forget! Let's be just memories to each other—Romola!"

Her face, too, had lost its color, like life fading from a rose when the stem is snapped. Her hand sought her throat and groped there, as it always did in her moments of nervousness, and she drummed on the cloth with a silver knife. She stared curiously at him, with the other light dying hard.

"Then I can only hope—a slender hope—to bring you back to the favor I asked you originally, and I place that before you now, my request for that favor—my last card, my final hope. You cannot refuse that. You cannot! You profess to be chivalrous. Now, let me—test you!"

CHAPTER XIV

THE DEVIL-WOMAN

"**ROMOLA, I SAID** no to Nara long ago."

She threw up her head.

"A woman should need to be informed but once that her love is not wanted. That is not what I meant."

"Ah! Another theme! Your little brain is nothing short of an idea machine. Remarkable! Go on."

"No," she said, rather sullenly, at this flow of bitterness, "a variation of my plan. If you will not accompany me to Nara, then I must go alone. I must have money. Do you understand? I am penniless. The *King of Asia* leaves for Japan to-morrow. It sails for the east at dawn. I will never return to China. Will you help me?"

"What do you mean by that? Will I break into the house and help you rob?"

"There is no other way. The money is in a desk, locked. I am not strong enough to break the lock. You can. Then, too, there are some papers of mine—"

"Romola, will this give you the contentment you desire?"

"I-I think so. I hope so."

"Then I will help you."

"Oh, Peter, how can I—"

"Not a word!" He lifted his hand. "You see, my dear, you can't frighten me—easily. You can't bribe me, Romola. But you can appeal to my weakness—"

"A woman in distress—your weakness!" But there was no mockery in either her voice or her eyes. It was more like a whisper of regret, the verge of a confession.

With the last decision behind them, they attacked the dinner, and by deft stages Peter led the conversation to a lighter vein. It was nearly ten when they left, the dining-room was all but deserted, and they departed in high spirits, her arm within his, her smile happy and apparently genuine.

"We must wait until midnight," she informed him. "He will be asleep; the servants will have retired."

Peter suggested a rickshaw ride through the Chinese City to while away the hours in between, but the girl demurred, and amended the suggestion to a street-car ride to Causeway Bay. He consented, and they caught a car in front of the hotel, and climbed to seats on the roof.

He felt gay, excited by the thrill of their impending danger. She was moody, In the bright moonlight on the crystal beach at Causeway Bay he tried to make her dance with him. But she pushed his arms away, and Peter, suddenly feeling the weight of some dark influence, he knew not what, fell silent, and they rode back to the base of the peak road having very little to say.

At a few minutes past midnight they alighted from sedan chairs in the hairpin trail beside the incline railway station at the peak, and as they faced each other, the moon, white and gaunt, slipped from sight behind a billowing black cloud, and the heavens were black and the night was dark around them.

She took his arm, leading him past the murky walls of the old fort, and on up and up the sloping, rocky road, dimly revealed at intervals by points of mysterious light.

They came at length to a high, black hedge, and, groping cautiously along this for a number of yards, found a ragged cleft. He held the branches aside while she climbed through with a faint rustle of silken underskirts. He followed after.

By the dim, ghostly glow of the clouds behind which the moon was floating he made out ominous shapes, scrawny trees and low, stunted bushes.

Hand in hand, with his heart beating very loudly and his breath burning dry in his throat, they approached the desolate, gloomy house—her home!

A low veranda, perhaps a sun-parlor, extended along the wing, and toward this slight elevation the girl stealthily led him, without so much as the cracking of a dry twig underfoot, Peering from left to right for indications that their visit was betrayed.

But the house was still, and large and gloomy, and as silent as the halls of death.

They climbed upon the low veranda. The girl ran her fingers along the French window which gave upon the hedged enclosure, and drew back upon greased hinges the window, slowly, inch by inch, until it yawned, wide open.

He followed her into a room, dark as black velvet, weighted with the indescribable, musty odors of an Oriental abode, and possessed of an almost sensuous gloom, a mystic dreariness, a largeness which knew no dimensions.

As Peter cautiously advanced he was impressed, almost startled, by the sense of vastness, and he was aware of great, looming proportions.

Close at hand a clock ticked, slowly, drearily, as if the release of each metallic click of the ancient cogs were to be the last, beating like the rattling heart of a man in the arms of death. This noise, like a great clatter, seemed to fill all space.

And he was alone.

Suddenly a yellow light glowed in the dark recesses of the high ceiling, and Peter sprang back with his hand on the instant inside his coat, where depended in its leather shoulder-sling the automatic.

Across the great room the girl raised a steady hand, indicating a desk of gigantic size, of ironwood or lignum-vitae.

He found himself occupying the center of an enormous mandarin rug, with letterings and grotesque designs in rich blood-reds, and blues and yellows and browns. He gave the room a moment's survey before falling to the task.

The walls of this cavern were of satin, mandarin rugs also, which hung without a quiver in the breathless gloom. Massive furniture, chairs, tables, settees, of teak, of ebony and dark mahogany, with deep carvings, glaring gargoyles and hideous masks, were arranged with an apparent lack of plan.

And against the far wall, with a face like the gibbous moon, stood a massive clock of carved rosewood, clacking ponderously, almost painfully, as if each tick were to be its last.

Peter crouched before the desk examining the heavy lock on the drawer, and accepted from the girl's hand a tool, a thick, short, blunt chisel. He inserted the blunt edge of this instrument in the narrow crack, and—

A muffled sob, a moan, a stifled cry!

He sprang to his feet, with his hand diving into his coat, and the fingers he wrapped about the butt of the automatic were as cold as ice.

Romola Borria was cringing, shrinking as if to efface herself from a terrible scene, against the French window, and staring at him with a look of wild imploration, of horror, of—death!

From three unwavering spots along the wall to his left glittered the blue muzzles of revolvers!

Peter dropped to his knees, leaped backward, pointed by instinct, and fired at the lone yellow light in the ceiling.

Darkness. An unseen body moved. Metal rattled distantly upon wood. And metal clanked upon metal. Darkness, black as the grave, and as ominous.

A white, round spot remained fixed upon his retina, slowly fading. The face of the clock. The hands, like black daggers, had pointed to ten minutes of one. Ten minutes of life! Ten minutes to live! Or—less?

Silence, broken only by the reluctant *click-clack, click-clack* of the rosewood clock.

If he could reach the window! Then a low, convulsed sobbing occurred close to his ear. The girl groped for his arm. She was shaking, shaking so that his arm trembled under it.

"Your final card!" he whispered. "The final trick! God! Now, damn you, get me out of this trap!"

"I can't. I-I—Oh, God! Kill me! I gave you every chance. They forced me—forced me to bring you here. They would have strangled me, just as they strangled the other!" She seemed to steady herself while he listened in growing horror.

"Safe!" he groaned. "Safety for you. Death—for me! You— you led me into their hands, and I-I trusted you. I *trusted* you!"

She laid a cold, moist hand over his lips, this devil-woman.

"Hush! If they, if he, so much as guessed that I cared for you, that I loved you, it would mean my death. I was forced—forced to bring you here. Don't you understand? And if he even guessed. But you had your chance. You had your chance!"

Almost hysterically she was endeavoring to extenuate her crime, her treason.

"Stand up and face them. Meet your death! Escape is—impossible! *Impossible!* They are watching you like a rat. In a moment they know you can stand this strain no longer! Face them, I say! Show them that—"

Peter pushed her away from him in loathing, and she lay still, only whimpering.

Yet the devils of darkness—where were they? And slowly, yet more slowly, the rosewood clock ticked off its seconds. It should be nearly one. At one—

A fighting chance?

CHAPTER XV

FLOOD TIDE

ON HIS HANDS and knees he touched, and began crawling, an inch at a time, toward the French window, dragging the automatic over the thick satin carpet. He reached the window. It was still ajar. Far, far below twinkled the lights of Hong Kong, of ships anchored in the bay, and the glitter of Kowloon across the bay. Out there was life!

A board creaked near him, toward the heart of that darkened vault. He spun about, aimed blindly, fired!

The floor shook as an unseen shape collapsed and writhed within reach of his hand. In his grasp was the oily, thick queue of a coolie.

And suddenly, as he groped, the wall spat out angry tongues of corrosive red flame.

A white-hot iron seemed to shoot through the flesh of his left arm. The pain reached his shoulder. His left arm was useless—the bone shattered!

Groaning, he pushed himself back. His knees struck the sill, slid over, and he felt the coarse, peeled paint of the veranda. He reached the ledge—dropped to the ground, and in dropping, the revolver spilled from his hand as it caught on a projecting ledge of the floor, bounded off into the darkness.

He groveled to retrieve it, muttering as his hands probed, through the tufted grass.

Light glimmered in the room above. There occurred sounds of a struggle, of feet scraping, a muffled oath, a short scream.

Peter leaped back, looking up, prepared to dash for the road.

A yellow light within the room silhouetted the slender figure of Romola Borria against the French window. Her arms went out in frantic appeal to the darkness, to him.

"Wait!" she cried in an awful voice. "I love you! Wait!"

At that confession, a hand seemingly suspended in space was elevated slowly behind her. The hand paused high above her head. A face appeared in the luminous space above her head, an evil face, carved with a hideous brutality, wearing an ominous snarl, and above the writhing lips of this one was a black growth, a mustache, pointed, like twin black daggers.

Emiguel Borria, ardent tool of the Gray Dragon? Emiguel Borria, husband of the girl, Romola?

Emiguel Borria, in whose lifting hand Peter now caught the glint of a revolver, attempted to crowd the girl to one side. But she held her ground, and then this woman who had on a half-dozen successive occasions tricked and deceived Peter, who had deliberately and on her own confession lured him into this trap, upset, womanlike, the elaborate plan of her master.

In a frenzy she spun upon Emiguel Borria, seized the white barrel of the revolver in her two hands and forced it against his side. Tiny red flames spurted out on either side of the cylinder and smeared in a smoky circle where the muzzle was momentarily buried in the tangled black coat. And Emiguel Borria seemed to sink into the great room and entirely out of Peter's sight.

Romola leaned far into the darkness.

"Run! Run! For your life!"

And as Peter started to run, out of the compound for the dubious safety of the cloistered road, other men of the Gray Dragon, posted for such a contingency, let loose a shower of bullets from adjoining windows.

But the gods were for the time being on the side of Peter. These shots all went wild.

Shuddering, with teeth chattering and eyes popping, Peter dove through the matted hedge, dashed into the street, and down the street, lighted at intervals with its pin-points of mysterious light.

He came to the incline station, and his footsteps seemed weighted, dragging. And the clock in the station, as he dashed past, showed one o'clock.

He plunged down the first sharp twist of the hairpin trail, fell, picked himself up dusty, and dizzy, with his left arm swinging grotesquely as he ran.

And behind him, riding like the dawn wind, he seemed to feel the presence of a companion of a silent rickshaw which rattled with a grisly occupant; and a voice, the voice of Romola Borria, shrill and terrible in his ear, cried: "Wait! Oh, wait!"

But the specter was more real than Peter could imagine.

It was quite awful, quite unreal, the way Peter stumbled and plunged and fell and stumbled on down the hill; past the reservoirs which glittered greenly under their guardian lights.

How he managed to reach Queen's Road in that dreadful state I cannot describe. He dashed down the center of the deserted road, with rudely awakened Sikhs calling excitedly upon Allah, to stop, to stop!

But on he sped, straight down the center of the mud roadway, past the Hong Kong Hotel, now darkened for the night, and past the bund.

Would the sampan be waiting? Otherwise he was now bolting headlong upon the waiting knives of the Gray Dragon's men. No sampan in the whole of Victoria Harbor was safe to-night, but one. Would the one be waiting? Upon that single hope he was staking his safety, his dash for life.

He sped out upon the jetty.

Where could he seek refuge? The *Persian Gulf! The King of Asia!* The transpacific liner lay far out in a pool of great black, glittering under sharp, white arc-lights forward and aft as cargo was lifted from obscure lighters and stowed into her capacious hold.

Yet he must go quickly, for in all China there was no safety for him this night.

A shadow leaped out upon the jetty close upon his heels. But Peter did not see this ghost.

The sampan coolie, asleep upon the small foredeck of his home, shivered and muttered in his strange dreams. By his garb—and by the richness of the large sampan's upholsterings Peter guessed this to be the craft sent to him by the small Chinese girl.

Peter leaped aboard, awakening the *fokie* with a cry.

Dark knobs arose from the low cabin hatchway, and by the yellow lamps of the jetty Peter made them out to be the heads of the maid from Macassar and her old grandmother.

A *dong* was burning in the cabin, and Peter followed the girl into the small cabin of scrubbed and polished teak, while the old woman gibbered in sharp command to the *fokie.*

Crouching like a beast at last cornered, Peter, by the shooting rays of the dong, glared dazedly into an angry red face, a face that was limned and pounded by the elements, from which stared two blue, bloodshot eyes.

The girl said nothing as she nestled at his side, and Peter permitted his head to sink between his hands.

Yet, strange to say, the red-faced did not fire, made no motion of stabbing him.

Peter looked up, snarling defiance.

"You've got me cornered," he whispered harshly. "It's after one o'clock. The parole is up. Why prolong the agony? Damn you, I'm unarmed!" He shut his eyes again.

Again there was no premonitory click, no seep of steel upon scabbard.

The red-faced man seized his shoulder, shook him.

"Say, you young prize-fighter," he sputtered, "You drunk? Crazy? Or just temporarily off your nut? Who in thunder said anything about prolonging the agony? What agony are you talking about? Why the devil've you been dodging me all over South China to-day? You dog-gone young wildcat, you! I've got an assignment for you. The *King of Asia's* wireless man is laid up in the Peak Hospital with typhoid. I want you to take her back to Frisco! Blast your young hide, anyhow!"

The wizen face of the girl's grandmother appeared in the hatchway. She seemed annoyed, angry. She said something in the Cantonese dialect, which Peter did not understand.

"A sampan is following," translated the girl in her tiny voice, "but we are nearly there. In a moment you will be safe."

"Where?" demanded Peter, staring over the red-faced man's shoulder for a glimpse of the other sampan.

"The *King of Asia*," she told him. "In a moment, *birahi*, in a moment."

Her tones were those of a little mother: she was mothering Peter, endeavoring to soothe him; and I must admit that Peter's agitated state justified her attitude.

But Peter was staring anxiously into the red face, trying to decipher an explanation.

"I told the red-faced one to be here, too, at midnight," the girl was whispering in his ear. "He came. He is a friend. Your fears were wrong, *birahi*."

The sampan lurched, scraping and tapping along a surface rough and metallic.

The yellow face of the old woman again appeared in the hatchway. A bar of keen, white light thrust its way into the cabin. It came from somewhere above. Peter could no longer hear the groan and swish of the sweep, and the cabin no longer keeled from side to side. He guessed that the sampan was alongside.

The old woman motioned for him to come out.

"I am not coming aboard; I am going back to my hotel," said the red-faced man. "You will not leave this ship? You will promise me that?"

"I will promise," said Peter gravely. "You, I presume, are Mr. J.B. Whalen, the Marconi supervisor?"

The red-faced man nodded. As if by some prearranged plan, Whalen, after slight hesitation, climbed out of the cabin, leaving Peter alone with this very small, very gentle benefactor of his. He wanted to thank her, and he tried. But she put her fingers over his lips.

"You are going to the one you love, *birahi*," she said in her tinkling little voice. "Before we part, I want you—I want you to—" and she hesitated. "Come now, my brave one," she added with an attempt at briskness. "You must go. Hurry!"

Peter found the side ladder of the *King of Asia* dangling from the upper glow of the liner's high deck. He put his foot on the lower rung and paused. A vast number of apologies, of thanks and goodbyes demanded utterance, but he felt confused. The slight relaxation of the past few minutes had left him exhausted, and his brain was like fog.

He remembered that the little maid from Macassar had wanted him to do something, possibly some favor. The glow high above him seemed to swim. His injured arm was beginning to throb with a low and persistent pain. And the climb to the deck seemed a tremendous undertaking.

"You were saying," he began huskily, as she reached out to steady the ladder. "You wanted me—"

"Just this, my brave one." And she reached up on tiptoes and kissed him ever so lightly upon his lips. "When you think of me, *birahi,* close your eyes and dream. For I-I might have loved you!"

Half-way up the black precipice, Peter stopped and looked down. For a moment his befuddled senses refused to register what now occupied the space at the ladder's end.

The sampan was no longer there; another had taken its place, a sampan long and as black as the night which encompassed it.

Wide, dark eyes stared up across the space into his, and these were set in a chalky-white face, grim, fearful—startling!

It was Romola Borria. Her white arms were upheld in a gesture of entreaty. Her lips were moving.

Peter descended—a step, and stopped, swaying slightly.

"What—what—" he began.

"He is dead!" came the whisper from the small deck. "I killed him! I killed him! Do you hear me? I am free! Free! Why do you stare at me so? I am ready to go. But you must ask me! I will not follow you. I will not!"

And Peter, clutching with a sick and sinking feeling at the hard rope, found that his lips and tongue were working, but that no sound other than a dull muttering issued from his mouth. Momentarily he was dumb—paralyzed.

"I am not a tool of the Gray Dragon," went on the vehement whisper. "I am not!"

And to Peter came full realization that Romola Borria was lying, or endeavoring to trick him, for the last time.

"Go back—there," he managed to stammer at last. "Go back! I won't have you! I'm through with this damned place."

Painfully he climbed up a few rungs.

Then the voice of Romola, no longer a whisper, but loud, broken, despairing, came to him for the last time:

"You are leaving me—leaving me—for her—for Aileen!"

Peter made no reply. He continued his laborious climb; first one foot, then a groping few inches upward along the hard rope

with his right hand, and then the other foot. Nor did he once
again look down.

He gained the deck finally. It was blazing, with incandescent
and arc-lights. Under-officers and deck-hands were pacing
about, giving attention to the loading. Donkey-engines hissed,
coughed, and rattled, as the yellow booms creaked out, up and
in with their snares of bales and crates, which vanished like
swooping birds of prey into the noisy hatchways.

Peter took in the bustling scene with a long sigh of relief.
He still heard that lonely, anguished voice; the black sampan
still rested on his eyes, heaving on the flood tide upon which
the great ship strained, as if eager to be gone. And out there—
out there—beyond the black heart of mystery and the night,
was the clean dawn—the rain-washed spaces of the shimmer-
ing sea.

But he could not look down again. He would not. For a
while—or forever—he had had his fill of China. Before him
now lay the freedom of the open sea, the sunshine of life—and
his homeland!

Peter the Brazen had drunk all too indulgently at the bitter
fountain.

ABOUT THE AUTHOR

THE DECISION TO become a writer of fiction was made for me by fate. In 1914, in Panama, where I spent a week when I was a wireless operator on a little steamer that creaked up and down the Central American coast, I met an author who painted the joys of free-lancing so vividly that I could not resist the call. We were drunk. I was twenty. Since then, I have been trying to catch up with all of those joys he mentioned.

Starting to write stories in 1914 and, four years later selling my first one, marks up, I suppose, a very poor batting average. But in those years I was getting experience, seeing the world, and acquiring knowledge. I "punched brass" as a wireless operator all over the Pacific. I entered Columbia University in 1915, and one year later left because I didn't believe in higher learning. I still don't believe in it. I became a newspaper reporter, later a magazine editor.

Then came the war, which I won practically single-handed by writing high-pressure publicity to induce patriotic Americans to send books to Washington for camp libraries for soldiers and gobs. Books came by the carload, by the ton: McGuffy's readers, old almanacs, spellers, arithmetics, out-dated novels and just trash. The soldiers and sailors who read those books soon hated the war so bitterly, that they promptly got busy and ended it. That's how I won the war.

After the war, I wanted another look at China, and was sent to the Far East by *Collier's* to write articles on China, the Philippines, India and Malaya.

251

The first story I sold was written while I was editing a motion picture trade paper. It was bought by the *Argosy*, and it was about a wolf named Murg. Don't ask me why. In the intervening years I have written millions of words. Perhaps it is Murg who sits so patiently at my door!

I started writing fiction under the pen name of Loring Brent, because it would have annoyed the owner of the motion picture magazine to learn that I was writing fiction out of hours. He thought I fell asleep at my desk because I was working so hard for him! When my income from fiction exceeded my salary, I quit the job. Since then I have been free-lancing exclusively, except for a two-year period when I lived in a Florida swamp town and added to my writing the duties of postmaster, game warden and deputy sheriff. Out of that experience came a long series of stories about a Florida town I called Vingo.

I have enjoyed most writing stories about certain established characters. Apparently the most popular of these have been the Peter the Brazen, the Vingo and the Gillian Hazeltine stories. I stopped writing about Peter the Brazen (a swashbuckling wireless operator on ships in the China run) about ten years ago. He was, incidentally, the subject of the only novel I have had published in America. I am now starting a new series about him.

When I am not traveling I live in Westport, Connecticut. My interests are horses, sailing and flying. I took up flying about a year ago to write some articles on how it feels to learn to fly, and was badly bitten by the bug. I can make a three-point landing about five times out of ten.

I like New York, but would prefer to live in Honolulu. I smoke sixty cigarettes a day. I like murder trials. I have never mastered the noble game of poker, although I once wrote a book about it. In my spare time I study law and medicine. I have two young sons and a still younger daughter; an able crew for my sailboat—except that there is usually mutiny aboard the lugger!

THE ARGOSY LIBRARY™

SERIES 2 INCLUDES:

* BRAND * BRENT * ADAMS *
* MacISAAC * ROSCOE *
* GIESY & SMITH *
* BECHDOLDT *
* MONTGOMERY *
* FARLEY *
* DAVIS *

THE BEST FICTION
FROM THE FRANK
A. MUNSEY LINE

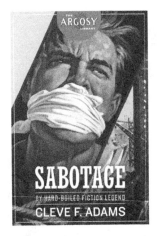

SABOTAGE
BY HARD-BOILED FICTION LEGEND
CLEVE F. ADAMS

CHAMPION OF LOST CAUSES
WILLIAM F. NOLAN
MAX BRAND

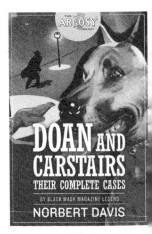

DOAN AND CARSTAIRS
THEIR COMPLETE CASES
BY BLACK MASK MAGAZINE LEGEND
NORBERT DAVIS

THE KING WHO CAME BACK
BY THE AUTHOR OF THE RAMBLER
FRED MacISAAC

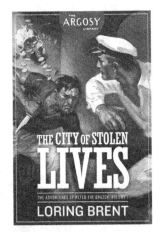

THE CITY OF STOLEN LIVES
THE ADVENTURES OF PETER THE BRAZEN, VOLUME 1
LORING BRENT

THE RADIO GUN-RUNNERS
BY SCIENCE FICTION LEGEND
RALPH MILNE FARLEY

BLOOD RITUAL
THE ADVENTURES OF SCARLET AND BRADSHAW, VOLUME 1
THEODORE ROSCOE

THE SCARLET BLADE
THE RAKEHELLY ADVENTURES OF CLEVE AND D'ENTREVILLE, VOLUME 1
MURRAY R. MONTGOMERY

SEMI DUAL
THE COMPLETE CABALISTIC CASES OF
THE OCCULT DETECTOR, VOLUME 2: 1912–13
J.U. GIESY AND JUNIUS B. SMITH

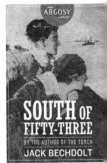

SOUTH OF FIFTY-THREE
BY THE AUTHOR OF THE TORCH
JACK BECHDOLT

SERIES 2 • AVAILABLE SPRING 2015

Made in the USA
Monee, IL
28 August 2024